SECRETS OF SKIN AND STONE

Chelsea,

Thank you for
all your help!
You are the best!

W.J. June
AKA
W.Sparrow

SECRETS OF SKIN AND STONE

WENDY SPARROW WRITING AS
WENDY LAINE

Entangled Publishing, LLC
2614 South Timberline Road
Suite 109
Fort Collins, CO 80525
Visit our website at www.entangledpublishing.com.

Entangled Teen is an imprint of Entangled Publishing, LLC.

Edited by Kate Brauning
Cover design by Anna Crosswell
Cover art from Depositphotos

Manufactured in the United States of America

First Edition June 2017

To my daughter, who gave me the strength to shine light into my shadows.

Chapter One

The last stretch on the motorcycle always seems the longest. Even the cooling breeze, rich with the scent of grassy fields and cedars, wasn't keeping me awake. I was dog tired. I stopped to stare at the sign leading to the town I'd be spending my next few weeks in. After taking off my helmet, I peered at the quaint sign with its fancy, uptight font. Hidden Creek, Population: 1136.

I snorted a laugh. How often did this spit-on-the-map Alabama town have to update that sign? Probably not often. Well, it'd have "1137" residents for as long as I was here—which was hopefully not long.

Stretching, I listened to the soft sounds I'd missed due to the roar of my bike. The hum of insects. Something scurried through the underbrush nearby. The light wind slithered across the grass with a hissing sound. My hair felt molded to my head from the long ride.

I inhaled, taking in the clean air. I could appreciate the

rural appeal, without wanting to put down roots. These 1136 people had been born here, grown up from those roots, and they'd die here.

Still, it did smell nice.

I shoved my helmet back on. Almost there.

How many fiends could be hiding in Hidden Creek? This was a crap job—a gimme. I'd do it, if that's what it'd take to prove to my dad I was ready to go solo at eighteen. You'd think there'd be enough need for my skills that I could at least get a decent assignment for my first on my own.

My relatives were probably making up stories about the town's fiend infestation so they sounded important. It was telling that they always visited us in the city, rather than the other way around.

The ride to my aunt and uncle's place took me through patches of neighborhoods leading to what I supposed was the town center. After spending so much time in cities like Atlanta, Savannah, Charlotte, and Tallahassee, this itty-bitty town was more constrictive than my riding leathers. The outskirts were scattered fields with obligatory trucks parked in the driveways of darkened farmhouses. What did these people do that they were all in bed by eleven at night? The town was nothing but porch lights and the scent of dinners I was too late for. Maybe my aunt would cook for me sometimes.

Two dogs ran to the edge of their fenced yards and barked at me as I passed. Inside the nearby house, a light flicked on. I was disturbing the peace already. My motorcycle *was* loud— that was part of why I liked it. But I didn't much care for everyone in town knowing Gris Caso was around. Drawing on my powers, I hushed the sound from splitting the night.

I passed into a less desirable part of town, if the abandoned, falling-down structures and overgrown fields were anything to go by. An ancient tractor was rusting to death and being overwhelmed by tall blades of grass. Beside it, a molding scarecrow looked down in judgement on the blight it was.

A tingling sensation running along my shoulder blades was my first indication that the area wasn't as still and deserted as I'd thought. The hair on the back of my neck stood up straight, despite its sweat-soaked condition.

The heaviness in the air and the screech of fiends were like a wall I plowed into. Holy hell. I skidded to a stop beside an old mill. Its weathered, gray boards were most likely a termite haven and even the attempts at graffiti seemed half hearted. It was eerie, even without its wispy occupants' screeching, providing a horror film backdrop.

Fiends. The damn place was full of them. Squinting, I tried to get a sense of how many were in there. Too many.

Okay. Maybe this job wouldn't be such an insult. Something must have happened there to gather so many of them.

Fiends were nasty creatures, half monster and half spectral. They were drawn to sites of violence and fear, to humans having nightmares, and to those practicing dark arts. They looked like insubstantial versions of Watchers—they could have been my ghost and it was creepy as hell. They didn't have wings, but their frame was similar. They clawed their way out of the shadows at night and crept and slunk around. If normal people could see them, they'd never sleep. Fiends' jaws would drop as they shrieked, and their shiny teeth were hideously long. That was even before you got to their talons. And while they could shrink down, it still seemed like there were a lot of them in that mill.

This was Hidden Creek. There shouldn't be more than a dozen in the whole town.

My back itched from the urge to shift into my gargoyle form. Fiends and Watchers were natural enemies. I was halfway off my bike before I shook off the urge and climbed back on.

Be smart, Gris. You'll live longer.

I'd find out the mill's history and then tackle it—when I was more prepared and after I'd slept. I'd learned the family trade from my father, and his strict set of guidelines hinged on knowing what he was walking into. Research. Hell, I did so much research on crime I was likely on watch lists.

Keeping my motorcycle hushed, I continued on. The draw of the fiends was intense enough that I clenched my teeth while tightening my fists on my bike's handgrips. Not right now. After about a mile, the pull was a background hum and the fiends' shrieks no louder than a distant bug-zapper.

I'd memorized the weird directions my aunt had given me. Small towns had odd points of reference: "when you see the green broken-down combine in a field, take the next left," or "Turn at the stop sign with the bullet holes in the shape of a peace sign."

My cousin was sitting on the front steps of his parents' house when I rode up. He was tossing a wrench in one hand with a lazy sort of grace that ran in the family.

"Problems?" Danny asked after I cut the bike's engine. "You're awfully late. Thought you'd be here hours ago."

"Late start and I hit traffic coming out of Atlanta." I parked the bike on the road.

Leaving behind the wrench, my cousin got to his feet, holding up a jingling set of keys. "Here they are. I wouldn't expect much. Mama went over and cleaned it up some, but it still looks like it was beaten with the ugly stick."

Across the street from their house was my new abode. The Ritz, it was not. My cousin's folks had bought the property with the intention of bulldozing the house, but they'd never gotten around to it. The house couldn't have more than three or four rooms. It looked blue, but even my Watcher's vision wasn't good enough to make out color at this time of night.

Why hadn't they turned on a porch light?

My aunt and uncle probably figured they were doing me a favor letting me stay in the house, but I was taking care of the town's fiend population without the usual paycheck coming my way.

My next job, I'd be on my own *and* earning a paycheck.

"Here, Grisham," Danny said, "catch!" He threw the keys wide so I dove and caught them with the tip of my finger. My cousin laughed.

"Thanks." I didn't call him on using my full name though he knew it annoyed me.

"Sure thing. Be sure to lock up. Wouldn't want the fiends to bite."

Shaking my head, I turned away. The house didn't look any better up close. I walked through the front gate and let it slam closed behind me. A wide yawn made my jaw crack. I was going to sleep as soon as my head hit the pillow…at midnight. Midnight! That early was unheard of for me. Watchers owned the night, but it had been a long ride. I'd stubbornly insisted on riding my bike rather than bringing my truck.

After walking my bike to the carport at the side of the house, I dragged what little I'd brought from the saddlebags. I pulled off my boots and left them and my riding leathers beside the bike. A decade of shifting into form every night meant I was more accustomed to walking around barefoot than not. The yard's overgrown grass tickled my feet as I strode through it to the porch. The stairs creaked loudly with each of my steps, but they didn't break.

The only warning I had was a hiss of wind as the shadow took form and slammed against me. My bag fell to the planks as I crashed into a rickety porch swing. One chain snapped out of the porch's roof, and the swing clattered against the boards. I shifted to form, my wings tearing through the shirt I was wearing. I dove at the fiend, meeting the screeching beast with my own roar. Its clawed hand caught the porch swing, yanking it clean out of the roof. We spun, banging into the railing and knocking a spindle loose. I grabbed the wooden rail and swung it like a bat, but it sailed through the fiend as if it were as ephemeral as a ghost. I tossed it aside and crouched down. "I've had a long night, so let's get this over with. This is my family's place, and you've already gone and broken their porch swing."

It shrieked at me.

"Oh, you think you've got problems? I was thinking this town would be a piece of cake. What's with all your buddies at the mill, huh? I thought my great-uncle was blowing things out of proportion."

The fiend made its move, going in high and casting its elongated body toward me. I reached out and grabbed its heart. The fiend disintegrated all around me, the scent of sulfur settling on me like perfume. Great. Fantastic.

I leaned up against the porch railing, breathing heavily. What was up with Hidden Creek? I could taste blood. Damn thing had busted my lip. I'd been sloppy. The porch swing had been in decent shape, too, but now it was kindling. Maybe I could rebuild it if I was around long enough.

With an exhausted sigh, I looked up, staring at the stars. At least I could see those clearer out here. Finally, an upside to this town. If I dragged the fight outside, I could see actual stars when I got knocked on my ass.

Far across the field, a dog barked, and I peered at the white farmhouse up the road. A lone light was on. Somebody was up late. Hopefully, this neighbor's dog was all bark and no bite. Dogs could sense fiends and got all uptight about them. If there were more fiends in this area, and I wanted a peaceful night's sleep, I'd have to deal with those around that neighbor's house first thing. I didn't want to get bitten by their mutt for my trouble.

I had enough things with sharp teeth in my life.

After wiping my dirty bare feet on the straw welcome mat, I pushed into the house and sighed. It wasn't bad. It wasn't good. The linoleum was far older than I was and proved that the seventies weren't dead. The ceiling had a few suspicious cracks that might not keep out the rain if it poured. Inhaling, I caught the scent of bleach and pine cleaning solution…and me. I reeked.

First, a shower. Then, a good twelve hours of sleep. Tomorrow, I'd find out what was dragging fiends to that mill. What…or who. The thought of somebody gathering fiends unsettled me. My fingertips itched to do the searches on my laptop, exploring the possibilities. I rolled the tension from shoulders and stretched. Not good. Drawing in fiends could turn nasty real fast. I'd seen it, and it made jobs like this worlds more complicated.

Chapter Two

PIPER

I walked out my front door, rubbing at the itch on my arms that came with it. Stepping outside was the hard part. It got easier after that. Usually. Not today. The itch only increased.

"Jester?" I shouted. A sour taste settled in my mouth, and my stomach ached.

The guilt came fast on the heels of everything else. Guilt was my closest friend. I'd yelled at my dog sometime after midnight. I'd been trying to get enough sleep before my ACT test, and he'd been barking his fool head off. When he'd finally stopped, it'd been a blessing. Now, I was back from the testing center, and Jester hadn't shown up for breakfast.

Even if dogs could feel sulky about being yelled at, Jester wasn't *that* dog. He was stupidly cheerful. He spent most days chasing either his tail or butterflies.

I shouldn't have yelled at him.

Stepping off the porch, I shaded my eyes and looked around. "Jester!"

He always, always came when I called, ever assuming I had food for him.

"Jester!"

Our yard wasn't so big, only a couple acres. We might even have one of the smallest plots of land in Hidden Creek. But if Jester'd decided to explore the whole town, well, I'd be spending the rest of the day searching for him. I headed toward the shed where Daddy kept the tractor. Maybe he was hiding.

Rubbing the itch from my arms, I stopped and turned. Somebody's eyes were on me, staring at me. Waiting. Watching.

"Hello?"

No answer. 'Course there was no answer. There wasn't anybody out there.

An ugly stain crept across the grass right in front of the cheery, yellow outbuilding. I stopped to blink down at it. It lurked a few feet from my white, white sneakers. My toes curled inside my shoes at the thought of that red staining my shoes, getting everywhere. The grass was painted reddish brown. My heart quickened, the thumping beat in my ears. My breath rasped in and out of my throat. I'd seen enough of my own blood to recognize the sight of it.

I rounded the corner and there was Jester, cut open. Everywhere, that reddish brown blood, coating fur and flesh. I'd stepped in it. I'd stepped in the blood. It was staining the tips of my shoes. My white, white shoes were covered in red, red blood.

The screaming started. It went on and on as I stood there and stared at my dog—the blood all over the ground.

Red stain on white shoes.

Red blood on white fur.

So much. So much blood. Tightness pulled at my chest as black dots shot across my vision. The earth rushed up and I fell to my hands and knees.

So much blood.

Mama's footfalls behind me broke through the screaming. She grabbed me 'round the waist, hauling me backward, dragging my shoes away from the staining red-brown blood, while she shouted for my brother. "Dale! Dale! Don't come out here! Don't come! Call your daddy. Just get him on the phone! Piper, it's gonna be fine. It's fine. Piper, stop your screaming. Hush now! Hush!"

I shut my mouth. The shrieking stopped. I gulped in deep breaths and the spots dancing in front of my eyes slowed.

Mama pulled me back to the house. From head to toe, I was numb, other than my throat, which burned. It stung like my throat had bled, too.

When we reached the porch, Mama shoved me at my brother who was holding the phone to his ear. "Dale, take her." Mama leaned over the side of the porch and retched into the rosebushes.

I sucked in deep breaths as I built my wall in my mind, barricading that memory in.

Jester. Jester.

There'd been so much blood.

One brick. Another. A row separated me from Jester—or what once was Jester. I couldn't see him from here—that was another row of bricks. Another brick and another brick.

A dark thought wriggled out of my brain: what had happened after I'd yelled at him? Had I gone back to sleep? All of the awful images of death, both accidental and purposeful rushed forward as if I'd called them. Had I done this? Somehow? Being able to kill and killing weren't the same thing. Being angry and wanting the barking to stop wasn't the same as ending it. I'd never killed anything—even though I could if I wanted to. I couldn't have done this. Could I?

No.

No. Never at my worst. They were just thoughts. Dark thoughts. But just thoughts.

I stared down at my hands. There was blood on them from when I'd fallen. Not much, but some. It hadn't been there before.

Dale shouted questions at Mama.

Water splashed on my hands. Tears streamed along my palms, catching in the creases as I stood there, staring. My numb thoughts were at odds with my stinging throat and the clenching, knifing pain in my stomach.

Jester. My dog. "Jester," I whispered. More tears filled my hands. They ran through the bits of blood, turning my palms into a pink sea. I cupped them so it wouldn't get all over the porch.

I needed to wash my hands. I had to.

I was in the bathroom washing them when Jem walked in, rubbing sleep from her eyes.

"It was so loud," she said.

I grabbed a nearby towel and wiped my eyes. "It was nothing, baby doll. Go back to your nap." The wall between me and what was once my dog was thick enough, now, that I could say that with only a small skip in my words.

Jem's lower lip stuck out in a pout. She was about to dig in and be stubborn. Even at three years old, she shared a stubborn streak with the rest of the family.

"If, um, if you go back to your room, I bet Mama will give you a cookie when you pretend to wake up."

Jem smiled and scampered back to her room. Once upon a time, a cookie would've bought my happiness, too.

I went to my room and locked the door. I could hear the mumble of Mama's and Dale's voices coming from the front room. Mama kept saying, "It was just an animal attack. You got me? An animal killed Jester."

Animals didn't kill like that. They didn't. They didn't cut

something open cleanly and just leave it. Daddy would tell her. Daddy might take a bit to get home from work—his Saturday schedule was unpredictable.

I pulled out the razor blade from the book in my bedside table.

That was the funny thing about blood. Sometimes, it made things worse. Sometimes, it made things better.

I checked again to be sure I'd locked the door, even though I knew I had. There were things that I didn't care to explain to anybody, let alone to my family—especially not to my family. Mama had her version of OCD, and I had this one. It wasn't clean. It didn't help me sort things like socks. It was in my head and heart, and it howled.

The blade was sharp, and I disinfected it regularly. I cut high across my shoulder. It hurt, and it felt right at the same time. Pain I could control. When everything else in my life flowed in opposite directions, and the itching threatened to eat me alive, I could still control the pain from the cuts.

It was my fault Jester was dead. I hadn't gotten up to check on him. And I'd yelled at him. The cut was a small payment toward a debt that loomed over me.

Daddy's car pulled up outside with a crunch of tires on our pebble driveway. Normally, he pulled in slowly so the pebbles didn't spray everywhere, but not today. He must've already been on the way home from Memphis if he got here this fast.

Mama knocked on my door a few minutes later. "Pips, Daddy's fixin' to bury Jester. Did you want anything buried with him? His toys? Anything?" Her voice was watery and sobby.

My wall was thick. I'd built it thick. "How about... everything?"

"Everything?" Mama repeated.

I shrugged, even though she couldn't see me. There wasn't

a reason to keep anything. It'd grow all moldy and vile. If all his toys were buried, I wouldn't have to look at them and be reminded there was no dog using them anymore. The guilt would still be there, no matter what, but maybe I'd forget now and again.

"Fine," she said eventually. Her footsteps retreated down the hall.

The light from the window slid across the floor as the sun moved through the sky. Outside, a shovel slid in and out of the earth with a *shoosh, shoosh*—like the ground was hushing the memory of my dog. The ground between Jester and me was another layer on my wall. When the noise stopped—when I was sure what had once been my dog was deep underground, I got up off my bed.

There'd been no sirens. In our family, we didn't talk about things we didn't want to believe had happened. It was like with the toys. They were gone. Jester was gone.

The itching, which the cut had pushed off, was coming back. The air around me was tight and dusty. The whispers came. In my head. The whispers screamed and filled my mind like a crowded room. *I'll never be clean again. I'll never be good enough. My fault. My fault.*

I changed clothes. Those clothes had touched death, and the red shirt reminded me of all that blood everywhere. Normally, I wore dark colors, or red in case my cuts bled, but I slipped on the farthest thing I owned from blood-red—a blue-checkered sundress. The thick straps might show my cuts if I wasn't careful, but I was nothing if not careful. Tragedies didn't happen to the things I loved 'cause I was so careful. Things didn't get broken, but Jester was good and broken—broken to bits.

It wasn't me. It couldn't have been me.

So, who was it?

I looked out my window. There'd been rumors the

Trunkers' old place was rented again. Hard to believe anybody'd want to live there. Maybe they were the type who liked killing animals. There wasn't a car or truck in the driveway. It still looked empty.

I left the house without running into anybody.

The Trunkers' property wasn't much of a walk away. I cut through our front yard, the Henleys' field across the road, the back lot of the Porters' machine shop, and then crossed the road again to get to the farmhouse. I *could've* followed the road in front of our house the whole way, but then it wouldn't have been a straight line, and I took a direct path whenever I could.

From above, our part of Hidden Creek looked like a wing in the way the roads crossed. I lived at the tip of the wing and the road in front of our house formed the underside. The Trunkers' barn and their dilapidated house sat at the top of the wing. The fields stretched across it, filling it in. 'Course it was too pointy to be a bird wing—it was more like a bat wing. The barn would've been like the finger of the bat—which was about right. The wretched thing darn near gave the whole town of Hidden Creek the finger with how ugly as sin it was.

I pushed through the gate of the fence that framed the yard and went up to the door. The porch swing was all in pieces. I knocked twice. And waited. Nobody answered. Shifting sideways, I peeked through the picture window into the front room. If somebody was living here, they weren't anxious to decorate. A couple of cereal boxes sat on the counter, but otherwise, the place looked empty.

What kind of people rented a falling-down house? Maybe they wanted to use the barn—such as it was.

My parents used to tell me never to go into the barn—or trespass. But there's a statute of limitations on things like that. In Hidden Creek, we're expected to trespass once we're teenagers.

A good breeze after a soaking rain would take the Trunkers' barn down. It was held up by termites stacked on top of each other and just plain stubborn Southern persistence. I touched the flaking red paint on the outside the barn and tore off a small strip to mark I'd been by. A one-by-one foot stretch of paint was already missing. It likely made the barn less stable, but I didn't care. Well, I cared a little, but not enough to stop doing it. Better to complete my patterns and keep the voices hushed, and my skin less itchy.

My family wasn't into farming and such, not like most of Hidden Creek. Daddy wrote computer programs for a company out of Memphis—though he telecommuted a lot, on account of the distance. We had three computers and only a couple acres of land. That was darn near unnatural in Hidden Creek. I'd never driven the tractor in our barn, and I'd never owned a horse—just a dog. Just Jester.

I guess I didn't really own him anymore. You don't own the dead. He belonged to the earth more than me.

The dusty stillness inside the barn suggested it wasn't an explanation for the new renters. It looked as ugly as usual. Rusty tools once hung on the walls of the barn, but I'd taken them down one day while wearing latex gloves and buried them near the fence. Having rusted metal tools lying about wasn't safe. Better to bury things like that—to hide things that shouldn't be seen.

I counted out the steps toward the hay bales, eight steps. Eight steps toward the first bale and then an even number between each one—sometimes, they were big steps to make it an even number. After touching a bale of hay, I brushed my hands off before pulling all my hair back and wrapping it in a knot to keep it out of my mouth. There was enough of a breeze that strands kept tickling my lips and cheeks.

"What are you doing?" a deep voice asked from the dim corner of the barn.

I jumped a foot. Squinting, I could almost make out a body lounging in the barn's inky black corner. He was only a shadow, but he seemed tall and long. "What am I doing? What are *you* doing?"

"Sweetheart, I think my question gets answered first." There was a smile in his voice. Yeah, I didn't trust that. Or him.

"You can wait all you want, but I don't talk to strangers." I put my hands on my hips before leaning over and touching one of the bales of hay real fast. Then, my hands were back on my hips. My hands itched. I tapped my middle finger and thumb against each other—it made the itch more bearable.

He laughed as he pushed up from the hay bale, then walked toward me. His voice sounded young—my age or thereabouts. But shoot, he was tall. Crap, if he fell over, he'd be halfway home. His walk had a hitch in it, like he rode something. A horse. A bike?

As he came closer, I backed away and put up my hand. "Stop!"

He stopped. The lower half of his body was visible in the sun cast through the door. His blue jeans had a hole in one knee. Rusty-brown splotches ringed the ripped denim. Blood? Probably his own blood from a skinned knee. It looked like an old stain—like it'd stubborned out a wash cycle or two. Black leather boots peeked from beneath the raggedy hems of his jeans. Not cowboy boots.

"Fine then, Dorothy, I'm stopped," he said.

Dorothy? I flicked my eyes down to my checkered dress. Maybe I looked a bit like Dorothy from *The Wizard of Oz*, but not more than a smidge. My hair was blond, not brown, and it was in a knot at my neck, not in braids.

"Easy. I'm harmless," he said, pulling a baseball cap from his head. His speech was too neat and tidy to be small town, but his drawl was smooth, southern, and sounded real sweet. "People call me Gris." He hit the red baseball cap against his jeans. Dust from the cap caught the light and sparkled.

"What kind of name is that?" I didn't trust him or the funny feeling in my heart and stomach.

"Short for Grisham, but only my mother and my birth certificate call me that. You always ask more questions than you answer?"

"You always ask questions of people when you're trespassing?"

His face was in need of a shave and a smudge of dirt graced his cheekbone. He grinned. That probably worked with everybody else, but not with me. I didn't take to charming boys.

"I'm not trespassing," he said.

"You sure are." I needed to get out of the barn, but I had one more hay bale to touch before I could leave. I took the steps, counting in the back of my mind.

His eyes followed me, and a frown pursed his lips. He had a cut on his lower lip. I shouldn't be staring. People didn't like it when I stared. But then, that mouth of his smiled, pulling the cut tight. 'Course he would prove to be the exception to that "staring bothering people" business.

"What's your name, sweetheart?"

"That"—I tapped the last bale of hay. Done. I could leave now—"is none of your business."

Gris flung his cap back on his head and blew out a sigh.

"And don't call me sweetheart." I edged sideways toward the door. My hand fingered the pepper spray in my pocket. I'd made it myself. My parents refused to believe shadows crept into my room at night, but they did. Plus, the world was filled with dangerous, ugly things.

"Give me another name, then." He watched my progress toward the door. Then he took a single step forward.

Whoa. I yanked out my bottle of spray. "Stop! Stop yourself right there!"

He held both his hands up. "I'm not trying to hurt you. I'd heard small-town people were friendly, but they sure don't mean you, do they?"

"I'm nice to people I trust...and who mind their own business." Not entirely true, but I wasn't mean to people, so it was near the truth.

That smile again. He probably got away with murder.

Murder. He'd darn near distracted me from my whole purpose of coming over here.

I frowned. "How long have you been around? Did you hear a dog bark early this morning?"

He tilted his head. "I'll answer your questions if you tell me your name."

It should've been a bargain, but I didn't give out information to people I didn't know. "I'm serious, Gris. Somebody murdered my dog."

His whole body went still as a statue. "Somebody killed your dog?"

I nodded.

"Who?" The cut on his lip stretched tight from his frown.

I shook my head.

"You don't know, or you won't tell me?" His words were clipped, without the smooth charm of earlier.

I shook my head again. I knew I was draining his patience, and maybe that's why I did it. I wanted to see how far I could push Gris before his control broke. I'd file it away with the rest of what I knew about him—which was precious little.

"You live in the white house over there?" He pointed.

It wouldn't be too difficult to figure out that's where I lived, but I still didn't want to tell him.

"Will you at least tell me your name? This is getting pretty damn ridiculous."

"Don't profane." *Don't profane?* I sounded like my mama, and I said much worse things in my head all the time.

His charming smile was back. I'd shown weakness, and now he reckoned he'd be able to pull me under his spell.

"I don't like charming boys."

"You find me charming?" He tilted his head again. "Could've fooled me."

"I *don't* find you charming. It won't work on me, so just knock it off." I let myself have two fibs a day before I cut myself. I'd have to tell a second one now.

"Settle down, sweetheart. You're in my barn. You've told me somebody killed your dog, and I think you're accusing me. I've told you my name and, in return, you've acted like I'm a walking disease that you're gonna spray with whatever that bottle holds."

My bottle held hot red pepper powder mixed with rubbing alcohol and baby oil. It was the first recipe I'd learned. The second had been chocolate chip cookies. I make a mean chocolate chip cookie…but not as mean as my pepper spray.

"Nobody owns this barn." A small fib, but it was still a fib. So, that's two. Somebody did own it. Though it hadn't been the Trunkers for longer than I'd been alive.

"I'm renting this place—so it's like I own it."

"You're the new renter?" He didn't look old enough to be renting a place and living all by himself.

"I am. Now tell me your name, and I'll answer any questions you have."

"Laura," I fibbed. Three fibs. I'd have to pay for that and tell another one. This fib was worth the cut. If Gris was gonna be around for any length of time, saying the name Piper Devon would give away my life history—and I didn't care for a stranger knowing that much about me.

His eyes narrowed. "Fine then, *Laura*." The heavy way he said the name called me a fibber. "My name is Gris Caso. I'm eighteen years old, and I'm staying in the farmhouse while I…take care of something in town. I got in late last night and went right to bed. I don't know what happened to your dog, but I'd be happy to help you find out."

"Why would you wanna help me? I've been particularly aggravating." Hanging my hands at my sides, I tapped my fingers again. *Tap. Tap. Tap. Tap.*

"You were trying to rile me up?"

I nodded. 'Course I was. He didn't think I acted like this with everybody, did he? I wasn't rude. Not usually. My mama had raised me better than that. "I wanted to see if you'd lose your temper."

"In order to figure out if I'd killed your dog?"

"No."

He waited for me to elaborate.

I didn't.

His eyes narrowed. "Are you sure it was a *person* that killed your dog?"

"What makes you think it wasn't?"

He shrugged. "I heard a dog bark after midnight. It didn't sound like it was being harmed. It was just barking. I imagine if it was an animal attack, you'd have heard that. But it still seems more likely than somebody killing it. What was it—poison?"

There was too much I didn't know about him. Ignorance was dangerous. Knowledge was power. I eyed Gris's cut lip. "How'd you hurt your lip?"

He ran his tongue along the cut, making me shiver. "Punch to the face."

"Does that happen often to you?"

"More so than I'd like."

I squinted. "Maybe you aren't charming *enough.*"

In the distance, two sharp whistles blew. Mama wanted me home. She could whistle loud enough with her fingers I could hear it over a mile away. "I should go."

"All right." His charm had fallen away and left behind

confusion. It was easier to talk to somebody when they were confused.

"I'm going to find out who killed my dog," I said over my shoulder. Jester deserved that, and I needed to know the answer if I was ever going to sleep again.

"And I meant what I said about helping you."

I snorted. "You can't help me. Nobody can help me." At the door to the barn, politeness dictated I turn and say, "It was nice to meet you, Gris Caso." My mama had drilled politeness into me. She said if we weren't polite, people and society all around would turn to anarchy. I didn't like anarchy, but I also didn't always like being polite.

"It was…interesting to meet you, Laura."

I shook my head. "My name isn't Laura. Please don't call me that." I spun and ran across the fields toward my house. With the machine shop and the tree line, it should've taken me out of Gris's sight long enough he'd tire of watching. But the truth was, as I walked into my house, I knew he was still watching me from the top of that bat wing. I didn't like it.

No, that was a lie. I *did* like it. Four lies. One. Two. Three. Four.

I shouldn't spend any more time with Gris Caso. Right there was serious harm waiting to happen.

Well, that and whoever had gotten to my dog.

Chapter Three

Moonlight bathed the old structure, turning it shades of blue and purple. The night had always felt welcoming to me; though, admittedly less so with the task ahead of me tonight. The closer we got to the mill, the heavier the atmosphere the fiends put off. Hopefully I didn't get my ass handed to me with my cousin just outside the door.

The rickety mill's door nearly fell from its frame when I opened it. I shifted into my Watcher form when I was out of my cousin's sight. The thought of tackling all these fiends alone had me jittery. Adrenaline stole my breath, from both excitement and a healthy amount of uneasiness. I winced at the loud creak as I slammed the door closed. It drew the attention of all the wispy creatures inside. The fiends turned toward me all at once. Oh hell. I'd just shut myself in and committed to a cage match that might kill me. The monsters never held with taking turns and rushed me all at once. Even with my armored skin, the jagged board that I slammed up against knocked the wind out of me.

"Sounds like there's a few of 'em in there," my cousin said from outside. Only Watchers could see and hear fiends so he was judging that based on the sound of me crashing around.

"Ya think?" I sprang forward with my talons extended. I grabbed a fiend by the throat, my long black nails gouging into its vapory substance. Throwing it to the old mill's floor, I plunged my other hand through its chest. A sting shot through me as another fiend latched onto my back.

"I'd help you if I could, but seeing as how I didn't get the birthright…"

Yeah, well, I might die for getting the birthright, so I wasn't about to cry over my cousin losing out.

Ducking, I yanked the fiend off my back like I was pulling off a shirt. Down it went, and then its heart was dripping through my talons. I shook the dissolving ooze off and moved on. These fiends were rabid, and I still had another four circling me. It was hard to bob and weave and still keep my wings tucked. The last thing I needed was to round off this night by getting my wings sewn.

"Why are there so many?" I shouted.

My cousin sniffed. "Well, like we told you. Strange things are happening here."

"Is somebody to blame for it? This kind of thing doesn't just happen." Groups of fiends were like the stench of fetid evil. You typically found a human at the heart of unusual activity, and what I was in the middle of was definitely unusual. "Give me names, Danny!" I jumped back, missing a swipe from one of the remaining four fiends.

"Hell, I don't know. That's why Critch sent for you. This is your job. If you can't handle it, we can always call Uncle Jack."

Like hell. My dad wasn't coming here unless I lost a limb.

I flung myself at another fiend and twisted to avoid its claws. With it wrapped in a chokehold, I drove my talons through its chest and caught another scrape to the back. Damn, these things were mean. If only something other than ripping out their hearts would kill them.

"Why are they even in here?" I yelled. Sulfur tinged the air. Possibly something had gone bad, but the place wasn't littered with beer bottles or trash. Research hadn't told me much about the place, as Hidden Creek wasn't on the cutting-edge of historical documentation.

"Everybody 'round here figures it's haunted. On account of somebody hanging themselves inside." He smothered a laugh before asking, "Was that you that just hit the wall?"

Dazed, I blinked. I'd taken the equivalent of a monster's right hook to the face. My lip felt really split this time, and I was seeing bursts of light. I held both my hands up to ward off a quick attack. In a stroke of pure luck, a fiend impaled itself on my outstretched hand. Not one to miss an opportunity, I grabbed its heart. Either I had two left, or I had one and that last knock to my head had me seeing double. "A suicide isn't enough. I'm looking for a bigger source. Who stands out in this town?"

"Now that you mention it, there is this one family. All high and mighty. Different from everyone else."

"Different how?"

Two years ago, I might not have survived this job. My great-uncle wasn't wrong in sending for a Watcher. I ducked a claw aimed right at my face. Nasty, ornery things. I'd fought rural fiends before, but these seemed more uncivilized than those.

"They're not a generations-old family, for one. And they just sit on their land, not doing anything with it. Mr. Devon is in computers, so they think they're better than everyone else. Piper especially."

"Piper?"

"The daughter. Remember that old lady I told you about

who went crazy and drove through the barbershop window? Well, last week, this guy shot up the library…and guess who'd just left? Piper."

Surging upward, I snagged the heart of another fiend. "So?"

"So, you wanted to know who didn't fit in? That'd be the Devons. Though, everyone is acting strange. Whole town seems bedeviled."

The final fiend paused, then its mouth dropped open in a screech that made its sharp teeth look extra long, even if they were vapory. The first time I'd seen one do that, I'd screamed right back. Now, it just seemed at odds with my cousin outside. "Why move to a place like Hidden Creek if you're fixin' to leave every day for work?" Danny asked. "And Piper *had been* in the library."

"So? Literacy hasn't been a sign of devil-worship since the Middle Ages." I circled the last fiend. The cuts on my back pulled as I moved. I'd gotten good and torn up this time.

"Librarian says Piper looks up all sorts of strange things."

"Define strange."

He snorted. "Reads about murder. Seems to focus on the occult."

Now we were talking.

"Town only puts up with the Devons on account of her mama being a church-going woman and involved."

I'd check out this family tomorrow. For now, I sucked in a deep breath and ran at the last fiend. It pulsed toward me, its long vapor arm outstretched like we were jousting. Ducking sideways, I avoided the fiend's claws while plunging my own talons through its body. And…silence. The mill was back to being abandoned and empty—and it really reeked of sulfur now. I leaned over, planting my hands on my knees as I breathed.

"Gris?" Danny rattled the door.

I shifted back to my human form. My skin tightened as my body twisted and warped. Somedays, I couldn't tell which side of me felt more foreign. The crackling of my body shifting and softening was uncomfortably loud when I knew I had an audience. "Yeah. They're gone. Come in."

He entered, squinting into the darkness. "How many were there?"

"Nine."

He nodded. "Is that a lot?"

"It's enough." I didn't want to seem as beat as I was, but, holy hell, nine had felt like a freaking army. And they'd been as ornery as I'd ever seen them.

Danny shrugged. "Critch did say we had problems here."

A month ago, Uncle Critch had sent an email saying there were fiends in Hidden Creek that needed taken care of. Seeing as he was a "retired" Watcher, he'd know. "Having *some* fiends isn't the same as having nine in an abandoned mill, plus one waiting for me on my porch."

"Is that what happened to the swing?"

I straightened and ignored his question. Pulling a flashlight from my loose khakis, I started examining the mill.

"A fiend took me by surprise." Crouching, I pulled up a suspiciously loose floorboard. "That's not normal, either, one waiting to attack a Watcher. They avoid us."

"I wouldn't know. Never seen the damn things. I have a real job." Danny worked at his dad's machine shop that was right across from the house I was renting. "It might not pay half as well as flying around and killing things, but we can't all be gargoyles." He leaned against the wall as I shone the light down into the dark recesses of the mill's crawlspace.

"Something smells," I said, but I made no move to go down there.

I could feel my cousin's eyes on the back of my head. "Too much of a city boy to get your hands dirty?"

Danny and I shared the blackish-brown eyes of our Granddaddy Trent, and we were close to the same age, but that was where the resemblance ended. Danny's blond hair was almost bleached white from time spent in the sun. I didn't see enough of the sun due to all my nights spent fighting the things in the shadows.

I yanked up another floorboard. "Hey, I met this girl earlier in that barn beside the house."

"I can't believe you went in that barn, what with you turning your nose up at the dust in here."

After pulling up another board, I lowered myself into the three-foot-tall crawlspace running under the mill. The flashlight's beam skimmed across the skeletons of more rats than I ever needed to see. There was a fabric-covered lump in the middle of the rat graveyard, and I tried to work up the desire to go grab it.

"So you're here less than a day and already meeting girls," Danny said. "Trying to show us up?"

"Ain't my fault you're so ugly you look like something the dog was keeping under the porch." We used to compete in insults whenever we'd meet up. We competed in everything over the years.

"You're so ugly your mama stuck a sack on your head as a kid." Danny's weren't always particularly witty.

"Yeah, well, you're so ugly you hit every branch of the ugly tree on the way down."

"Gris, you're so ugly, when you look in a mirror, your reflection turns to stone."

I winced. That one hit too close to home. "If I had a dog as ugly as you, I'd shave his butt and teach him to walk backward."

Danny said, "You're uglier than the east end of a horse headed west."

I took a quarter out of my pocket, acknowledging he'd

won, and set it on the floorboards before ducking back down. Here went nothing. Damn, it smelled bad. I *was* a city boy. "So this girl from the barn, you with me, Danny? She's about five-two—maybe shorter. Blond hair. Green eyes." I banged my head on the floor above me as I tried to avoid kneeling in rat bones. To hell with it, I was too tall. Luckily, a box of clothes had arrived from my mom today. I could burn these pants. Putting the flashlight between my teeth, I crawled toward the sack that'd been thrown down here.

"How old?" Danny asked.

"Don't know." I tried to mumble a reply around my flashlight before sighing and propping it in the dirt. I had incredible night vision, but I'd just as soon not accidentally stick my hand on one of the broken beer bottles. "Might be young—ish. Probably not too young."

"A bit twitchy and mouthy? Watches you like she don't trust you an inch?"

Not quite the adjectives I'd use, but I could see what he was saying. "Sounds about right. Beautiful…uhh, cute."

"That, Gris, was Miss Piper Devon."

"That was Piper?"

"Yep. Should've guessed she'd trespass in our barn."

I rolled my eyes and picked up the sack. It wasn't covered in dust like everything else down here. It was fairly clean. "She seemed all right." Not that I spent a lot of time with anybody my age. The birthright had sort of killed all hopes of being "normal."

"She's stuck-up. Thinks she's smarter than everyone."

"Is she smarter?"

"Well, it's a given that she's valedictorian—has been for a while."

I opened the sack and scooted back toward my flashlight. The scent was potent—sulfur being the strongest.

"Find something?" Danny asked.

"How long has the town seemed bedeviled?" I didn't want to share what I'd found until I knew what it meant.

"Year. Year and a half. Folks started talking about bad dreams and ghosts. Then, some just started to snap—like they couldn't control their impulses."

"How long have the Devons been your neighbors?" Not that I wanted Piper to be the one planting curse sacks like the one in my hand, but I was here to do a job, and it might be over fairly quick.

"Oh, eight or nine years."

Closing my eyes, I tried to find some inner reserve of patience. I'd forgotten how some small towns didn't accept newcomers. Something was wrong in Hidden Creek. Especially if someone was killing dogs.

"Don't underestimate her," Danny said. "Piper is creepy. She watches things. Watches people. She stares at you with this devil look and don't ever blink. You put her in a horror movie and people'd know right off the bat she's evil."

"Only on account of her being the last person you'd suspect. C'mon, Danny, she weighs like one-ten soaking wet and she's sweet." Sweet as sugar, sassy as tart lemonade.

"She stares, Gris. Stares."

Likely imagination on Danny's part. He and his parents were wired to be suspicious because they knew what lurked in the shadows, even if they couldn't see it. They weren't wrong about Hidden Creek, so far. But Piper? She wore cheery, checkered dresses and had a dusting of freckles spread across her face. Evil people didn't have freckles. I tucked the curse bag into one of my pockets and made my way through the crunching, fragile rat bones.

"When you catch her watching you, judging you… She sees things. Knows things. She gets in your head. But maybe you reckon you got nothing to hide. Hell, Gris, you always did act like the sun shines brighter for you. Always getting above your raisin'. It's like you think…"

He muttered a few things under his breath as I reached the break in the floorboards.

"You kiss your mama with that mouth?" I pushed out of the nasty, dusty hole.

Danny raised his eyebrows.

"We've all got something to hide," I said. Most of the people around here were hiding a little shoplifting or maybe some drug abuse in the ugly corners of their souls. My dark corners had wings. "She said her dog got killed this morning."

He stopped what he was doing for a breath, but then he went back to it. "So?"

"That happen a lot?"

"Some. You aren't in the city anymore. We don't dress up our pets like they're kids or paint their toenails. They roam around like animals are supposed to. Shoot, that barn used to have cats until they got into some antifreeze in our garage. We got a decent amount of meaner critters in the woods nearby, too."

"She said somebody had done it—not another dog or another animal. A human did it. *That* doesn't happen all that often, does it? People killing pets?"

He shrugged. "It was probably her."

"You seriously believe she killed her own dog?"

"Hard to say," he said finally. "People are different from how they look sometimes. Even girls. Especially girls." He nodded down at the floorboards that I didn't bother putting back. "What did you find?"

"Nothing." The lie was sour on my tongue. I didn't even know why I was lying. Danny was my cousin.

I'd gotten the birthright and he hadn't. Some part of me knew that was a problem. It was a problem for Critch. Old fool figured I'd stolen the birthright from him. There were only ever two Watchers in a direct line at once, so he'd lost his powers when I'd gotten mine.

"Do you really think one of the Devons could account for the town being bedeviled?" I asked. "Do you think Piper is doing something? You have enough of our Watcher blood to sense things." It was stupid, but I liked her. On the other hand, I was charged with killing fiends, and if she was calling them somehow...

Danny shrugged. "Not all evil looks the same, Gris." He spun his truck keys around a finger and shook his head. "Asked her out once—little over a year ago. On great granddaddy's grave, she looked right through me and said she'd rather not. Who was she waiting round for? Believe it or not, I do all right with girls, but Piper wouldn't give me the time of day. You'd think she'd be less choosy but, no, she shut us all down. Like she could do any better. She'd have been lucky to have Jimmy, and I swear that boy has lice every few weeks."

No wonder she'd been irritable with me. She'd probably seen a lot of the local "charm" played out over the years. At least she hadn't gone for Danny—that suggested she had good taste. I examined the rest of the mill, looking for more sacks. There had to be more. No matter the contents, a single curse sack wouldn't drag in nine fiends.

"She lives in that white farmhouse up the road from your place?" I tossed aside a broken table.

"Yep. You gonna go watch her?"

"I'd like to know what killed her dog." From all Danny had told me, the bedeviling of the town hadn't reaped any human causalities. Some joker might just think it was funny to throw curse sacks around. Hell, Critch might do that just to get back at me.

"Maybe fiends killed the dog. Maybe the whole town is a time bomb. Tick. Tick. Tick." He kicked a bottle and it broke on the wall opposite him.

Hopefully, my cousin hadn't seen me jump. "Fiends *can* kill, but since they feed on people's dark thoughts and nightmares, it'd usually be through collateral damage. Sometimes an animal might be in the way—or if the bedeviling has gone on a while, a person's mind is so far gone, they'll kill others or animals themselves."

"Which is what has been happening here."

"You mean with other animals?"

"There've been a few other issues with animals. Might've been related to fiends—one way or another. This old farmer slaughtered like half his cows one night six months ago. Hasn't been the same since—jumpy. Some said drugs. Some said he just snapped. Some of the guys at school reckoned he sold Piper her dog when it was a pup so she cursed him and made him go mad and kill those cows."

"She cursed him for selling her a pet?"

"The dog *did* bark."

"Piper had nothing to do with this. And there's no real reason for a fiend to kill an animal just to kill it. Animals don't feel fear or anger or pain the way we do. I won't say it's impossible they killed her dog to bedevil her—the fiends here aren't like anything I've ever seen. The way they're behaving means something *is* happening in this town." Hidden Creek had hidden depths—that was for certain.

Danny's eyes were on me when I looked up. He'd complained that Piper stared, but I felt like he was staring at me in a way I didn't care for.

"What?"

"There *is* something about this place. Critch says so anyway. He says Watchers are born where Watchers died. That's how he got the birthright. That's why he lived here. The birthright lingers, haunts, maybe even taints the soil."

A chill ran up my spine, and I abandoned my bag search. "A Watcher died here?"

"Sure did. A whole family line died in Hidden Creek.

Fiends ripped a Watcher to shreds. He's buried in the cemetery on Old Hill road." He shrugged. "That sorta violence don't let up—maybe it makes people crazy—do things they might not normally. And Critch says that Watchers and fiends are drawn to each other." Danny continued spinning the keys on his keyring as we left the mill and walked toward his truck. "There are things here in Hidden Creek, Gris. Things that won't go quietly. You're in over your head. You better watch yourself or Hidden Creek will get you, too."

I didn't like his smile—didn't trust it.

Maybe there was something wrong lurking in Hidden Creek. Something dangerous and evil. But it wasn't Piper.

It couldn't be.

Chapter Four

Gasping, I sat up in bed, clutching the sheets to my chest. Inky darkness hung around me like fog. My nightlight was out. Out of habit, I listened for Jester's barking before realizing he was hushed forever. He'd bark on nights like this when I'd woken up from a screeching nightmare with the room feeling extra dark. Normally, there was still some light. The room was usually shadowed and dim, not dark.

I shivered. I missed Jester. Poor dog. Poor dog in the cold ground.

I swallowed thickly. My fault. My. Fault. I should've taken better care of Jester. It'd hit me a million times today. I'd be doing something and the guilt and grief would threaten to drown me. I bit down hard on my lower lip; the pain pushed my grief back. If only it could erase the memory. Or, better yet, bring him back. A great cosmic do-over for Piper Devon.

But the universe wasn't granting favors in Hidden Creek, lately, and neither were any deities. If anything, we'd been cursed and forgotten.

The least I could do for Jester was find out who'd done it. Work through my list of suspects.

With a shaky exhale, I fumbled on my nightstand for the flashlight I kept there. I swept my hand across the top. What the heck? It was gone. Maybe I'd knocked it off while I was sleeping.

The night felt like it had eyes, despite the darkness. "Is somebody in my room?" I inched my legs out of bed.

Was I really expecting somebody to answer?

Then somebody did, and I realized I would've preferred them not to. "Piper?" a raspy snarl asked. Whatever was out there wasn't human. It sounded like it had teeth. Maybe big, sharp teeth.

I scrambled backward toward my headboard, swallowing. "Who are you?"

"Who do you think I am?"

"I asked you first."

There was a snicker, and the voice hissed, "Don't you ever answer questions?"

I scowled in the direction the voice was coming from. "I'll answer reasonable questions put to me face-to-face by people not afraid to show themselves." Why was I talking to it? It was a lot harder to pretend something didn't exist after you'd talked to it. My fingers clutched the sheets.

"No, you don't." The voice sounded…reptilian.

A shiver whispered up my arms. "Where are you, and who are you?"

"What's happening in this town?" it asked.

"What do you mean?"

"Your dog. The cattle. The library."

It was asking the same questions I'd been asking tonight. "Are you real? Or is this more of my nightmare? Show yourself."

"There are things you don't need to see or know. Tell me about your nightmares, and I'll hand you the flashlight and be gone."

"Fine!" I went still. Somebody else in the house moved in their sleep, and a headboard scraped the wall. I couldn't get anybody else involved in whatever this was. After it was quiet a bit, I whispered, "In my nightmares, I'm walking in a forest with a wind pushing against me. At first, it doesn't bother me, even though it's loud—like a screeching banshee. Then, I look down and it's as if black waves of wind are stealing pieces of me. I start screaming and wake up."

"Have you always had nightmares?"

"Doesn't everyone?"

"Have you always had *these* nightmares?"

"You said you'd give me my flashlight if I told you about my nightmare. I did. Now, give me my flashlight."

"You really are something else, Piper Devon." It was amused, this far-too-real dream-monster. The air stirred as it prowled my room, but it didn't bump into anything. It smelled less like sulfur than the creatures I usually sensed when I was halfway between nightmares and waking. This one smelled deeper and richer, like a freshly-turned field.

"You're different than the others," I said, mostly to fill the silence.

"Others? You've seen something else?"

"After the scream, as I'm waking up, I do. The room is cold, but the wind is there. The dark wind. It knocks things over and moves things."

"And you're sure it's not part of the nightmare?"

"At first, I thought it was just me. I think it's real, though, what's happening. It's not just happening to me. Some other girls at school have talked about it, but I'm the only one in my family with the nightmares. I keep quiet about them, and shut my door so they don't bother anybody. Usually my nightmare

monsters don't talk. You're sorta breaking the rules here."
Now I was lecturing it? *Shut up, Piper.*

"I'm not one of them."

Whatever that meant. It wasn't exactly comforting to
know there were different sorts of monsters living in my room
at night. "Did you kill my dog?"

"No." The end of the word trilled as if its tongue was long
and thin like a snake's.

My hand stopped searching, and I had to know. I had to.
"Did I kill my dog?"

"Shouldn't you know that?"

It was mocking me. I swung my legs back into bed, and
laying back down, I closed my eyes. It would leave or it would
kill me, but there was no way I'd let it make fun of me. I had a
funny type of pride, but I did have it. Now, I'd need to ignore
this monster. Two. Four. Six. Eight.

"Shouldn't you?" it repeated.

"Go away. I'm pretending you don't exist, and it's far
more difficult if you're talking. So, either kill me or go away."
Hopefully, it wouldn't take me at my word and kill me. That'd
be messy at the very least.

"Damn it, Piper."

"Don't profane." Why'd I keep saying that?

"You could make a preacher cuss."

"I haven't yet. Now go away."

"I'm on your side."

I snorted. Right. I was alone with my guilt and my
thoughts and all these regrets that now included Jester. "No,
you're not. Nobody's on my side," I whispered.

"Maybe that's because you won't trust anyone."

"Trust a person…or a monster?"

"What if I'm both?" it hissed.

Something heavy fell at my side, making me jump.
Cool metal. The flashlight! I snatched it, and a rush of wind

fanned my face as I slid my thumb along the switch. The light illuminated my empty bedroom and the curtains blowing around my window. *Pop!* The nightlight flooded the room with its pale blue glow.

Holy crap, what had just happened? Darting the beam of the flashlight around, I searched the corners of my room. Empty. It was gone, whatever it was.

I was awake, and there'd been something here, something that hid in the shadows and snapped off my lights. I got to my feet and closed the window.

The room felt darker now than it ever had, and emptier, too.

I grabbed my list of suspects from my desk, took it back to my bed, and added "creature" to the bottom of it. If anybody came across my list, they'd assume it meant animal. If only.

Hidden Creek—where my nightmares stalked me. I had to get out of this town.

• • •

The ground was soft, but undisturbed. If not for the claw marks around my window frame, I'd have guessed my late-night visitor was a figment of my imagination. I'd decided that a human being had killed Jester, but it was hard to stick by that when a genuine monster had come out of my closet. Well, okay, maybe not my closet. Could monsters even hold knives with their claws? Or maybe it'd been a claw that had done that to Jester.

I swallowed. I had to stop picturing that. My throat burned like acid, and I fought gagging.

I'd even gone to church that morning to do a sort of penance for Jester. Sitting there, with half the chapel staring at me, had felt like a punishment—especially when all the dark, ugly thoughts crept in. Thoughts as black as tar and as filthy. I swore I didn't think of them…they just appeared like waking nightmares. Indecent and vile…and counting only held them off for so long. I wanted to stand up and scream that I didn't belong in there. Church made my head so crowded.

It'd made Mama happy at least. And wasn't I supposed to be miserable? My dog had died. I should be miserable. I hadn't decided how miserable—it was difficult to quantify it, but I deserved misery. It'd be even that way. Unhappiness and pain. It'd balance the scale.

"Hey," a voice said behind me.

I jumped a foot in the air. Crap. That'd taken almost a year off my life. He moved real quiet for somebody so tall. "Hey yourself. Can't you make some noise before you scare a person half to death?"

"Now where's the fun in that?" Gris asked, stepping forward to stare down at the ground below my window. "What are we looking at?"

"Nothing, and I don't talk to strangers." Shuffling slightly in the soft grass, I stayed focused on the ground in front of me.

"Your name is Piper. My name is Gris. We're not strangers anymore."

That caused another jolt, but this time it was my stomach jumping around. He knew my name. I glanced up at him. His cheeks looked less hollowed out here in the sun. His eyes were brown, dark brown, and he had crinkles at the edges like he smiled a lot, probably to get what he wanted.

"I told you, I don't like charming boys." I shaded my eyes. The sun hung behind him like a shimmery outline. A devil wearing an angel's halo—a white, white halo.

"I wasn't trying to be charming." He tipped forward on his feet as if he'd been telling me a dire secret. Clearly, he couldn't help being charming. "So, what are you looking at?"

"Nothing." It wasn't a lie 'cause it was nothing I felt like sharing with him. It was near enough the truth.

He frowned down at the grass under my window and tilted his head.

I followed his gaze, but it just looked like grass to me. Green, green grass. The stain on the grass near the shed yesterday flashed in my head, but I pushed it away with a wince. "What are *you* looking at?"

He crouched down and touched the grass with a finger.

"What is it?" I eased down beside him, watching his face rather than the ground.

"What happened to your dog?"

"Why?" Why did he care what had happened to my dog? "And how do you know my name?"

His head swung my way, and a grin widened his lips. "Are you completely incapable of answering a question?"

The words so closely resembled those of my visitor last night it was eerie. "No," I said, raising my chin an inch. Hah! Gotcha, charm boy.

"Hmm." He looked back at the ground. "My cousin told me your name after I described you. He said he went to school with you and once asked you out."

Whoever his cousin was, Gris had probably heard an earful about me. Maybe Gris coming here was a joke. "Who's your cousin?"

"Danny Porter."

I couldn't stop the grimace. Danny was careless about people's feelings. He'd made a friend of mine cry. It was enough for me to tell him thanks, but no thanks.

What few boys there were at my school always acted like they were doing me this huge favor by asking me out. Hidden Creek was a small town, and they didn't have a lot of options. Dating me wasn't a huge favor to me; it was simply a poor male-to-female ratio.

Although, dating Danny would've been a favor, but not in the way he saw it. He hadn't even bothered taking the ACT 'cause he didn't wanna go to college. What kind of person would rather be stuck in Hidden Creek for the rest of their life? Apparently, I was strange in this, too—I was gonna blow out of here after graduation. Nobody looked twice at you in the big cities. That was a dream come true. I could fade into the crowds.

"You don't look much like Danny," I said.

"We're not much alike."

"But you asked him about me?"

"Uh-huh."

"And he told you?"

"Yep."

I rubbed my shoulder against the itch of a scabbed cut. I felt naked and raw in front of Gris. He knew what they said behind my back, and I didn't.

Just as I was fixin' to stand up and walk away, Gris spoke. "You look tired, Piper. Did you sleep okay?"

That sure wasn't what I was expecting him to say. "Why would you ask that?"

He reached out, and I jumped back, falling to the ground in my rush.

Gris frowned and held up his hands. "I was just about to say you have shadows under your eyes." He gestured at my face. He stood up and offered me a hand, which I ignored and got up on my own.

"I don't always sleep well." Thoughts of Jester had kept me up late. I kept turning over and over my list of suspects. "It takes me hours sometimes to get to sleep and when I do, dreams wake me up." It was a dream last night. It had to be. In the light of day, it was too strange, too unreal. The monster had spoken. Unless they were inside my head, my monsters kept quiet. I brushed the dirt from my butt. Why had I chosen today to wear light-colored cut-offs? I normally prepared for a multitude of possibilities, but it was difficult to account for something as far-fetched as Gris.

"Dreams? What kind of dreams?"

"Maybe I dreamed about you," I said tartly to put him off balance.

His cheeks went pale. "What?" he blurted out, his mouth hanging open. Recovering, Gris snapped his jaw closed as his face went blank.

What had his cousin told him about me? I'd been messing with Gris when I'd said that. I cleared my throat. "It was a little like *The Wizard of Oz*. I was Dorothy and your barn fell on top of you…so you can imagine who you were."

It startled a laugh out of him. Still, why had he acted like me dreaming about him would be a fate worse than death?

"What are you doing here?" I tapped my fingers together. I could usually tell what people thought of me, but I couldn't make hide nor hair of Gris.

"I want to figure out what happened to your dog."

"He's dead. That's what happened. And I don't need your help figuring out how that came to be."

"You said somebody killed him?"

I shrugged. It wasn't any of his business.

"Let me help you, Piper. I swear I can if you'll let me." His drawl made his words even softer, and they curled around my heart in a way I didn't trust.

"I don't need your…whatever this is." I gestured between us. I did just fine without a boy in my life making it all sorts of complicated. I didn't *need* him.

"Friendship," he said.

I snorted. It sounded awful, but it was a near gut reaction. Friendship. Not a single boy in town had bothered with that route. Not that I'd buy it if they had. Gris was a smooth one, all right. 'Course, he was related to Danny which probably meant he was looking for a way to score with the crazy girl— which was probably how everybody thought of me. I saw it in their eyes sometimes, felt it in their treatment of me. If they could see inside my head, they'd think even worse things, but, for certain, I was crazy.

My shoulder itched again, but I was ignoring it. If I stopped thinking about it, it'd stop itching. I rolled my shoulder. *Stop. Just stop.*

"Show me where you found your dog's body," Gris said.

Fine then, I could do that. I led him past the house toward the shed that held our tractor. We didn't have much of a field, but my daddy insisted on owning a tractor. Then again, we didn't do much camping, but we had an RV parked on the other side of the house. My daddy liked to own things, just in case we needed them.

When I reached the spot behind the shed where a pile of hay had been brushed across the stain, I stopped and pointed. "It isn't pleasant."

"Death usually isn't." Gris continued forward and crouched beside the hay like he had beneath my window.

"Somebody'd split him open. There was blood all across the grass here. I'd just gotten back from taking my ACT, and my mama said she hadn't seen Jester all morning."

"Was he a family dog or your dog?" Gris pulled aside the hay to reveal a red patch of grass.

I turned away. I was working on disassociation. I could disassociate myself from just about anything. But it was harder when you were faced with something tangible like the grass that was still stained. *Jester, you poor, silly dog.* They'd probably killed him 'cause he belonged to me. Maybe I'd said "no" to one too many guys. Maybe they just didn't like me. I felt the weight of everything that'd gone wrong—that I'd done wrong, but Jester was a debt that I'd never repay.

"He was my dog. I've had him for three years now. I *had* him, I mean. I *used to* have him." There was no way to define his presence in my life now that he was an absence. I inhaled deeply before breathing out through pursed lips. Then, I built up my wall of detachment—brick by brick. My fault. I clenched my fists, my nails biting into my palms. I could do this. The pain in my palms helped.

"It's awful that you were the one to find him."

"She threw up. She retched in the rosebushes," I said. Hopefully, Daddy had taken care of cleaning that up too. I hadn't dared look.

"Uhh, are you talking about yourself, Piper?"

I rolled my eyes and sniffed back the tears that had almost escaped. "No. Mama did when she saw it. I don't blame her. He was all laid out, and then the blood…"

"So, it definitely wasn't an animal that did this."

"No. It was…neat. Animals don't kill that way. Only human beings kill cleanly. Also, Jester would have made a racket if another animal came after him, like you said. One moment, he was barking—then he wasn't. There's something dark and filthy about that." I lifted my hand to my necklace and ran the locket at my throat back and forth, back and forth. It was my mama's and empty, but there was something soothing about the weight of it around my neck. "Mama has been trying to convince everybody it was an animal. She thinks if she tells my brother enough times, it'll be true. But it wasn't an animal." My voice wobbled.

"There are animals around here that'll attack livestock and such."

"The edges of where he'd been torn into…" I swallowed. "It had to have been done with a knife. A sharp knife. I mean, I only saw him for a few seconds, but I remember." I'd always remember. "He'd been barking around midnight. I'd heard him. I yelled at him. I can't take that back. Ever. When he stopped, I was happy." My voice cracked on the last word. I paid for being happy more than I ever paid for being sad.

His hand touched my shoulder, firmly and briefly. "I

covered it back up. The police must've had something to say about…the way he was."

"My parents didn't call them."

"Why? Because they really believe it was an animal?"

My thirteen-year-old brother, Dale, would think it was a cool story, but I wasn't sure if he'd hold to Mama's version of events. He was in this morbid phase where dead things were cool and all of his online games included shooting zombies. By school tomorrow, everybody would've heard something from him and come to their own conclusions. Small towns sometimes sucked eggs in that way. Everybody knew everybody's business. "They want to believe that. Sometimes, that's the best way to deal with unpleasantness. You move on."

I hadn't planned on telling anybody that. It was his charm. No, it was something about the way he looked at me that had me wanting to tell him all my secrets. Plus, he always looked at my face, and not my legs or my chest. It was different—like he did actually want to be my friend.

"Sometimes, it is easier to move on," he agreed.

"I never move on from anything," I whispered, staring at his shoulder. He was over a foot taller than me, so his shoulder was closer to my eye level.

"If you're going to find out who did this, I'm going to help you. Whoever did it might be trying to send you a message or planning to do worse." A heavy sigh made his black T-shirt rise and fall. "I'm hungry. Let's go grab some lunch. I brought an extra helmet."

I blinked up at him. We were going out to lunch?

All right. Yeah, I could do that.

His body went still, and he looked in the distance. "I hear sirens. Hurry, and we'll go see what they're up to."

I didn't hear a thing, but I nodded. "Fine then, I'll go tell Mama."

Chapter Five

GRIS

With Piper pressed up against my back, every rise and shallow of her body brushed mine as the bike bumped along the dirt roads around Hidden Creek. She had her fist bunched up in the fabric of my shirt. Was she scared? Her sudden burst of laughter ratchetted up my body's temperature and then she yelled, "Go faster, Gris!"

I went faster. Her excitement was nearly tangible. Her fidgety shifting was for a whole different reason. A good reason.

The sunlit fields full of blooming wildflowers seemed to match Piper's new mood. She was carefree—something I hadn't seen in her yet, and I liked it. That I'd thought of this and dragged my bike over made me like it even more. It was feeling more like a date and less like an attempt to interrogate her.

Piper laughed again, tightening her legs on either side of me.

Even though it was still cool and not even noon, I started to sweat under my helmet. The humidity and heat of summer would be unbearable, but I planned to be long gone before this spring season had passed. I shouldn't get too attached to the girl with me.

I was up to about 95 percent certain she wasn't roping in the fiends—purposefully. The curse pouches I'd removed from her room last night had different ingredients than the one I'd found at the mill—nothing uncommon or unusual. But they still drew in fiends. I'd killed three outside her room and shoved two more out her window.

Piper somehow managed to scoot even closer. Her legs were right up against my thighs, and I could see her knees out of the bottom of my helmet.

I went faster.

I slowed down at the end of the short road and stared down Old Hill Road at the flashing lights in front of a cemetery.

"What do you reckon happened?" Piper pulled off her helmet and stared hard down the road. "That's the cemetery. Why would the sheriff be at the cemetery?"

I shrugged. I almost didn't want to know.

"Should we go ask?"

I smiled. "How would that go? 'Yeah, sheriff, I'm new to town, but I see you're investigating a crime, and I'd like to know more about it.'"

She slapped my shoulder. "Maybe we don't have to ask then. C'mon, I know a back way in." After she put her helmet back on, Piper directed me down a few narrow roads then motioned to leave the bike. We crept along another winding path and emerged behind a tall stone mausoleum on the edge of the cemetery.

"That's in the old part of the cemetery," Piper said. "Real old. Nobody there is fresher than the fifties."

I peeked around the mausoleum and asked, "Do you

come here often?"

"This is where our history is. The people who are alive today have nothing on those buried here. They have stories the years are eating away. Sometimes I come here to listen to the dead speak in dates. Agnes Phillips, beloved wife, mother, knitter." She pointed at a nearby grave. "Horace Turner. Died December 7th, 1941. Pearl Harbor. I confirmed it in the library 'cause I wanted to be sure."

I tried not to stare at her. Piper had to be one of the most fascinating people I'd ever met.

"Anyway, I read the dates and guessed at how they lived and died."

"Do you know whose grave they've cordoned off?"

"No, but give me your phone." She stared at the image of a gargoyle before handing it back. "Unlock it."

Right. Something about Piper scattered my wits. After unlocking it, I swiped away the gargoyle screen and handed her my phone again.

Piper held it up and used the zoom feature on the camera. Squinting, she said, "Oh, I do know that one. Silas Beaumont. I was totally wrong about him. It was a bad year for the Great Depression, but that was right before prohibition was repealed, so I thought, what is a desperate man in Hidden Creek going to do to earn a living?"

"Leave Hidden Creek," I suggested.

"That's my plan, but I figured Silas probably died from a bad batch of moonshine." She wrinkled up her nose. "It was an animal attack. There was an article about it in the local paper. I looked it up at the library." Chewing on her lower lip, she shifted the phone up and snapped a picture. "But here's the really cool thing. You're not the only one who likes gargoyles."

I snatched the phone from her hand and stared at the photo. It was a little blurry, but there was unmistakably a sculpture of a gargoyle perched on top of the grave. Oh, that wasn't good. I'd been to enough of my family's graves to recognize signs of a Watcher's burial plot.

"What is it?" Piper asked.

"Uhh, nothing. Just surprised to see gargoyles in Hidden Creek." Danny had said a Watcher died here. And if the birthright really did linger and haunt the way Uncle Critch claimed, then it wasn't a stretch to assume this grave was connected with the rabid fiend population.

There are things here in Hidden Creek that won't go quietly.

"Why would somebody dig up such an old grave?" Piper stood on her tiptoes.

No good reason. Still, to distract her, I asked, "Do you want me to put you on my shoulders?"

Piper blushed bright pink and sent me a repressive frown.

I needed to get back here, but not with all the police around—and certainly not with Piper. It'd probably be clear after dark. "I'm starving. Let's get out of here."

Her green eyes narrowed. "Don't you have any natural curiosity?"

Oh, I was real curious. "You're half my size, so you can't possibly understand how much energy I need just to stay standing."

Laughing, she shook her head. "Fine. But something is going on in Hidden Creek, and I'm going to find out what it is."

I couldn't disagree with that. In fact, as we rode toward town, I had to face the fact that I'd practically encouraged it. I shouldn't let her get involved. I was used to hunting monsters; she wasn't. Jester's death could be part of an escalation. Maybe somebody just hated the Devons—and the tiny blonde behind me in particular. Hard to believe, but plausible.

"I don't suppose that diner on First is any good."

Piper slapped my helmet this time. "'Course it's good. Good enough for civilized people."

Alrighty then, Dick's Diner it was. Every small town had a diner like it. Joe's. Moe's. Fred's. Half the time, they made grease run through your veins. The other half, well, they weren't any good.

"So, I take it you've eaten here before?" I asked as we walked in. I ineffectively tried to rub the helmet look out of my hair.

Piper ignored the question, just like she'd ignored all the previous ones.

Dick's Diner had two dozen red vinyl booths and Formica tables. There was a counter around the grill where a few older folks were eating, and a group of jocks in the corner booth scowled at me. The menu had weird items like "Ethyl's special chicken covered in Judy's sausage gravy"—a private joke against outsiders. I'd eaten at a Joe's Diner in a town outside of Tampa after a job and "Tom's special chicken" had turned out to be alligator.

"I've never gone that fast," Piper said, pulling strands of her hair from her face. The wind from our ride made her skin flush pink and her eyes sparkle. She looked more like a pixie than ever. A patch of light freckles dusted her thin nose. She had freckles on her knees, too, a thought that made me uncomfortably warm. "That was amazing. Sorta like flying."

Not quite, but close, and as close as most people would ever get.

I forced myself to look at her face, and not just at her mouth. I didn't want to be too obvious. Making eye contact was good, so I stared at her green eyes, trying to figure out their exact color. Not grass green, more of a light mossy color. Maybe the color of mold on bread? Wow. I'd need to think of something better than that.

At least I wasn't focused on the same parts of her as the

idiots behind me, placing bets on whether or not I'd get "into" her. They were quiet enough that she wouldn't be able to hear, but I wanted to punch them. The cook behind the grill had glanced their way a few times. Maybe somebody else would tell them to shut their big mouths.

Our waitress came up and watched Piper arrange her silverware in front of her.

Piper refolded her napkin into a triangle after sliding the silverware out. Everything was exact and everything had a place. Every motion she made was controlled and just-so.

She met my eyes and smiled tightly—as if waiting for me to comment.

I didn't.

I turned into a gargoyle. She only liked things a certain way. There'd be no judgement from my side of the table.

"The usual, Piper?" the waitress asked.

Piper nodded. She smiled, a real genuine smile. Her upper lip had a freckle on it, near the corner. I'd been staring at it earlier, fantasizing about how her lips might taste. All the shadows were gone from her green eyes when she smiled, and that freckle hovered in the corner of her mouth, tempting me.

"What'll you have?" the waitress asked me.

"Whatever she's having." I handed back the menu. I could eat everything and anything.

Piper's green eyes met mine, and a challenging look replaced her amused one. Yeah, I needed a better way to describe her eyes than bread mold—they were sharp and intelligent.

"A Piper's Special? You sure about that?" the waitress asked, her pen poised.

Piper's eyes dared me. Her special must be more than a straight burger and fries.

"Yes, ma'am. Whatever she's having." I never backed down from a challenge, and I was practicing a new kind of charm on Piper.

"Fine then. Two Piper Specials." The waitress drew out the words, and the implication was "it's your funeral." She walked away, shaking her head.

"I feel like I'm not in on a joke," I said.

Piper's pointed chin firmed as her jaw tightened. I'd got this same reaction earlier when I'd mentioned my cousin's name. "Yeah, I get that feeling a lot." She glanced behind me at the pack of boys.

I turned. The five boys made a big production of *not* looking at her, but whispering just the same.

"Why did you have an extra helmet?" she asked.

"Borrowed it from the Porters. They fix bikes in their shop and had one for test rides."

"So, you came over to take me on a ride?"

"I was hoping it'd help get your mind off things."

Her nose wrinkled up as she tilted her head. Maybe she wasn't used to the attention. She'd better get used to it. I planned on giving her a lot of attention—for as long as I was here.

"Though I hadn't intended on the extremely cheery side-trip to the cemetery."

Her gaze shifted to stare unfocused over my shoulder. "Just another mystery for this year."

Another mystery—or a clue to the murder of her dog?

Remembering all the blood beside the shed was enough to freeze my veins. It was cold. Cruel. There'd been enough there to paint the shed. And it wasn't fiends. When they harmed or killed outside of a swarm, it was to torment the mind of their intended victim. This had happened too far away from Piper. Fiends were more immediate than that. This had been calculated and must've taken some time. Then, there had been tiny drops of blood beneath her window. Somebody'd killed her dog and then gone to her window and looked in.

Nothing in the nature of fiends fit this.

Hidden Creek was spitting out uglier things than I usually handled. For once, I wished it was fiends; I could predict them.

Piper's fingers darted out to adjust my knife a hair. Then, her eyes flew up to meet mine, partly nervous, but also daring me to say something. I tried to keep my expression blank. There was a fierce aspect to her, even when she was vulnerable. Like how last night she kept searching for the flashlight while giving me a tongue-lashing. She'd kept her composure while conversing with a monster.

Piper rearranged the salt and pepper shakers, ketchup, and maple syrup. She'd moved on to aligning the local advertisement for a community play with the napkin dispenser when I said, "I once had this ferret named Fred, smartest critter I'd ever met. He got out of every cage he was put in. I'd had him two years when he decided to take a stroll outside. He fell into this bucket right below my window. It'd been collecting rainwater. The edges were too slick for him to climb, and he drowned."

For all her forced detachment, Piper looked tragically upset on behalf of Fred. "That's awful."

"It was like six years ago, but I remember hating myself because my mom had asked me to dump the bucket earlier that day. So, it took me some time to work through that before I could even begin to hate him for dying on me."

"Hate him?"

"They're supposed to live forever." I sat back, giving her room to think it over.

Boys around here'd certainly done a number on her willingness to trust another soul. Luckily, I was patient. Well, sorta patient anyway. I wasn't gonna be in Hidden Creek forever. But I wasn't looking for a quick score. Not that I was looking for a relationship, either; that wasn't an option for me. I clenched my jaw. Damn, maybe I was being as bad as the locals.

I smiled. "If we're both looking into this, seems convenient if we work on it together then, doesn't it?" After seeing that her dog's murderer had stopped by her window, no way was I leaving her to investigate this alone. And I was going to be dropping by to check her place in my rounds of Hidden Creek. The only one stopping by her window was going to be me.

The waitress set plates in front of us and then waited. Clearly, a response was expected to whatever I'd ordered. It was a burger. A burger that smelled funny. Plus, my fries were on an entirely separate plate with something white. Mayo? Tartar? Ranch dressing?

I lifted the top bun of the burger. Huh.

Piper grinned before she took a bite of her burger.

"Is that what I think it is?" I asked the waitress, pointing at what sat atop my burger.

"I reckon it might be. Crunchy peanut butter with pieces of bacon mixed in on the top bun only. Sesame seed bun toasted just past tan. Two pieces of lettuce underneath the burger. Fries on a separate plate with tartar sauce."

"Same as me," Piper said. She was enjoying the moment.

The waitress waved a hand at the shake she'd put directly below a long spoon. It looked like an exclamation point. Piper's matched in position exactly. "That there's a banana caramel shake with chocolate chips on top." She snorted a laugh before deadpanning, "Enjoy."

I'd never eaten anything so strange. Crunchy peanut butter? Who put that on a burger? The rest wasn't quite as unusual, even if it was more specific than I'd ever ordered it. I generally ate what was on the menu or what was put in front of me. It was the only way I'd ever even skirt the edges of a full stomach.

"Was this on the menu?" I picked up the burger.

"Nah, that's why it's the Piper Special." Piper took

another bite and closed her eyes with a sigh of appreciation. She even made eating sexy.

I took a bite.

Everybody in the diner was waiting to see my reaction. Their gazes made the hair on the back of my neck stand at attention. Small towns.

The peanut butter blended with the bacon and burger. There were enough flavors all at once that I was surprised at how good it was. "Did you come up with this all on your own?"

Piper shrugged. "I'm special that way. It actually started out with Dick saying, 'Piper is special, so she gets her fries on a separate plate, and she gets the best-looking lettuce so I don't have to deal with her complaining.' Now he just calls the whole thing Piper's Special. He was gonna put it on the menu as Piper's Special, but I told him I didn't want…that."

She didn't want the attention.

"You're a genius," I said.

She smiled while pressing her napkin to her mouth. I loved how polite she was. My mom would love that, too. Mom hadn't been impressed with the girls in Atlanta I'd dated. She said they had the manners of badgers dressed up to look like humans.

Piper put her napkin down to the side of her plate. She had another on her lap that she'd unfolded and kept ironing the wrinkles out of with her hands.

"You like the burger?" she asked.

"Best thing I've ever eaten."

Another round of betting took place behind me. If I was laying down money, I'd bet whatever Piper wanted, Piper got. Including me…if that's what she wanted.

Leaning across the Formica table, Piper whispered, "You'll have to leave a decent tip when you ask for it, though. Dick isn't above spitting in food if you annoy him, and I'm not so sure he'll go to all this trouble for somebody new in town."

I glanced over at the older man at the grill. He was in his forties, a big man with shrewd eyes that were watching me. He either wanted my response to the burger or to Piper. Both were good, but he'd probably appreciate me lusting after the burger more than Piper. He flashed her a rather paternal smile when she gave him a thumbs up.

"Especially someone renting," she added, frowning.

I saw the moment it occurred to her that I might not be anything more than a transient person in her life.

"I have family here." It might be the one and only time I claimed Danny.

And it backfired. She nodded, and her spine stiffened.

Behind me, a chair scraped the floor as one of the jocks got up from their table. The heavy tread of boots thudded on the diner's floor, heading in our direction. Great. Just what the moment needed.

"Hey, Piper." The guy's hair was brown, but buzzed short, and his nose looked like it had been broken once. He was bulkier than Danny, but shorter than me. "Who's he?" He nodded at me with a flat expression that his tight-muscled stance contradicted.

Piper eyed him warily, but she hadn't heard the betting behind me—she didn't look pissed enough. "This is Gris, Hank. He's...uhh, Danny's cousin." Not how I wanted her defining my place in the world.

"You're Danny's cousin?" Hank asked. "Danny says you hunt monsters and ghosts."

Thanks, Danny. Real nice. I couldn't punch Hank for that. I might punch Danny instead. My business was my business, and it should've been my right to spread it around.

"Pretty much," I answered.

Hank laughed and called to his friends, "He really does. Danny weren't messin' with us."

They all laughed.

Piper retreated even more—either because of their laughter or because it was obvious she knew very little about me.

"He said you're like Batman, too. You have all this money and you sleep during the day."

I ignored that. I had to. Danny hadn't just been referring to money and my sleeping habits when he'd brought up Batman. I sipped my shake and took another bite of my burger. "Does it taste as good if it's not crunchy peanut butter?" I asked Piper.

She shook her head. "Plus, there's the texture."

"He says you're rich," Hank interrupted us. "Are you rich?"

Piper froze like a statue again.

I shrugged. "Inheritance." It was my standard answer. I'd inherited being a Watcher and money came with it. It was the way my funny little world worked. I'd had a career at six years old.

"Why are you here in Hidden Creek?" he asked.

"Seemed like the thing to do and the place to do it." Then, because he'd pissed me off talking about Piper earlier, I added, "My aunt thought it might be nice for Danny to have a good example around for a bit. She says he hangs out with jerks who aren't worth a girl's time." I looked at Hank. "So, you're friends with Danny?"

It was worth it to see Piper hide a laugh by turning away and covering her mouth.

I darted sideways quick so that Hank's fist hit a metal bar on the back of the seat. It was likely pissing painful even before I swept his legs out from under him. He fell flat on his back with a loud *swack* that got everybody's attention.

The cook jumped from behind the counter right as Hank's friends stood up.

"All of y'all, cool it," the cook said to the others. He was my height with an additional hundred pounds of bulk from eating the same food he cooked. He reached down a hand to help Hank up before asking me, "You fixin' to make trouble?"

"He was defending me," Piper said just as I opened my mouth.

The cook, whose name badge proclaimed him to be "Dick—Owner" smiled at Piper, before frowning at Hank. "What's the matter with you? Your daddy know you're still picking fights?"

"He told me to make sure I win 'em." Hank rubbed his fist while scowling at me.

"Not in my place." Dick gestured at the door. "Pay your bill and stay away for a week, or I'll have a talk with him and spit in your food."

Hank nodded. "We was leaving anyhow."

His friends shuffled by. One of them, tall, sharp-eyed, mouthed, "You're dead." I didn't like the way his gaze lingered on Piper. They paid their bill, grumbling, but under Dick's watchful eye.

When the door shut behind them, Dick turned to Piper. "Sweet Pea asked if she could come play with your dog sometime this week."

Piper wiped her mouth with her napkin, and this time I saw tears flood her eyes.

"Somebody killed her dog yesterday," I said.

Dick's eyebrows rose, and he looked to Piper for confirmation. She nodded, even though she had closed her eyes, keeping her body tense and shut-off.

"*Somebody?*" Dick repeated.

Piper covered her face with her hands, and her shoulders shook in silent sobs. Our waitress came over and hugged Piper.

I swallowed. I'd thought her control was unnerving, but

seeing her cry tore at my heart.

Dick stared out the diner's windows where engines revved as Hank and his friends took off. He frowned, but muttered, "They're stupid, but I can't see them killing a dog."

What was I supposed to say? I agreed, but I didn't have a better answer. Telling him that wasn't likely the answer he wanted from the new guy around.

"Hank used to be better," Dick said. "I mean, he's a bully like his daddy, but he got much worse after what happened to his sister last year."

I filed that away. Another unusual occurrence within the last year.

He tapped his fingers on the table twice. "You let me know if you need any help…uhh…"

"Gris. Gris Caso, I'm staying in the house across from the Porters for a bit." I shook the hand he held out.

"I don't like this business with Jester," Dick said. "It's ugly in ways we haven't seen here. This ain't that kind of place, you know? Didn't used to be, anyway. Been full of surprises, lately."

Piper pushed out of the waitress's hug with a stoic smile stretching her mouth. "We saw the police at the cemetery. I figured you'd know what it was about." She sniffed and bit her lip—hard. It seemed to give her a measure of control, and she sat a little straighter.

Dick snorted. "I probably knew before the sheriff. Everybody's been talking about it up until you two strolled in. Somebody dug up an old grave." He gave me a suspicious look.

I shook my head. "Not me." I'd been up to other things last night, other things I wouldn't be sharing.

Piper glared at him, and she punched his shoulder. "Dick! It wasn't Gris." I liked how quick she was to defend me.

"I heard he's some kind of ghost hunter. Maybe he went

to the source." Dick rubbed his shoulder where she'd punched it.

I held up my hands, flipping them side-to-side. A night of digging would've shown under my nails.

Dick grinned. "You've got city boy hands."

I shoved my hands back under the table. When I was in Watcher form, I had claws and hard-shelled skin, but he was right about my human hands.

Shrugging, Dick added, "Besides they're not sure it was dug up last night. It was in a quieter part of the cemetery— could've happened a few days before." His expression said I wasn't off the hook.

The door opened. Dick and the waitress both called greetings to the older couple who strolled in. The waitress squeezed Piper's shoulder before heading to get the newcomers' orders.

"Your heart attacks are on the house. Least I can do for Jester," Dick said, going back behind the counter.

"So, umm, you're a paranormal investigator?" Piper exhaled. "That's…" I waited for her to finish, but she just shook her head as if she couldn't find a polite word.

"Yes."

"Like a medium?"

"No. I research paranormal events."

"And you're here."

I cleared my throat. "I have family here."

"You're not here on a job?"

I couldn't lie to her. "I *am* here on a job."

She nodded. "I know absolutely nothing about you."

"That's not true."

"You're right. I know I can't trust you. I don't know if you'll be here in a week, or that you're not like your cousin, or that you're not just interested in me 'cause I'm weird and strange things have happened." She pushed to her feet. "Excuse me. I see someone who can give me a ride. It was nice meeting you again, Mr. Gris Caso, paranormal investigator."

I swore under my breath.

"Don't profane." Piper shook her head and called out, "Lorna, are you headed home?" to someone leaving. She was gone a moment later.

I tightened my fist around the napkin in my hand before forcibly relaxing. Piper wasn't wrong and, hell, she didn't know the half of what I was keeping from her.

Don't get too attached, Gris.

Dick sat down across from me a second later. "Struck out pretty hard there."

"Thanks for noticing."

"What was it? If you don't mind me asking."

I did mind, but I also didn't want to alienate everybody in town. "I think it was…everything actually. I'm still going to find out what happened to her dog."

Dick started in on the remainder of Piper's fries. "Want some advice?" He dipped a fry in her tartar sauce, then ate it. It was probably very "city boy" of me that it seemed kind of unhygienic.

"Sure."

"I don't know if this paranormal investigator shtick is some sort of snake oil business."

"It's not." I was saving their town from being bedeviled into madness—and not even getting paid. Unbelievable, but not a con.

He waved that away. "If you want to know what's happening in this town, you'll make nice with Piper. Piper waited tables for me over the summer, and she pays attention. I mean, she really pays attention, and nobody knows the dirt on a town like the people who are hovering nearby to see if you're ready for your check yet."

I looked out the window where Piper was chatting

amiably with one of the servers while heading toward the woman's car. Just before getting in, Piper looked at me. Her jaw tightened, and she slid into the passenger seat.

Dick laughed. "I'd meet her on neutral ground, though."

"Where's that?"

"Her second home."

"Here?"

"The library." He got up from the table with Piper's plate. "She's there nearly every day after school. Good luck."

I wiped a hand down my face and stared out the window. Piper was an obstinate, complicated, beautiful puzzle, and she had a point. This place would be in my side mirror in a couple weeks. Though I wasn't leaving until I was sure Piper was safe. Someone had been putting curse bags in her room for a while. Killing her dog had been an enormous escalation.

Pulling my phone out, I started making notes of situations and people to check out. Suddenly, Hidden Creek had way too many people, and the only person I was ruling out as a suspect was Piper Devon. Ninety-seven percent sure.

• • •

It was difficult to tell whether Piper was awake or not. It was late, but she slept with at least one of her lights on. Her breathing didn't seem slow or deep enough for her to be asleep. I wasn't going inside, not tonight.

I tackled a fiend outside her window, muffling the sound as it turned and tried to claw my eyes. I drove my fist into its chest and ripped out its heart. The fiend dissolved with one last shriek only I could hear. I shook the sticky guts off my fingers, even though they disintegrated, too. Their insides were the consistency of wet sand. It got underneath my claws before they dissolved. Danny and his mom might think the birthright was a blessing, but we earned the money we made.

Most jobs, you could take a day off. If I did, fiends had an extra day to get into a person's brain and drive them mad with nightmares. Other cities contacted us. Cities and governments. Small towns like this one usually didn't know or worry about their fiend population. Of course, most other rural farming towns likely didn't have relations to Watchers living there to recognize things had gone wrong.

I'd cleaned out Piper's room and yard of fiends last night. Tonight, there were just as many as before, as if I'd never done it. I must've missed a curse bag…or two.

Behind me, a fiend shrieked in the air, diving at my back. I swung around as it shot from the roof straight at me. Ornery things always tried to tear my wings off. Its momentum knocked me to the ground. My outstretched claws plunged into its chest. Greasy and gritty fiend gore dripped down all over me, and I turned my face away, even as it sizzled and disintegrated. It was like a gross form of pixie dust. Only these Tinkerbells were six and seven feet tall, reeked of brimstone, and had fangs and claws.

I lay on the ground for a minute, catching my breath. If it'd managed to tear my wings off—wings which were very much a part of me—and there were other fiends waiting to attack, it might be easy enough to kill me. I'd never imagined such a thing, but that Watcher's grave and Danny's story about the Watcher dying here had gotten into my head.

After shifting back into human form, I inhaled shakily and got up. It was rare fiends managed to break any of my bones, and I did heal faster, but I was feeling unusually fragile tonight. My Watcher body had a hard shell, more muscle mass, and I had talons of my own. Feeling my own mortality like this was ridiculous.

I reached into my pocket and pulled out my phone. I'd gotten a bulletproof case because my phones didn't seem to care for crash landings or being slammed into things at high-velocity. This phone had lasted six weeks now—a new record.

I added to the notes on my phone as I walked back home. I never wore shoes or a shirt at night because my Watcher form would split both, but I drew the line at pants. I wore pants. They were loose, and I tore through them fairly regularly.

The cemetery would have to wait a night. I'd flown by there earlier and there was a sheriff's cruiser hidden in the nearby bushes—probably hoping the vandal would come back to check things out.

There was still plenty of research to be done, and my laptop was one of the few things I was never without. Since Hidden Creek didn't put so much as their newspaper online, visiting the library tomorrow had a two-fold purpose.

I sensed their presence in the bushes the second I stepped onto my property, but it was too late to wrap the night around me and muffle my approach. Hell, I'd be messing with the demonic *and* dumb tonight.

"You guys might as well come out. I hear your breathing," I shouted, stopping in the middle of my front yard.

Their shadowed forms fanned out as they walked toward me. It was Hank from the diner, and he'd brought along four little friends. It wasn't a fair fight, but I'd never held with fighting fair. Hopefully, their vision wasn't anywhere near as good as mine. I planned to keep my wings tucked in, but once it was five against one, my talons might come out.

Hank swung a sledgehammer in his hand—a one-man welcoming committee, even without the other four.

"You couldn't take me by yourself so you've brought that rockbreaker with you as well as your pack?" I asked.

Snorting, Hank gestured behind him. "No, they're here to clap when you're down. And this"—he held up the sledgehammer—"well, I helped you get a start on breaking up your firewood." He nodded at the house.

I'd picked up wood because I was planning to rebuild the

swing I'd broken. Now it was all the size of splinters. "Damn."

The guys snickered. Hank handed off the sledgehammer to his closest buddy and dropped into a crouch with his fists up.

"I'm not about to fight you," I said. If it was only Hank and me, it wasn't fair, and I might not be able to prevent myself from transforming. "Y'all are trespassing and you vandalized my property. Clear out before I call the police."

I knew it wouldn't work. I knew it even as I said it. Hank had lost face in front of his buddies, and he wanted to get revenge. I wasn't expecting him to move so fast. He ducked down and barreled into me before I had a chance to do more than brace myself. Hank was solidly built, and I rolled before he landed on top of me. He knocked the wind out of me, but fiends did that nightly. My wings shivered as my skin pulsed, begging to transform. But I could control the monster inside me. I'd had enough practice. I stayed Gris.

He swung a fist at my face, but I moved out of the way. "You're quick." Hank threw himself toward me. He had no idea.

I moved again. One of Hank's friends dove at my back, trying to pin me down, but I dodged him, too, and he ran into Hank's fist.

"Stop it, Jared!" Hank yelled.

"I was trying to hold him for you." Jared clutched his nose. It looked and sounded like a bloody nose, if not a broken one.

Somebody else dove for my back, and I ducked down and flipped him overtop me so he landed on Hank.

"Dammit, Carl!" Hank yelled after he bounced up from the ground.

Carl was down on the grass, moaning and clutching his ribs. "I think you might've broken something, Hank."

"It weren't my fault you flew into me!"

Hank managed a solid punch to my stomach. I doubled

over and considered tossing him, too, but his laughter stopped me. If this made us even, it was worth faking his punch had done more than a fiend managed on an ordinary night. I groaned.

"That's what you get!" Hank said.

Sure enough, his buddies clapped and whooped—those who didn't have a broken nose or fractured rib.

Footsteps came running behind me, and Danny appeared. "Y'all better get the hell outta here. My crazy uncle called the police."

They bolted, dragging Jared and Carl, to where they'd parked beside the Porters' machine shop. In a rush of tires in dirt, they were gone, laughing and shouting. The sledgehammer lay on the ground in front of me, dropped in the rush.

"They're gone. You can quit faking," Danny said.

I stood up straight. "You could tell?"

Danny rolled his eyes. "You're a Watcher. If you couldn't take them, then you're a right sorry Watcher, and you wouldn't still be alive. I sorta hoped you'd change when they rushed you."

"You were watching?"

"Sure was."

"Aren't you friends with Hank?"

Danny shrugged. At least he'd gotten rid of them. I wasn't sure exactly why he'd done that, but I was obliged to him for it. I picked up the sledgehammer and hefted it. This might come in handy, and it was one less weapon in the wrong hands.

"Why didn't you fly home?" he asked. "They might not have seen you that way."

Danny followed me onto my porch. He was right. They might not have. Or they might've seen me and had strange stories to tell. I wasn't sure why he was asking. Maybe he'd been hoping to see me fly, too. I wasn't used to so many people being all in my business.

"It uses a lot of energy, and sometimes I get bugs in my teeth." I stared down at the wood. I'd have to borrow my uncle's truck again.

"I figured Hank'd be by after what you did at the diner," Danny said. I should've figured as much, too. Hank wasn't the type to let things go. "Why were you at her place tonight?"

"Piper had some fiends around that I took care of."

Danny turned and stared at Piper's house. "How many?"

I lied. I didn't have much of a reason to, other than Danny knew fiends were drawn to evil at times, and I didn't want him thinking Piper was dangerous. "Just a couple. Not a big deal."

Danny continued staring at Piper's house.

"Where you been tonight, Danny?" His red pickup had been gone earlier.

"Out. With a girl. Just got back." He smiled in the direction Hank and his friends had gone.

"Is that a fact?"

"Turns out being kin to somebody as ugly as you doesn't make that impossible."

"Yeah, well, you're lucky being ugly isn't a crime because that face would earn you a life sentence," I said.

"You look like your face caught on fire and people tried to put it out with a fork."

I reached into my zippered pocket and pulled out the quarter for that one. I flipped it in the air and then winked out the porch light with my powers before the quarter reached Danny. He caught it anyway, but he had an odd look on his face when I let the light come back on.

"Cool trick."

It was—absorbing the light was one of my more awesome abilities, but it wasn't like me to show off. "It's not all eating bugs."

He nodded and stepped off the porch to walk home.

"Hey, Danny?"

He turned.

"Do you know anything about that grave that was robbed?"

"I heard it was some dead guy's."

I should have expected that. Being a smart-ass was practically genetic in our family line. "Thanks."

"No problem."

"Hey, hold up."

He turned.

"*Did* Critch call the police?" I still didn't hear any sirens.

Danny snorted. "For you? No way." He turned back toward his place and walked off, whistling.

Chapter Six

Shouldering my backpack, I strolled toward the microfilm readers. Knowledge always made me feel like I was donning armor and, dang it, I needed that. Sitting in school helped, but not knowing who might've killed Jester left me feeling exposed. The long silences among friends at my lunch table eventually drove me to go eat in my car, just for a break from their pity.

Since Dale was taking the bus home, I was free to go figure out why somebody would rob a grave.

What was left in a grave after that long anyway?

I blinked and stopped, staring at Gris, who was sitting in the seat in front of the microfilm reader. Nobody ever sat there but me. It might as well have my name on it. Plus, he'd pulled up the very thing I wanted to look at.

"What are you doing?" I asked Gris—Gris of the suspicious job and even more suspicious motive.

"Looking at that newspaper article you mentioned." He

didn't look up.

"I told you it was an animal attack." I grabbed another chair and pulled it over next to his.

"And I believed you. I just wanted to see what else it said." He jotted something in the notebook on the table beside him.

I craned my head to see it, but he flipped the notebook over.

"How was school?" His dark eyes focused on me. It was unnerving.

"Fine," I lied. Shoot. One lie. I looked him over. "I heard you got into it last night with Hank, but you seem pretty much how you did yesterday."

"Oh, you can't see the burn?"

"What burn?"

"I got it from a short blonde in the diner. Darn near broke my heart at the same time."

I pinned him with a glare. "I'd accuse you of being charming again, but I've been called nicer things—worse, too, but still." A short blonde? Really? "Jared looked like he had a broken nose and Carl acted like his ribs were in pieces." I'd been genuinely worried about Gris, thinking he'd gotten beat up for defending me. But here he was—looking right as rain with that cocky smile. "They said they won, but I have my doubts."

"Oh, they did that to themselves."

Uh huh. Sure. "You're really okay?"

"You sound like you care about me."

"As much as I care about anybody."

"Maybe a smidge more."

"Getting to be a smidge less." I cleared my throat. "You must've graduated last year?"

"Three years ago actually. Homeschool." He shifted to face me. I'd read a book about body language, and his posture said I could ask him anything. His expression said we weren't done, not by a long-shot. Walking out on Gris yesterday hadn't deterred him. I should've guessed as much. Gris Caso wasn't just stubborn. He was stubborn squared.

"You graduated when you were fifteen?"

"About that."

I tried not to find that sexy. "'Cause school bored you?"

"Because you can go much faster if you take twice the course load and never date."

"*You* didn't date?"

"You're wrong about me."

"You're not a charming player who'll be gone in a week after you've done whatever you're here to do?"

Gris continued to meet my eyes, stare for stare. He flipped the notebook over on the table. "I have questions. But you don't ever answer questions."

"You didn't answer mine." And it was kind of an important one. I wasn't about to be his diversion. I moved to get up, but he put out a hand.

"I'm here because strange things have been happening in Hidden Creek, and my aunt and uncle were concerned. Since 'strange' is my area of expertise, I agreed to come here and try to solve what's happening. I assumed, when I arrived, that'd take a couple weeks. Then, I got here and everything changed."

"Define 'everything changed' for me."

"I met a girl in a barn who plans on chasing danger."

"How long are you staying?"

"As long as it takes." There was a lot of gray area in that reply, and I still had more questions.

I set my backpack on the floor. "Why were you looking at that newspaper clipping?"

He leaned closer and dropped his voice. "I'm worried that maybe your dog's murder and the grave-robbing are related."

My jaw dropped. "Gris!" I hit my fist on the table beside

him. "You were investigating Jester's death without me?" How dare he! The nerve!

The librarian shushed me.

I pursed my lips and cast a look her way. Give the woman a little power, and she'd act like she owned the place. We were the only ones in the library. Who were we disturbing?

"If you get us thrown out of the library"—Gris relaxed in the chair—"I'll be able to cross that off my bucket list."

"Do you believe in ghosts?" I asked abruptly, in a much softer voice. Some folks in Hidden Creek might not mind a ghostbuster around. A few of them had their businesses blessed by Pastor Green before they'd even think about opening up.

"I believe there's a lot more than what meets the eye. I believe people can be haunted."

"By ghosts?"

"By a lot of things."

When I looked up, he was staring at me as if he knew. He couldn't. I was being paranoid and stupid. But his gaze fell to my shoulder as if he could see the cuts through my shirt. Nothing had made me feel more naked than his piercing eyes on my shoulder. I covered my shoulder with my hand.

Maybe he was psychic. That made me even more uncomfortable. The things that strayed through my brain everyday would scare a saint.

"Are you haunted?" I asked him, trying to shift his attention.

His lips tipped up on one side and he gave me a considering look. "Sure am. Not as haunted as some around, but you live long enough and see enough, you get ghosts and memories following you that'll make you shiver on dark nights. I imagine there are a lot of older folks in this town who are good and haunted."

When you notice everything, you notice when a casual

comment isn't casual. Gris was fishing for information. He'd thrown out a line to see if I'd bite. Maybe this was why he was paying attention to me, trying to charm me. He wanted information. It made my heart sick—which was ridiculous. Knowing why Gris was interested in me was useful and kept me from getting in too deep with him. "You mean like by *actual* ghosts?"

"Maybe. Maybe just by dreams. Maybe it's sickness. Maybe it's bad luck. People explain things in all sorts of ways. My cousin says weird things happen here. Sometimes."

I wanted to call Danny a liar, but I shook my head instead.

"You're saying they don't?" Gris's eyebrows raised.

"I'm saying it's not *sometimes*." I flipped his notebook my way. His notes were an indecipherable bunch of chicken scratches. It figured. Straightening the notebook, I lined it up with the corner of the table and then moved the pen to be parallel. It was better that way. Easier to grab. You wouldn't lose it. "A foul wind is blowing through town. It's increasing in strength and tearing up folks like trees as it does. The weeks when nothing happens are an eye in a hurricane."

"I'm looking for abrupt changes in people. One minute they're one way and the next they're another. Danny said a guy lost control last week, here in the library. Now, there's your dog and somebody digging up graves."

"I was here at the library that day. Actually, I'd just left. I was the last to leave—aside from the librarian." I really shouldn't sass her, seeing as how she'd had to deal with that mess. "Phil came in and shot up the reference section."

I felt Gris's gaze burning holes through me. "You'd been in the reference section."

"This place isn't that big. He kept screaming that he'd been cursed and that's why they're all dead." I rubbed my arms. The librarian had warned me of that. She wasn't sure if it was some sort of threat aimed at me or just a sign that he'd lost his mind. "He lost a slew of cows and horses a month ago—basically all the animals in his barn. It'd been locked for the night, too. It was like somebody had shut up a cougar with them. The next morning, everything was dead and there was blood all over. From what I heard of it, it was amazing Phil lasted as long as he did before breaking down."

"Danny didn't mention that."

"Danny hadn't just been here. The sheriff's wife attends church with my mama and this happened on a Saturday night. It was fresh in Mrs. Rollins's mind, and she doesn't much care for me, on account of me correcting her a time or two in, uhh, discussions. If Pastor Green hadn't interrupted their little 'talk' and taken Mrs. Rollins aside, it would have been an old-fashioned cat fight in the chapel." Mama hadn't balked about taking my side, not for a second.

"I hope they've got him locked up. Phil, I mean."

"I've heard they've got him in a mental hospital, but I'm not sure how long he'll be there, seeing as how he only shot books. He even put the gun down when the Mrs. Carson asked him to. Also, there's the extenuating circumstances of him losing most of his livestock. Grief can do funny things. There's been talk he didn't pass a drug screen afterward." I tilted my head. "I can't imagine they'd just throw him back out on the street. Especially since this is a federal building—being a library. I'm not sure how that'll factor in, but he probably would've been better off killing books in a bookstore."

"If only that'd occurred to him. Besides, that's not the only thing that's happened. You can explain a few things away, but eventually all these instances pile up and equal something."

I wrinkled up my nose and turned to face him. "You really are serious in thinking Hidden Creek is haunted, then?"

It felt like he was examining me, trying to judge exactly what he dared say. "You mentioned having nightmares about things coming after you."

Had I? Strange that I didn't remember telling him that. "Phil said he'd had dreams, but wouldn't you after seeing what he had?" I'd nearly fainted after seeing Jester. Even thinking about it made the acid rise in my throat. "Besides, the town is getting older. Some of what's happened would seem natural without the other things. Like the school's old principal. He'd always had a temper—so him screaming and screaming at the 4th of July festival wasn't too strange."

"I heard it was more than that."

I shrugged. "He threatened to light himself on fire, but he didn't actually *do* it." Of course, the pastor had darn near tackled him to prevent it. He hadn't taken the lid off the gas can, so there was that. "And he had a stroke a week later so it was probably something related. You know how it is with superstitious people; a story grows as it gets passed along. Events with a perfectly logical explanation are made into something supernatural. Curses and demons. Mrs. Carter wasn't possessed—she was just old. Her doctors are saying Alzheimer's." Though, truthfully, it hadn't settled in—it'd roared in—like she'd roared and raged. "And we'd always known Greta Mellor was strange even before she drove through the barbershop window."

"What about Hank's sister? Dick mentioned something had happened to her."

"Trina was always saying she wanted to leave. She might've just left." Trina's disappearance was the least unusual thing that had happened in the last year, but it did seem to be around when everything went wrong—with me, with everybody. I wasn't about to tell him about my sleepwalking, though.

I didn't know Trina very well. She was a year ahead of me in school, but we didn't have any of the same classes. Trina always took the classes that required the least amount of effort.

"And nothing's been heard of her since?"

"No."

"So, she disappeared."

"People do that, Gris. They leave Hidden Creek and never look back. You've been here a couple days, so you know what we have to offer."

"Hidden Creek isn't looking all that typical and some of what's here—I don't mind so much." He spun his pen on the table.

I slapped my hand down, to stop the pen mid-spin and straightened it. I couldn't read anything into his flirting. Flirting was like breathing for somebody like Gris.

"Then, there's your dog."

I didn't have an answer for that. He knew I didn't. What happened to Jester would haunt me til I died. Most of the time, it didn't even seem real. Nothing could be that horrible. Then I'd close my eyes and he'd be there...bloody, broken, and my fault. "Maybe somebody blamed me for something that happened—like Phil might've, though I don't see how."

"Yes, and that's why I, uhh, we need to figure out who did this."

"I don't need or want your help." His motives were suspect. *He* was a suspect.

"I'm planning on helping you, like it or not. I'd rather you be aggravated than dead." Gris said it all calm and firm...like it was a fact.

He wasn't afraid of either bullies or scary stories or superstitions. That might come in handy. Besides, I was stubborn, not stupid. And if he could help, maybe I could *let* him help. "So long as we agree that a real, live person killed my dog, not a ghost or a boogey monster...or whatever."

"Oh, I believe it was a person. In fact, I've found at the heart of most hauntings is a human who's a little dead inside."

I nodded. I might let him help, providing this wasn't some

trick and he wasn't running his own agenda.

"That doesn't mean they're not doing other things to stir up folks," Gris said.

"Like what?"

"On the nights you've had those nightmares about being attacked, have you found anything in your room?"

There it was again. I felt exposed at him knowing about my nightmares when I couldn't remember sharing it. "When did I tell you about my nightmares?"

Gris's forehead scrunched up for a second. "Right before we went out to lunch."

I still didn't remember that. That wasn't like me. I didn't "share."

"Sometimes," Gris added, "to spook someone and to give them nightmares, a person will place these bags in their victim's rooms."

"Bags?"

"Little pouches filled with ingredients that'll give them bad dreams. Have you found anything like that when you've cleaned?"

"I'm not really a clean person."

His gaze drifted to the pen. He spun it again.

I slapped my hand on it. "Stop it. Okay. I can't think when you…" I clenched my teeth. "Look, things should be a certain way. That doesn't make me clean, it's sensible. So stop it. Just stop it."

"Fine." He held up his hands. "I'll stop."

I nodded. He was getting under my skin, making me itchy and uncomfortable. I needed to leave. I tapped on the notebook. "What does this say?"

"I made a note to find out more about the Beaumonts— find out what you knew about the ones still around." He pointed at the scribbled words. "See, there's where I mentioned you. Ask the beautiful blonde beside you what she knows."

It was an improvement on "short blonde," but I still wasn't falling for it. I squinted at the notebook, willing it to make clear words. "Looks more like 'what made fiends attack,' but your handwriting is really poor. Poor handwriting can lead to mistakes. You should consider using a tablet. Or, I should take notes." I picked up the notebook and flipped to a new page. Eyeing his pen, I put it back down and pulled my own from my backpack.

"You don't like my pen?"

"Mine is blue so we can tell the difference between my notes and yours. Also, the contrast between blue ink is better on photocopies and that way you know it's handwritten."

"Here I thought maybe it was cooties. Let me see that." He took the pen from my hand, managing to brush his fingers along mine as he did. It made my foolish heart flutter. It was just my fingers!

"Give me that back." I reached for it.

Gris held it out of reach for a second—which got me in closer to his body than I was comfortable with.

Sitting back, I sent him a heavy frown.

With a grin, he handed me back my pen. "Now, it has cooties."

I fought the urge to wipe it off. He didn't have cooties. "I once had a pen by that brand." I nodded at his pen. "It leaked and ruined my purse." I wrote "Beaumonts" at the top of a clean sheet of paper and underlined it. "Okay, so there aren't Beaumonts around anymore. Not any that I've met. 'Course folks change names and marry and so on." I slid closer to the microfilm reader and examined the newsprint. "Now, that's interesting." I wrote Phil Laramie on the notepad. "Silas's body was found by their neighbor, Paul Laramie. I would bet that's Phil's father, seeing as how Paul is a family name. It says they were trying to contact Silas's relatives. They found some apparently—as somebody must've paid for the tombstone, right? If the estate paid, it wouldn't be as ornate."

"The gargoyle, you mean?"

I nodded. "It's one of the nicer gravestones in the cemetery, even if it's outside the regular section. There is another Beaumont in the cemetery with the same style, so I'm assuming that's family, even if they're not buried together. I can't remember his name, but he died young too."

"Another gargoyle?"

"On the tombstone? Yes." I added "gargoyle" in the notes. "That's strange, isn't it? Normally I wouldn't make much of it, but maybe someone has a fascination with things like that. Gargoyles and the occult and…"

Gris snatched the notebook out of my hand. "I'll check into it." He got up abruptly. "I'll let you focus on this." He walked off.

It was probably fair, since I'd done that to him yesterday, but I still glared at his back as he left. Fair or not, he'd left me with more questions than he'd answered again.

• • •

That night, I couldn't sleep. It was nearing midnight, and I had school tomorrow. I needed to stop thinking about Gris and everything else, but I couldn't shut off my mind.

A pouch? What had Gris meant by that? I looked around my room. My mom was always getting after me to clean up, but that was her thing. She liked things clean and in patterns. I liked patterns, but her cleanliness was sharp and unfriendly. It made the voices in my head shout louder. I tried. I swear I did, but no one could keep things that sterile. My room's clutter was like a nest. I knew where everything was—that was enough.

I dropped down and looked under my bed. Books and dirty clothes were piled underneath. I pulled everything out and fished around until my hand touched rough burlap. No way. I straightened up and stared at the bag in my hand.

Somebody had been in my room. That was violating. And creepy. They'd put a bag in my room. Who'd do such a thing? I couldn't decide if I was more angry or horrified. Maybe I was equal parts of both. Opening it up, I peered inside. Weird grass and a sulfury smell rose up. Gross.

I made sure nobody was around as I snuck into the hall. Then, I went into the bathroom and flushed the whole thing. There—if that thing supposedly attracted ghosts, they could haunt our septic system.

What did it mean that Gris was right, though? Was somebody trying to give me nightmares?

I climbed back into bed and tucked my flashlight under my pillow. Taking a deep breath, I turned off my bedside light.

The shadows shifted and inched closer. I closed my eyes, shutting them out, trying to turn off my thoughts. A breeze fanned my cheek, even though my window was closed. I knew it was closed. If I kept my eyes shut, I could pretend it was all in my mind. Heaven knew my mind was a scary place on its own, but I was at least used to that.

The dark thoughts crawled into my brain and made themselves a nest of other ugly wriggling thoughts—thoughts that bled and bred until my mind was full of them. So many. I'd done so many things wrong. Jester. Jester was at the top, but there were others—so many others. It'd become this chant in my head every night as I rewound and remembered all my sins and mistakes.

The silence of the night without my dog would be a permanent reminder of that mistake, but thinking about Jester made my stomach clench and tears leak out the corners of my eyes, so I tried to push it back. I hated crying.

Other dark thoughts moved in as if the gate had been opened.

What if I'd had something to do with Trina's disappearance? She'd disappeared the night of a rainstorm. It was the night Dale had said I'd sleepwalked out to the fence for the first time. My brother had come looking for me when he'd woken up and found the front door wide open. I was soaked to the skin. Things had changed after that night. The nights had teeth.

Our town was haunted—Gris was right about that, and, maybe I was helping that along. Strange things happened around me.

Mr. Foster, the old principal, had thought I'd cheated once on a test. He'd said I'd been staring at another student's paper, but that was just the way I concentrated on things. I'd been staring off into space. The new principal was nicer, less focused on me.

Then, there were all those thoughts—the thoughts that were evil and ugly that I had to cut out. Something ferocious and harmful lived inside me that was stronger than I was. I felt the roar of it at times—in my head and under my skin; it was as if my body couldn't contain it.

Greta Mellor told me I was a wicked, wicked girl a few weeks before she'd crashed into the barbershop. She'd looked at me and said she'd seen my soul, and it was hideous. Her daughter had rushed her away, apologizing, telling me her mama wasn't well, but I thought maybe Greta was the first person to see the real me. She saw the part of me that was diseased and rotten.

Reaching out, I fumbled for the flashlight and flicked it on, waiting for the odd hiss as the cold withdrew before I opened my eyes. I didn't wanna know what was out there. I truly didn't.

After I'd counted to twenty by twos in my head, I opened my eyes. I kept the straight razor in my bedside drawer hidden in a copy of *Little Women*. I always cut the shoulder I slept on.

The pain had presence that way, and, if my parents walked in, they wouldn't know. The cut wasn't deep, just enough to bleed out the bad thoughts and do right by my wrongs. To pay for things like Jester and not getting up to check on him. To pay for yelling at him—since I couldn't take that back. It was to pay for a lot of things.

I *am* wicked. I think of people dying. I fantasize about stupid Hank Jr. getting run over by the train that he and his friends play chicken with. I imagined something awful happening to Mr. Foster long before his stroke, and to Greta Mellor after she'd said that about me being wicked. I'd wondered what Mrs. Mellor would do if I pushed her into the street. She was standing too close to the curb, and you never knew how dark the person beside you was. It wasn't sensible to stand that close to the curb, ever.

The blood thickened and crusted in the light of the flashlight. One cut tonight. So I could sleep. I exhaled shakily. For a moment, there was peace…and quiet. I was in control. I was here, not in the past. I was here.

The cuts were getting more frequent. Maybe I was losing my mind…maybe it was lost already.

I wiped the straight razor on the inside of my black tank top before putting it away. No more cutting this week, not until this healed. I imagined the bad thoughts seeping out of my body through the blood. It was sick and wrong. I was sick and wrong. Sometimes, I thought about quitting but it made a panic rise up in me. What would I do if I couldn't pay? How would I cut through the crowded thoughts in my head?

Every cut reminded me I wasn't strong enough to quit, and was a reason to cut again in the future.

I'd paid for tonight, and for Jester. I should pay and somebody else should pay, too. Maybe finding out who'd killed Jester would be part of my penance. Another swipe of a slate that hadn't been clean for as long as I'd lived.

As I turned off the light, and I felt the monsters crawl across my body to lick my cut and tease at my blind eyes, I knew, even with them here, I was all alone. It was better for me to be alone. I couldn't hurt anybody but myself. I had more control when I was alone. Control was all that I needed.

No more time with Gris. I could figure this out all on my own.

The rush of a fresh cut healed my soul. I'd paid.

I closed my eyes against the darkness with its shadowy monsters and their frigid, sulfurous breath. Demons. They might be demons.

One of the demons whispered in my mind that I was strong enough to kill, if that's what I wanted. I could hide it 'cause I was so smart. I pinched my shoulder hard where I'd cut the one inch gash. It hurt, but the pain felt right. Pain could heal. Pain could silence the demons. Both inside and outside. For tonight.

Chapter Seven

GRIS

I sat on the mattress in the corner of the room and stared at my laptop screen.

Normally, I didn't sleep at night.

Normally, I didn't have both steroid-jacked jocks and fiends using me as a punching bag. Hidden Creek was exhausting me. I also had spent more of today than I'd planned looking for answers to what was happening in this town—and I'd spent less of it in the company of Piper than I wanted. Hell, she'd spooked me with the whole "gargoyle" talk.

Guys like me were better off steering clear of girls like Piper, who deserved a fair amount of attention and honesty. I couldn't be honest about my birthright.

I needed to do the job and get out of here and, tonight, that meant checking out the grave.

Yawning as the drag of the day pressed on my body, I leaned my head back and closed my eyes. I'd wait until midnight, and then I'd go check. I'd just catch a quick nap first.

The soft click of a door shutting cut through a frequent nightmare I was nearly glad to end. What the hell? I got up quickly and moved through the house.

The sledgehammer I'd inherited from Hank was beside my bedroom door. I grabbed it as I eased the door open. If Hank and his buddies were back, I wouldn't fake getting injured. Coming inside the house was a whole new type of trespassing.

I stood in the hall and waited, listening. My chosen bedroom was halfway down the hall in the empty house. I turned toward the back of the house and heard movement behind me. Spinning, I caught sight of a wisp of clothing as somebody crossed my front room.

A strange scent hung in the air. Sulfur. Hank had smelled more like ineffective deodorant and BO.

"Whoever is in here better clear out before I call the sheriff." I held the sledgehammer like a bat as I edged toward the intruder. "I'm not messin' with you!" I jumped into the room only to find my great-uncle Critch standing in front of the big picture window that overlooked the porch, the yard, and at the machine shop.

He didn't turn to look at me, but stayed staring out.

"Sir?" I set the sledgehammer to the side. As much as we didn't care for each other, we were family. I turned on the kitchen light. I preferred leaving things dark since I could still see well, and the lack of curtains on this place would make me feel like a free peep show otherwise. But there was something wraith-like about my uncle that begged for the lights to be on.

His breath wheezed in and out. Critch once was Danny's height with Danny's blond hair and fair complexion. He'd shrunk with age and now his hair was bone-white and stuck up at weird angles as if he'd licked a live wire. Despite it all, there was this stubborn lean look to his frame. It wasn't impossible to see the Watcher in him, even if his powers had passed to me.

"Used to be, things were different," he said finally, still staring out.

"You mean in Hidden Creek?"

He didn't answer.

"Why are you in my house, Uncle Critch?"

He looked around, blinking. "Oh, are you staying here?"

I rolled my eyes and rubbed a hand down my face. "Cut the crap. I know you're not as senile as you pretend." He couldn't be. It was a hunch, but I was sticking to it. Since I was up, I might as well have food. I'd bought a few boxes of cereal to get me through when Hidden Creek rolled up its sidewalks.

"No respect for your elders," he said under his breath as I went to get a bowl out of my cupboard.

"No respect for those who don't respect a locked door. You want cereal?" I held up my only other bowl.

His rheumy eyes stared at the large, orange bowl in my hand.

My aunt said she used the bowl normally to hold candy for trick-or-treaters. It had a giant skull on the side, maybe that's what he was staring at. I held up the bowl I'd been planning on using—it was bigger, but no skull. "Or you can have this one."

He shook his head. "Don't eat as much as I used to. Not since you stole my powers."

I put the orange bowl back. "Yeah, well, I'm beginning to suspect I'll be anxious to retire myself when the time comes." The fiends at the mill would have killed my great-uncle. Hell, if I'd stopped on my way into town when I'd been so exhausted, they would've killed me.

He glanced around my living room. "You know who used to live here?"

"Uh-huh. The Trunkers."

Letting out a frustrated hiss, he said, "Not the Trunkers.

Everybody remembers the Trunkers. They were only here a few damn years. No, the Beaumonts. The Beaumonts! Two generations of them lived in this house."

I froze. "The Beaumonts lived here? In this house?"

"That's what I said, isn't it?" His face took on a wistful expression. "Tawna Beaumont. Was she ever a looker."

"I heard you used to live here in Hidden Creek way back when." I poured my cereal. There was a rumor that he'd gotten a girl pregnant, too—maybe that had happened here. Weird to think I might have a relative around here if that was true. Of course, responsible guy that he was, Critch had deserted his supposed child and wandered all over for decades before coming back here to live with my aunt and uncle just recently—after all the adults had decided he'd gotten too senile to live alone.

"'Course I did. I wanted the birthright, didn't I? Watchers are born where Watchers die. Like I told Jess, right here. Right here is where you need to be." He stomped a foot. "Right here."

"Aunt Jess? You told my aunt that her kids would get the birthright if she lived here?"

"She didn't listen, though. Left on that trip when she was about to deliver and ruined everything."

I held up a hand. "Hold on, Critch. Are you saying you told Aunt Jess that because Danny was born in Chicago on that trip—that's why he didn't get the birthright?"

Critch's eyes surveyed me before he turned back to the window. "I used to live right there." He threw a hand in the direction of the machine shop. "They razed my old house and put up that. That!"

"You don't like the machine shop?"

He shrugged.

"If you lived there, did you live near the Laramies?"

My uncle's unfocused gaze sharpened and cut to me.

"Why'd you bring up them?"

"Phil Laramie's dad was the one who discovered Silas's body after he'd been killed by fiends."

"You've been busy. I bought the place from the Laramies. When I moved out, they razed it." He stabbed a finger in the machine shop's direction. "It shouldn't be there. Danny shouldn't be…" His words hung between us. "All of y'all shouldn't be…but it's full circle, isn't it? And Hidden Creek… the pull…the pull is just so damn strong." He shook his head.

"Why is that?" I'd started feeling it, started noticing the pull of it, like he said. It's almost as if I was stronger here.

The silence stretched and it had teeth. If he was going for creepy old geezer that you crossed the street to avoid—he'd nailed it. I was good and spooked.

I cleared my throat. "So, Tawna Beaumont? Is she still around?" Maybe she might have more information on Silas Beaumont.

Critch snorted and turned to stare out the window again. "Gutless." I wasn't sure who he meant by that. "Everybody's changed names. As if the name they were born with had something tainted stitched to it. It's funny that people in Hidden Creek have such a long memory except for things they'd rather not know about. Didn't work then, though… didn't work then. Won't work now." A long, wheezed breath hissed out of him. "And it isn't right."

"What isn't?"

"Getting her involved. Or him. But especially her. Shouldn't have gotten her involved." He was really getting worked up. His breath was coming faster and faster. Was he still talking about Tawna? "She shouldn't have been involved!" He slammed a hand against the window frame with each word.

I blinked. Was any of this supposed to make sense? "Who? Who shouldn't have been involved?"

Minutes went by with only his heavy breathing as a response.

Finally, I said, "I went to the mill a couple nights back. You're right that something is happening here. You were right to ask me to come." Maybe that'd appease him.

He snorted. Maybe not. "Was I right? They didn't kill you so it's difficult to say either way."

The spoon paused halfway to my mouth. "Was that the plan? That they'd kill me?" Hell, how involved was my uncle in all this? He couldn't possibly be summoning all these fiends to kill me. No. No way. He was old. Possibly senile.

I ate the cereal on the spoon. No use letting it get soggy.

"Not sure what the plan was or if there was one. Cerberus seems like it'd go for brute strength."

"Cerberus? Are you talking about the three-headed dog that guards hell?" I wasn't especially fond of Hidden Creek at this point, but calling it a gateway to hell seemed a bit extreme.

He barked what sounded like a laugh. "Maybe I am, and there's no controlling it or what it might unleash. One head is better than three." He tapped his head. "One head."

More like no head. "Were you talking about Piper earlier—when you said 'her'? Do you know who killed her dog?"

He squinted at me. "Tawna had hair the same color as her—as bright and sunny as a spring day. Ugly way to go… bedeviled mad."

"Is that a threat?"

"How could it be? Tawna's gone." He went to the door, shaking his head. With his hand paused on the doorknob, he muttered, "Have a little respect. You're walking on graves." Then, he was gone.

What the hell was that? What did any of that mean? For all I knew, he might've been saying that Piper was Tawna's grandchild or great grandchild through him.

She couldn't be, though.

She wasn't.

While eating my cereal, I watched Critch through the picture window as he shuffled across the yard to the Porters'. My aunt and uncle had built a room to the side for him. Dad said Critch had paid for it. Maybe there was a retirement program for old Watchers. I finished up and washed my bowl while it all swirled around in my head. Critch could bedevil better than fiends.

Since there was no way in hell I'd fall asleep after that little visit, it was as good a time as any to go check out that grave.

Stepping outside, I inhaled deeply. The time I'd spent in cities did make me appreciate some of the scents of nature here, like the smell of freshly turned earth. Shifting into my gargoyle form, I flexed the muscles in my back, sweeping the air with my wings. My face stretched, pulling at the skin on my cheeks. I flew slowly, gathering darkness to mask me as I approached.

The cruiser wasn't at the cemetery anymore.

I landed and wandered over to the grave. There was something eerie about the gaping hole. The plot was beside a clump of bushes in one of the older sections of the cemetery. All the other graves around it were nearly a century old. The hole itself was shallower than I'd have expected. That, and the fact the bushes obscured its location likely helped the grave robber get what they needed without being discovered.

The stone above the open grave was rounded other than the gargoyle perched on the corner. It called to me, drew me. It was as if Hidden Creek was some sort of link between birth and death, old and new, Watchers and fiends. I felt a connection to the grave, same as I did to this place. "Silas Edward Beaumont. RIP Born March 18, 1896, Died May 13, 1933. Beloved Husband and Father." And the former owner of my house.

So much was rattling around in my brain. Too much. There were too many players and too much information. I needed a sounding board. Especially since I was now staring down into a damn grave.

Screw this. It's not like I was asking for help. It was brainstorming.

I called Dad.

He answered immediately.

"I'm looking at a Watcher's grave. Silas Beaumont's grave, to be exact. He came from a line of Watchers that once lived here in Hidden Creek. But I think they died out, or their birthright did." I circled the grave. "I'm staring at it because someone dug it up."

Dad swore. "And you're sure it's a Watcher's grave?"

"Yeah. I mean, I think so."

"Okay, if it's a Watcher's grave, it would be off to the side of the cemetery—nearly outside of it."

"Yes, sir. It's the farthest to this side. Why is that?"

"It's old?"

"Yeah."

"They didn't let us be buried on hallowed ground back then, and it was more common for local religious leaders to be aware of a Watcher's presence in a town." He snorted. "We could clean their town of fiends but not be buried beside them. We were cursed and linked to fiends. They painted us with the same brush. Is our inscription on the bottom?"

I crouched in front of the headstone while trying not to get too close to the hole. I should have checked this earlier, but it felt like I was staring down my own mortality by doing so. Pushing the grass away from the base, I read, "Ever Watchful."

He swore a full-on blue streak. He was so thorough that if Piper had been around she would've insisted he wash his mouth out.

"Why would somebody steal from a Watcher's grave? Was there something buried with him?" I asked.

"Possibly. It's not tradition if that's what you're asking. We're not exactly pharaohs or kings. No fancy scepters or jeweled gargoyles."

"I get it. I get it."

"What's left in the coffin now?"

I looked down into the shadowed recesses of the casket. They'd broken clear through the pine box he'd been buried in. "I don't know." I pulled a flashlight from one of the pockets in my cargo pants and shone it down. There was dirt inside the casket but, beyond that, the shadows and the remainder of the casket obscured its contents. I couldn't even see any bones.

"Well, get down in there and find out."

"Oh, hell no." I'd never said that to my dad before, but if ever a time warranted it, this was that time.

He sighed—loudly. "Gris, if it just happened, the police are probably trying to find his living relatives to fully exhume that coffin. We don't have time for you to be prissy."

"Prissy? You want me to climb down into the grave and root around through his corpse, and you're calling that prissy?"

"Sounds like it fits. You wanna be a full Watcher and hang with the big dogs—you gotta do nasty things that you hope you can forget. It's why we get paid the big bucks. Stay in Watcher form if it helps."

"Fine. Hold on." After switching my phone to speaker, I tossed it to the side and bit the flashlight between my teeth.

Taking his advice, I shifted into Watcher form and even flew into the hole. I tried setting down gently, but my weight on the partially broken lid of the coffin collapsed it entirely. I let out my own slew of curses. I didn't need the flashlight to see the talons on my feet had torn through the bottom of the coffin. Moist dirt squished between my toes, even the armor of my skin couldn't mask that sensation. Hopefully it was dirt. It had to be. Either way, I'd caught my balance, but I was leaving some strange traces behind for whoever did exhume this grave. Great. Freaking fantastic.

"Is everything okay?" Dad asked. I didn't bother answering his amused question. Real funny. He wasn't ankle-deep in either dirt or dead guy.

I pulled the flickering flashlight from between my beak-like lips and discovered my teeth had broken through portions of the metal Maglite so the batteries were visible. This couldn't get any better. It just couldn't.

I crouched down and looked at the wreckage around my feet which were buried deep in the dirt beneath the coffin. I exhaled a puff of breath. Just dirt.

"Casket looks empty," I called out. "Either the police or the grave robber took everything." That was a relief. It would have been real nasty to find my foot through another Watcher's rib cage.

"Hell." Dad groaned.

"Will whoever took them be able to tell they have the bones of a Watcher?" I hadn't ever gone to regular doctors, not since the birthright had chosen me—my wings made that impossible. They looked like ribs if you didn't examine an x-ray too long, but not enough to fool a doctor.

"Much of it might have decayed. It's an old grave, right?"

"Yep. About eighty years old." Around the same age as Uncle Critch.

"It's hard to say how much would be left, but we need to be worried about what our robber is doing with Watcher bones if he knows he has them."

"What might they be doing?"

"I don't know. What else is going on? I thought I'd hear

from you before this."

"I've been busy. There's more here than I expected."

"More fiends?"

I didn't want to tell him. This was my job, and I was feeling downright possesive of the town and some of its residents. On the other hand, if anything happened to Piper because I was too stubborn to see reason, I'd never forgive myself. "More everything. This town is not at all normal. It's bedeviled beyond anything I've seen. I took on nine fiends in an abandoned mill over the weekend. Somebody is planting curse bags, messing in the dark arts. Then, I'm checking out this neighbor girl, Piper, and…"

"You're checking out a girl?" The amusement was back in his voice.

"No, I'm checking things out for her. For her."

"Not what you said."

"Somebody killed her dog."

That sobered him up real fast. "Somebody? Somebody bedeviled?"

"I can't tell. I can't figure out who did it. Piper is trying to help, but I'm worried she's in danger because somebody is planting curse sacks in her room, too. I keep thinking I've gotten them all, but there's still fiends there."

"Same as whatever you found at the mill?"

"Different. But I don't know if I'm dealing with different people or they're evolving. The fiends at the mill were mean as hell." I gestured at the grave, even though he couldn't see me. "Then, I've got a grave dug up and, oh, Crazy Critch got into the house I'm staying in. I'm not sure how he got in. I know I locked the doors."

"Oh yeah? What did he have to say for himself? Is he proud that he was right about the number of fiends?"

"I don't know. He mentioned the Beaumonts who lived in the house and at least Silas died there."

"In your house?"

"From the newspaper report, I know Silas did. Critch told me I was walking on graves. I don't know what happened to the rest of them, aside from another one who's buried somewhere around here—who also died young. You don't think Critch meant other Beaumonts were buried underneath the house, though, right?"

"Maybe it was meant to be metaphorical."

"Because Critch has been known to get all poetic at times." I shook my head. That bit about Cerberus was weird. "You're not allowed to do that, are you? Bury people on your property? That's against code or a health violation or illegal, right?"

Dad's cough sounded suspiciously like a laugh. "Listen to my urbane, sophisticated son getting his panties all bunched up over staying in a house that might have bones buried in the yard."

"The yard's fine." It wasn't. Not really. "I just don't want to open a closet and have the Beaumonts spill out." There'd been renters, but what if they hadn't poked around much? What if there were bones in the walls? Or floors?

"Is there a cellar? I'd bury annoying relatives in the cellar if it was me, rather than spring for a funeral. You're lucky you're the favored son; we might get you a pine box."

"Whatever, Dad. Remember, I'm your only child and responsible for picking out your retirement home."

"Noted." Sometimes I had to rein him in.

I cleared my throat. "Dad, did Aunt Jess want the birthright?"

There was a long pause before he said, "Yes. She talked about it all the time when we were kids. She told her husband that it'd go to them because it usually doesn't pass directly like it did with us." Another pause. "Why? Has she said something to you about it?"

"No." I didn't want to cause strain between him and his sister. Besides, as much as Aunt Jess might want the birthright, it was too late and my aunt was a very pragmatic woman.

"Do you need me to come there?"

"No! I'm doing fine. I got this." I just needed to talk this out. That was all. Physically, I could handle this.

"Gris, they've dug up a Watcher's bones, killed a dog, and it sounds like they're flinging curse bags around like they're at a Mardi Gras parade. I can try to rush things along here."

"How's your job going?"

"I took more hits than the agents protecting this diplomat. I'm glad he's going back to his own country soon. He's dragging in a ton of fiends. It reminds me of New York after 9/11. Diplomats from war-torn countries are like bait."

"It sounds like you couldn't come here anyway."

"If you need me, I *will* be there."

"I don't. It's fine. I got this." I just had to keep saying that. "Do you think there's a chance Uncle Critch might be doing some of this to get his powers back or to get rid of me for taking them?" I couldn't picture him taking on the more physical aspects of this—the graverobbing or killing Jester— if that was related.

"I don't think he'd be ambitious enough nor does he have the knowledge."

"You make it sounds like it's possible."

"It's been attempted, but I don't know if it's ever been successful. With great power comes greater temptation. Watchers have often tried to manipulate or control who gets the birthright or to give it to those who don't have it. It's also possible this grave robber could be trying to revive the Beaumont bloodline using the bones, but I suspect you'd need the blood if not the life of a living Watcher for that."

"You suspect?"

"Well, most of that knowledge has died off because

Watchers who go that route have a high mortality rate. They also might be trying to pry a gateway open and flood the town with fiends."

"There are a lot of fiends here."

"Are you safe?"

"Dad, I'm fine. I can handle the fiends, and if it's Critch coming after me, I like my odds against an eighty-year-old who breathes louder than Darth Vader."

"I'd bet on you."

"It might just be some psychopath who likes playing with bones," I suggested. "If that's the case, would they know what they have—what we are?"

Dad sighed. "Maybe. Most of what looks decidedly different about our bodies would've decayed away, but it'll look…fishy. An anthropologist might call it a strange medical anomaly. So, at best, if knowledge of the bones surfaced, you're exposed—our secret is exposed. At worst, someone with the right knowledge might try to revive a dead bloodline by killing a live Watcher."

Until I knew who'd done this, my secret was vulnerable to exposure with all of Hidden Creek. Anybody could have those bones. They could know about me, know what I was. My so-called job would make it obvious.

"Heaven help us." I surged out of the grave with a swoop of my wings and dropped down beside my phone.

"Heaven won't even let us be buried in the same cemetery. For hell's sake, I hope our grave robber keeps those bones to himself."

• • •

I'd stopped by Piper's, intending just to check on her, and there were more fiends than ever. I must've missed some curse pouches—or someone had been in her room and put more in.

I couldn't let fiends prey on her for another night. Piper didn't need any bedeviling from outside sources.

I gathered the night around me. I'd need to transform completely, rather than just making use of my powers or shifting without my wings emerging. This number of fiends would require my full strength. My wings shifted and shoved their way out as my bones creaked and warped. My talons broke through; their bone pallor absorbed the blackness of the night instantly.

The wispy spectral forms of the fiends slithered around her house like writhing snakes. Hopefully, none of the curse sacks were buried. It wasn't only on account of me being a city boy that I didn't relish digging. It might take a while to find any buried sacks—like the worst sort of treasure hunt ever devised.

Holding the darkness around me, I inched her window open. I'd nearly suggested she stick a pipe in the window well to secure it when I'd been here before, but keeping others out would keep me out, too. Her curtains brushed my face as I slid in.

Holy hell! There were more fiends here in her room tonight than last time.

I might be in over my head. This might be the definition of in over my head.

The ghostly shades ate the light as they prowled her room. They hovered around her sleeping form, hissing at me. At least they weren't as aggressive as the ones in the mill—the ones in the mill had converged on me all at once. These were passively hostile. Killing them all would be too loud—and once I attacked, it was likely to get nasty. I'd never thought of myself as outnumbered before, but I was most definitely eyeballing that scenario. A dozen fiends against one Watcher. Those odds weren't pretty. I'd still dive in and hope for the best, but not with Piper in the middle of this storm of vapor. That many fiends with her fragile mortal body in the eye of the storm…no way. Too loud. Too dangerous.

Leaving the window open, I shoved against them with the darkness I could command. Propelling them away took more effort than killing them, but made them less mean, and it was quieter. It took me ten minutes to rid the room of all but two. Sweat dripped down my face. I was gonna have to eat several meals and sleep all day to make up for tonight.

The last two fiends clung to Piper's body, snarling. One had wrapped itself around her neck tighter than the bark on a tree, and its great mouth was attached to her shoulder, the one I'd seen the cuts on. The other was prone across her body. Hell, this was new. Their gray-green bodies shimmered and tightened around her possessively. They weren't going and, no matter how many times I pushed at them, my powers wouldn't dislodge them.

I'd have to kill these two. Piper squirmed beneath them as if under the influence of a nightmare. Bedeviled. She wouldn't wake up until they left. She muttered under her breath—numbers. Weird. Only even numbers—weirder.

Approaching the bed, I shook my hands out. It was true I hadn't done this *exact* thing. Normally, fiends didn't wind themselves around a person. They didn't need to get that close to feed off their minds. Okay. Okay. I shook my hands out again. I'd been killing fiends for a decade. This wasn't much different, other than it being Piper, and they were much closer than usual. I could do this. I'd grab their hearts and be done. Piper wouldn't feel a thing if I was careful. I could be careful. Very careful.

I dodged toward them, reaching out, but they both twisted away from my talons, and I pulled up short so I wouldn't harm Piper. Damn.

The fiend prone across her wriggled upward, elongating

into a rope that crept into her mouth. She gagged and shivered.

Aw hell. I paced back and forth in the room. How was I supposed to get this out of her? What if the other one went in? I stopped and took a deep breath. I could bang my head against this wall and hope for the best or I could ask for help. Again.

Piper shuddered.

It was Piper.

Yanking the darkness around the room to shroud the noise, I redialed. Dad had more experience, especially in dealing with bedevilings. I'd had to partially shift back to use my fingers, and the strange mixture of Watcher and Gris made me feel more unnatural than ever. I was split between my two worlds.

"What happened?" he asked.

I swallowed, concentrating on forming my human tongue in my Watcher mouth. I caught a glimpse of myself in Piper's bedroom mirror and turned away quickly. "I stopped by Piper's house to clear it of fiends and one slithered into her mouth." I enunciated slowly. My mouth felt like a beak instead of lips.

"Aw hell," Dad said. "This was supposed to be a simple solo job. I didn't deal with this level of bedeviling until I was in my thirties. Okay, You'll have to kill it." I heard my dad leaving a room and the rustle of fabric as he pulled on clothes. He probably didn't want my mom to hear about this.

"Them. I'll need to kill them."

"More than one?"

"The other one is wound around her neck and body. I didn't want it going in, too."

Silence. Dad must be stunned. I waited for him to recover. "This has escalated. You're dealing me in after this."

"Maybe."

I heard what sounded like a cross between a growl and

a groan from my father. "Fine. This is how you do it. Kill the one around her neck first because, you're right, it might go in, too, and then you're screwed. After you've done that, pull the fiend out of her using your palm over her mouth."

"Pull it out?" I repeated.

"Use the same energy you use to turn off the lights inside a house from outside."

"She won't be able to breathe." I'd be stealing the breath right from her lungs. It'd choke her.

"No, she won't be able to breathe, so do it real fast. Then, kill it quick before it dives back in."

"I've never seen this before." I'd never even heard of it.

"Because it hardly ever happens. They don't normally do this unless they're older, and I'm guessing it was summoned by something in the room. You've got more curse bags to find. But get it out first. It'll eat her mind from the inside if you don't."

"Eat her mind?"

"She won't wake up outside of this nightmare—she won't be able to. Bedeviling from the inside locks in the fiend until she dies so they don't normally do this unless they're baited with some strong emotions."

"Her dog *was* just killed." I paused. "Maybe this was why." Somebody had turned Piper into living bait. I watched her shiver on the bed. Damn. I had to find out who was responsible for all this. "But, you've done this before? Pulled a fiend out from inside a person?"

"Once. Successfully. Normally, we're too late. It looks like an exorcism—feels like one, too. Send me a message when you're done."

"Okay." I turned off the phone and slipped it into my pocket.

The fiend twisted around her neck was wholly focused on her shoulder. I waited until I was a foot away and plunged my talons through its torso, grabbing its heart. It screeched as I yanked the pulsing black mound out. Everything dissolved a moment later, turning to oozing black blood. It dripped through my gray fingers down to the floor—a murky puddle that melted out of sight.

One down.

I climbed onto Piper's bed. I'd never even thought to pull a fiend out of somebody, nor imagined it would come to this.

Her quilt was checkered patterns of red and white material with hearts quilted in—strangely grotesque given the circumstances. As I peeled the quilt away from her shivering body, my claws caught in the cotton fabric, and I kept dropping it. Dammit.

I could do this.

I could.

I needed to. She didn't have much time, and I'd been the fool who'd spooked the fiend into her.

She seized as the shudders from her vapory inhabitant rattled her frame. Her muttering increased. More even numbers. She skipped backward and forward but always even numbers. "No more," she hissed, shaking. "Cold. So cold. Six. Four. Twelve."

I had to stay in full transform to use all my Watcher powers. My slick-skinned body, normally so agile, was awkward and bulky as I straddled her slim frame, trying not to press too firmly. She was so tiny.

There was a new cut on her shoulder.

Damn. I'd wondered. She had more bedeviling her than just fiends. I shook it off. Time to get that thing out of her.

"Fourteen. Fourteen." Her body shook so abruptly I damn near slid off.

I took a deep breath and let it out slowly.

I covered her mouth with my hand, but drawing the darkness out using my palm made her gag as she inhaled through her nose. Oh hell, that wouldn't work. I'd need to cover both her nose and mouth. Wrong. So wrong. I'd be smothering her.

Sitting back, I tried to work up to it. I could do this.

After a cough, she murmured, "Eight" and then moaned as her body arched beneath a violent shudder from the fiend. Her eyes twitched behind her lids as she jerked and twisted.

I covered her nose and mouth with my palm and pulled at the fiend's vapor inside her. Her body contorted under mine, and I put a leg against hers as she bucked. One of her hands wriggled free and yanked at mine, breaking my concentration. The fiend slid back as she gagged and turned her head to the side. I pulled my hand away from her face again.

She took gulping breaths and coughed out, "Eighty-eight. No." She shook her head. "No. No. No."

Hellfire, why didn't I know how to do this? I couldn't concentrate and restrain her.

New plan. Lying across her as the fiend had been before entering her, I trapped her torso and pinned both of her arms. I lay my palm over her nose.

This had to work.

Her body was a violent tornado under mine as she panted hoarsely through her mouth.

Just because I didn't use my mouth like this normally, didn't mean that it wouldn't work. Fiends couldn't get into my mind. That was another edge we had on the rest of the world—besides our Watcher bodies. So, this plan was logical. Terrifying, but logical.

It had to work.

I had to do this.

I was out of options. After a deep breath, I covered her mouth with mine, inhaling the darkness from inside her and pushing it out my nostrils. She twisted and bucked, her neck arching, struggling for breath.

This was disgusting. I was a monster, but I couldn't stop. I was too far into the process to stop.

The fiend filtered through me, scalding my throat and nose. Beads of sweat collected on my skin, and my eyesight went red and then black as I felt the last wisp of the fiend draw through me. I surged up, reaching blindly in front of me as stars burst across my vision. I could feel the fiend—could feel the blackness. I plunged my talons through its chest and groped for the thick blob.

My hand finally found the fiend's heart, and I yanked it out, squeezing it tighter than I normally did. Bastard had gone inside her—it deserved more than just death. Its heart drizzled through my fingers. My vision flashed, bursts of bright stars against a midnight black. My body transformed back so quickly that my muscles stung.

"Piper?" I whispered.

For a moment, it seemed as if she wasn't breathing. I froze. I held my breath—needing her to take one of her own. Then, she inhaled deeply and coughed.

Chapter Eight

I woke up coughing with my throat on fire. A dead weight sat on my chest. I'd had this nightmare before, many times. The dead weight. The darkness. Usually there was screeching. At least there wasn't screeching this time.

Suddenly, the weight lifted.

Cutting the silence, a voice asked, "Are you okay, Piper?"

I jumped up and slammed my back against the headboard of my bed.

"Hush, Piper, it's me, Gris."

His hand touched mine. Knowing it was him was only slightly less terrifying.

As my mind bounced around in time with my raspy breathing, I heard footsteps out in the hall. Oh crap. The hall light turned on, and a rectangle of light appeared underneath the door. Somebody was coming. Gris was in my room, and somebody was coming. They'd wanna know what a boy was doing in my room in the middle of the night which, admittedly,

I'd like the answer to as well.

Something, presumably Gris, hit the floor right beside my bed as my door opened.

Gris. Gris was in my room.

The light from the hall blinded me as my mama looked in. I covered my shoulder with my hand.

"Are you okay, Piper?" she asked.

My breath came out in quick gasps. I swallowed my panic in a thick gulp. Ouch. That stung. What was up with my throat?

I could handle this. Gris didn't scare me. My mama finding out about Gris being here…that put the fear in me. "Nothing, Mama. Nightmare. It was nothing." I'd managed to sound almost calm. My voice came out croaky, but that would fit with the nightmare story I was selling. I swallowed again. Ow. Ow. Sandpaper would have gone down softer than that gulp.

"You feeling okay?"

The light from my nightlight and the hallway was enough for me to see the bottle of water at my bedside. Turning so the cuts on my shoulder weren't visible, I smiled tightly and grabbed my water bottle. "Just thirsty."

While drinking, I slid my hand under my pillow, searching for that flashlight. Oh, I'd be seeing Gris's face when he explained. And, there *would* be an explanation this time.

He was in my frakking room!

My room.

Okay. Okay. Be cool, Piper.

Mama ran a hand through her hair. She took a deep breath. "Do you want me to lock you in, sugar?"

My dad had installed a deadbolt lock over the summer for those nights I was prone to sleepwalking. Sometimes, I'd ask to be locked in, knowing in a true emergency I could always climb out my window. Mama would unlock it in the morning before I got up.

I nodded in quick jerks. "Sure, that's fine." It would

reassure her I wasn't about to run out and create more problems.

She closed the door, and I flicked on the flashlight, tiptoeing over to the door to lock it from my side. After the sound of her footsteps had died off, I approached my bed at a slow pace.

For once, something in my bedroom might be even stranger than I was expecting. I crawled across my bed with the flashlight. My quilt was completely off, but I wasn't cold. I was always cold. Then again, it wasn't often I had a tall, half-naked boy lying on my floor with a concerned look on his face. Very tall. Very half-naked. Very concerned-looking.

"Are you okay?" he whispered.

"Am I *okay*?" I half whispered between my teeth. Of course I wasn't okay. He was in my room in the middle of the night, and I'd woken up with my throat on fire. Good night, was he for real? "What are you doing in my room?" And why wasn't he wearing a shirt or shoes? I blinked. Wow, he had a really strong chest for being so tall and thin. He should *never* wear a shirt. I shouldn't have noticed that, but it was right in front of me. How on this great, green earth did he manage to have such a nice chest when he looked ready to disappear if he turned sideways? It was as if all he owned was muscle.

"Sorry, forgot. The question thing," he mumbled.

Fine. Whatever. He was answering my questions—for certain. I wasn't accepting vague answers, either. I was gonna have a full explanation this time. "Okay, but, seriously, what are you doing in my room?"

Gris stood and pulled a phone out of his pants pocket. He tapped in a text while searching the corner of my room near the door. I followed his body with my flashlight. He had thin red scratches all over his back. I squinted. It was a good thing I'd already made sure he hadn't killed my dog—though the scratches looked around a week old.

"And why aren't you wearing a shirt? Or shoes?"

"I'm looking for those sacks I mentioned earlier. They're causing your, uhh, nightmares."

"That's why you're not wearing a shirt?" I'd been expecting a rational explanation. I don't know why. Nothing else in my life made sense these days. I shuddered. Not a good feeling.

"Shirts are too constricting," he whispered. "Help me look. Look in the corners of the room."

"Fine." I scrambled out of bed and went to a different corner. I was a sucker for a plan. If somebody had a plan, I was almost always willing to hear them out. "I found one earlier under my bed."

"What did you do with it?"

"Flushed it down the toilet. Do you need a flashlight?"

"No, I can see in the dark."

Of course he could.

There was no sack in the corner where my backpack and schoolbooks were sitting.

Gris moved on to a different portion of my room.

The remaining corner had my closet in it. I'd taken the sliding doors off, as I didn't like having patches of shadows in my room. My flashlight ran across some pink lace on the floor, and I shoved the bra under some dirty clothes nearby. If I'd known Gris was gonna be around, I might've tidied up.

'Course, this whole thing was weird and awkward especially since I wasn't wearing much, and I could feel the itch of the latest cut. I yanked a sweatshirt off a hanger and pulled it on to cover my shoulder. If he hadn't seen it, I wasn't about to let him.

My coats and a few dresses hung around my head as I crouched to search in the closet corner. Shoes littered the floor: a pair of well-worn tennis shoes, my boots, some slippers, and a few others.

I reached out to move them when Gris knelt beside me. His naked shoulder brushed my clothed one. Gris moved like a cat—he was so quiet. His hand stretched into the shadow my beam hadn't cut through and pulled out a sack.

"This is what we're looking for," he whispered.

He opened the purple sack and held it so I could shine the flashlight beam in. Strange flat leaves and blades of grass were in there as well as a sprinkling of yellow sulfur powder. He shifted the sack in his hand before lifting it to his nose.

"That looks different than the one I found earlier," I whispered. "It was in a different kind of sack."

"Canvas, burlap, silk?"

"Burlap."

Gris nodded. "This one's stronger. Either they're escalating or there's two people doing this."

"So somebody keeps breaking into my room to plant these bags full of powder and grass to give me nightmares?" My life kept getting weirder. Especially since it seemed to have worked. I'd been having a nasty nightmare when Gris woke me up.

"There might be another." He got to his feet and ran a hand through his hair as he scanned my room. "If they went with the most hidden corner and don't know you well enough to recognize items of personal value, maybe under your dresser?"

Sure enough, Gris pulled a sack from under my dresser, too, and opened it to peer in. "That's wormwood." He lifted up a blade of grass and sniffed it before dropping it back while shaking his head and frowning.

"Fine." I sat down on my bed and pointed the flashlight at him. A strange mark on his shoulder caught my eye—a one-inch golden brown mark that looked like a bat wing. "Is that a tattoo?"

"Sort of. Piper, I think somebody is trying to harm you.

Besides yourself."

What did he mean besides myself? "Just 'cause they're trying to give me nightmares?"

"They do more than that. These pouches are like curses for drawing bad spirits to you."

Bad spirits? He had to be kidding, or think I was ridiculously gullible. I waited, staring. He didn't smile at all. Sincerity was etched into his gaze and the lines bracketing his flat mouth. Okay. Spirits. Maybe he would know about such things due to his job.

"So, this is what you do?" I asked. "Catch bad spirits? Or get rid of them?"

Gris had to be the most secretive person alive.

He shrugged and walked over to the window. He was leaving?

"Wait. You can't—"

He dropped the pouches outside, then returned to sit on my bed. Oh. His scrutiny when he sat there was enough to make me wish he'd left. I kept the flashlight trained on him, and the shadows on his skin gave him a sinister look.

"It feels like we should be telling scary stories." Gris reached out to tap the flashlight. A scowl deepened the shadows beside his mouth. "Actually, tonight was the scariest thing I'd ever seen." Leaning in farther, he touched my shoulder, right on the latest cut. "Piper, tell me why you cut yourself."

I opened my mouth to deny it, and he must've expected it, 'cause his eyebrows raised in a dare. Fine. I knew nothing— *nothing* about him, and he knew one of my deepest secrets. This was so uneven and so unfair.

"I'm crazy," I snapped. "Isn't it obvious?"

Reaching out, Gris removed the flashlight from my hand and propped it up on a pillow so the beam pointed toward his face. "You're not crazy. You can't sell me on that—so don't even bother." Reaching out, he said, "Your hands are freezing," as he wrapped both his hands around mine. His hands were so warm—mine felt bony and cold in comparison. Lifting my hands to his mouth, he blew his breath on my skin. Warm steam slid into my entire body.

This was nice. I'd still like an explanation, but I'd never had a boy be like this around me. "The doctor said OCD," I said softly, watching my hands in his.

He nodded.

I narrowed my eyes. "But it's not the normal kind. My mama has that and mine is…darker. Like it's deeper. I'm not clean like her. I'm not like her in a lot of ways. Half the time I'm not convinced I have it, not her kind anyway." My thoughts were worse and worse every day. Feeling the spiral and knowing I couldn't control it was hell. It was swallowing me up.

"I think you still have it, Piper. It just looks different. I, uhh, researched it a bit after I saw you earlier."

I yanked my hands from his. No, he didn't get it. Nobody knew how deep the darkness ran inside of me. It was soul deep. It was too deep to cut out. "You're not an expert after reading a few websites, Gris. You don't *know* me." I got up to pace. "It's not something nice that fits in a box and can be defined. You have no idea what I'm capable of. If I run mad, watch out."

He stood in front of me, right in my path. "You're not dark or going mad, Piper."

"I think of awful things." I closed my eyes. "I think of them all the time. At night. In school. When I'm alone, they're so loud and clear and…" My arms shook as I wrapped them around my waist. Why was I saying this out loud? He couldn't possibly understand what it was like to be evil inside. It was a rage, a temper in my soul—sometimes I heard it scream. I didn't tell people this. I never told anybody this. My parents only knew a little from before I started hiding things.

His arms went around me—loose at first. Then he hugged me, and my cheek rested against his bare chest. My arms were trapped between us, so I let them drop to my side. I tapped my fingers together. The rhythm soothed me as much as his arms.

Gris's skin felt so warm, and he smelled salty and earthy at the same time. I'd always figured sweat was vile and disgusting, but the warm, musky scent of Gris spoke of activity and heat. It wasn't disgusting, not by a long shot.

"I'm gonna leave you alone to get some sleep, Piper. I wanna see you and talk to you tomorrow."

"Fine."

"I'm gonna sit outside your window and keep the shadows away tonight, so you can sleep. If you need me, you can lean outside, and I'll be there."

"And these bad spirits…they're real? The ones that those pouches are luring in? They exist? You're not just messin' with me?" I'd never even considered the possibility that other people might see the things that moved in on me from the shadows.

"They're real. You're more haunted than most right now."

Oh. Right. That's why he was here. He took care of ghosts, and I was haunted. My room felt bare other than him. It never felt empty like this at night, not anymore. It never felt warm, either. Though the fact that he was still holding me probably contributed to that.

"What are these things in my room? How did you get rid of them? I don't understand any of this, and you never answered my questions—not really."

"Can't we put this off for another day? I'm fairly exhausted."

Hmm, or he didn't wanna answer my questions. On the other hand, my room felt empty, and it hadn't for a year—I owed him for that. Gris, with his secrets, was good at whatever he did.

"You can stay inside my room. It's cold outside." As an afterthought, I added, "And there are bugs."

His amused chuckle shook his chest. "Will you be able to sleep if I hang out on your floor?"

"I'm not sure if I'll be able to sleep anyway." I leaned back. "You have secrets, too, don't you?"

He was staring at the window and grimaced before looking down. "I do."

"Will you tell me about them?"

His frown spoke loud and clear. He had some dark secrets. If he understood mine, even a bit, but didn't want to share to his own, what did that mean?

"I don't know," he said.

"Will you tell me about the ghosts you hunt? Whatever these bad spirits are?"

"Aren't you afraid?" Brown eyes searched mine. Did he want me to be afraid?

"Not really. I can think of a hundred things more terrible than spirits."

"I'll tell you tomorrow during the day. They aren't around as much during the day."

I was pressed up against his chest, and he still had his arms around me. I stepped back, wrapping my arms around myself and looking at the shadowed carpet at my feet.

"Fine then, so…you'll get back into bed, and I'll sit over in that corner." His discomfort was palpable, and it made mine bearable. We were just two human beings partially-clothed in a room at night that had a bed in it. It was fine.

As he was walking toward the corner, he stopped by my desk, frowned, and picked up the clipboard on it. "You made a list."

"It's a list of suspects. I told you I was gonna figure out who killed Jester."

"My name is on it." He pointed.

"Yes, but I crossed it out." I went to his side and traced the line through his name.

"Because you trust me."

I shook my head. "No, 'cause you told me you didn't do it, and you weren't lying when you said that."

"Gee thanks." His tone was bone dry.

"My name is on there, too."

He picked up the pen and struck a line through my name with an exasperated look at me. He flipped through the pages behind. "I didn't take this many notes for my schoolwork."

"This is a little more important than school, and the proper way to run an investigation is with thorough research."

"I've done research, too, but I've been focusing on the grave robbery today." And on OCD, apparently. He went to my timeline on the fourth page. "You've got the grave robbing on here."

"I can't rule out that it's connected. If I didn't have a Human Biology test tomorrow, I might've borrowed my daddy's laptop to see what's online." I tapped the circled numbers. "I've rated the events by how they might relate to Jester's murder. One is probably not related and ten is almost certainly related." The only thing with a ten beside it was Jester's murder 'cause that was the only absolute certainty.

"You didn't rate Trina's disappearance."

"I didn't know how to. If we're saying something sinister happened to her, then that changes the probability. What are the odds that we have multiple people willing to harm a dog and Trina?"

"Hopefully low, but Hidden Creek is full of surprises." He returned to the list on the first page. "My cousin and his dad made your list. Danny's dad might've killed Jester?"

"It's my suspect list and this is all about my dog. You can create your own. I went for the most plausible suspects. Your cousin doesn't much care for me—plus, there's proximity for him and his daddy."

"I can't imagine his dad not liking you."

I wrinkled up my nose. "Mr. Porter is close by and Jester would go to him. Also, he's strong and quiet. There's something…unsettling about him, if you'll pardon my saying so." His intensity spoke to a potential for heavy feelings, possibly for violence. I avoided him as much as I could. It was hard to judge somebody who rarely talked. I tried to believe that Jester had better instincts on Mr. Porter than I did, but I couldn't dismiss him as somebody I never wanted to be alone with. Ever. "Proximity and strength are significant factors I can't dismiss."

"Hank made your list—along with his father. Call me a liar, but I'm guessing he'd be more into kicking dogs than making friends with Jester."

"Well, if you gave Jester food, he'd be excited about that and fairly forgiving. If the food was poisoned… Do you see what I mean? I can't rule out Hank Jr. 'cause Jester might've been nice if food was involved. His bark might've been his 'happy to have a midnight snack' bark." It seemed like a betrayal to admit that, but it had to be how Jester was lured in. "And Hank Sr. is everything his son is. Besides, he didn't much care for his daughter. He thought Trina was a shame to their name."

"This Jared must be Hank's friend."

Nodding, I tapped his name. "He's a follower and anything Hank told him to do, he'd do. Also, I've heard of him drowning barn cats. It might just be a rumor, but it wouldn't surprise me. Some folks have this nasty, mean look in their eyes from the time they can walk—that's Jared. You know, he once ate a live fish on a dare?"

Gris shook his head. "Phil is on here."

I bit my lip. I'd hated to put his name on there, but it

made sense. "Well, I need to confirm that he's still in a mental hospital to do my due diligence. I can do that tomorrow."

It took him a minute, but then he nodded. "Coach Laramie? I'm assuming a relative of Phil's since they share a name."

"Okay, you might laugh, but Coach Laramie came to town 'cause his daddy, that's Phil, wasn't doing so well. But the coach hates this town. He's hoping that with his record as a coach and, well, Hank's athletic record that he'll be able to move. If Phil stays in an institution, the coach gets control of his daddy's money which I've heard is no small amount, and he doesn't have to stay in Hidden Creek. So, I can see him convincing Phil to do something crazy."

"But Jester was killed later."

"Yes, but the coach really doesn't care for me. I swear he's tried to kill me by making me run. It's a less obvious method for murder, but effective."

Gris grinned.

"I'm serious."

"No, that's both brilliant and sort of sweet."

I shoved his shoulder.

"But your last three…"

I rolled my eyes. I knew he'd have to comment. "I know they're vague."

"So, you have 'unknown enemy,' 'a creature,' and then just 'a woman.'"

I went to take the paper from him but he jerked it out of reach. "It's my list. I can put whatever I want on there. Besides, in an investigation it's important to account for two variables: the unknown and the unlikely. Too often folks jump to conclusions with limited facts when you discount those things. Like I said with Mr. Porter, you don't always know who hates you, and I knew even before you told me that there are dangerous things out there."

"But 'a woman' fits under unknown enemy."

"No, she wouldn't. A woman isn't necessarily an enemy."

"So, you have no female enemies?"

"I didn't say that, but if I did, they'd fit under the other category. Women have strange motives at times. Mattie once dumped an entire Coke on Felicity at lunch 'cause she had the same shirt at home and Felicity looked better in it. And they used to share deodorant in gym…so they're close…and also that's vile."

He blinked. "Men can have strange motives."

"But they typically don't. If I'm going to consider a woman, I'd have to think more outside the box for why she might kill Jester. Women are complicated. If a woman hated me, I'd assume she'd come after me, not my dog, but if she is my enemy, she's covered under the other designation." My logic was fairly sound.

"But an 'unknown enemy' opens up the field to everybody in Hidden Creek." He was determined to see this conversation to the bitter end.

"Of course it doesn't. Dick didn't kill Jester for example."

"But my name is on there."

"It's my list," I reminded him. "And it's been crossed off."

"Did you make the list before or after we went to lunch on Sunday?"

"I don't see how that's at all relevant." After. But sometimes it was good to show on a list things that had been eliminated. It was motivating, and it showed the process. It was like showing your work in math.

"Critch isn't on this list," Gris said.

"Nope."

His expression said it should be.

"My list of my suspects," I reminded him.

"Okay, so I'll take my relatives on your list to question. You can find out more about Phil and this coach. I'll take

Hank Jr. and Jared. I'll ask Danny about them. Both are violently stupid. I can research Hank's possible motives by finding out more about his sister's disappearance while you're in school."

"And you'll be sure to take notes? Though I think I should transcribe them." I should be more polite, but his handwriting was horrifying—there was no getting around that.

"Or I could just tell you."

"Methodical, Gris. We have to be methodical about this. It's the only way." It was the proper way to do an investigation. I should really be in charge.

"It's cute that you think so." He eyeballed my desk, and his hand went to one of the drawers.

"What are you doing?" I slapped his hand.

"Copying your list. Do you have another piece of paper and a pen?"

"Would you put your name on the copied list?"

"'Course not."

"Then it's not a copy," I pointed out. "Also, then you'd have eleven names. What kind of list has eleven names? Ideal lists have ten names, but I couldn't rule out two names when I made this list."

He stopped searching to stare at me. "I'd take your name off, too, so there'd be ten."

That'd be better. But still. "Whenever you're investigating something, you need to see the progress and the eliminations you've made. It's more sensible, Gris." I grabbed his phone from his hand, switched to camera mode, and took a picture. "There. Now you have an exact copy. See. Done. Also, it's legible." The value of legibility couldn't be discounted.

He was trying not to smile. I could tell. His lips twitched. "Thanks." Clearing his throat, he added, "You should probably go to bed before your mom comes to see who you're talking to."

Nodding, I climbed back into bed, setting the flashlight, still lit, on my bedside table so it illuminated the ceiling. I could see his shadow over in the corner. He texted another message as he dropped onto the beanbag. The screen illuminated his face. "I wonder if killing Jester is related to the curse sacks, which were part of a plan to drive you insane through nightmares.." He threw out these words like it didn't matter…like we weren't talking about my sanity or my dog.

"Was that what might've happened? Me going mad?" That nightmare had been one of the worst I'd ever experienced. I still felt shaky.

"Yes."

I waited for him to explain. He didn't. He just kept typing on his phone.

"Don't you need sleep?" I asked.

"I usually sleep during the day." His tone was matter-of-fact, as if nothing was unusual about him being in my room half dressed.

It was unusual though. Very.

I tucked my quilt around me, covering as much of myself as I could. Awkward. "Sometimes I talk in my sleep."

"Count."

"You want me to count?"

"No, you count in your sleep. Well, you throw out even numbers. You also say a few other things, but mostly you count."

I ducked farther under the blanket. I'd counted to get to sleep since I'd learned the difference between even and odd numbers and figured out on my own that even numbers were better. And sometimes I counted when I was awake. Even numbers were better all day, too. The counting ran deep—through my dreams, through the nightmares.

He might very well be the first boy my age I'd met who didn't try to score with me—probably 'cause he knew too much. Could he still be interested in a girl after he found out she cut herself on purpose, counted in her sleep, and did patterns for no reason at all? He knew all my secrets and I still knew nothing about him. In fact, I felt like I knew even less the longer I knew him, but now we were partners in finding the truth.

He'd acted concerned, but he likely saw me as a kid sister or something. Just what I'd always wanted. I flipped to my other side. Staring at the wall was a better idea. I'd forget he was here. I could do that. Easy as pie. I'd concentrate real hard on forgetting.

I clenched my eyes closed. Inside my head, I started over with the only thing that should matter—things that were absolute and clear and not harmful. Two, Four, Six, Eight, Ten, Twelve, Fourteen…

Chapter Nine

Worst. Night. Ever. Staying all night in a girl's room, when all you want to do is crawl all over her and kiss her, makes for a hellish experience.

I'd never wanted anybody half as much as I wanted Piper. Even her counting was turning me on by the end of the night.

When the sun rose, I bolted through her window as fast as I could. My Watcher powers were nothing to speak of during the full light of day, so I ran home. I couldn't even cloak myself in darkness. Of all the times for the residents of Hidden Creek to be up and going about their business. Danny and my aunt waved to me when they saw me. At least they knew why I was barefoot and without a shirt. I tried to tell an older man watering his grass I was out running, but he'd eyed my bare feet and grumbled about "kids and fads."

Still, I'd stayed all night, like I said I would, and that would earn points with Piper. I'd kept my promise. I'd pushed out nearly a dozen fiends during the rest of the night. The sacks had still been drawing them to the area, and Piper's emotional thoughts were pulling them in. Since I'd brought the pouches home, I'd see what was normal for her to attract tonight.

I might need to stay the night again. It would be preceded by a cold shower, which was the first thing I did before crawling into my own bed.

Piper might dream of counting, but I dreamed of Piper counting, and it was much less soothing for me, but not a nightmare. Definitely not a nightmare.

• • •

Working on the porch swing was a bust. I'd need new boards, and I didn't relish a trip into town with how nosy everybody was.

So instead, I did research on Trina and her boyfriend.

Social media had done me a favor there when the local newspapers fell short. But things weren't adding up. Sure, everybody said she was the local wild child, but running away in the middle of the night for no reason? Nothing had set her off, like a fight or other trouble from what I could tell. Her profiles online just dropped off. For a girl who posted selfies every few days, it was a significant absence. She'd just up and disappeared. Plus, it didn't sound like she'd taken anything with her. How far could a runaway get with no clothes or money? She'd had a boyfriend from Memphis who'd disappeared around the same time, but that didn't quite add up, either. Perhaps if her parents had spent more time worrying over their daughter than they had showering their son with attention…

In the one article in the area's paper, her dad was quoted as saying, "At least we still have Hank Jr. Did you see him in last night's game?" They quoted Hank's stats in his sister's disappearance article. Damn, that was messed up. Her mom kept referring to her as "deeply troubled." Maybe Trina was better off wherever she was. The only one in the family who seemed to grieve her disappearance was her brother, who'd insisted she wouldn't just run away.

Except she wasn't better off. Instinct told me she was dead—especially after I did more searches on the boyfriend. Nothing since the night she went missing. There was no reason for both of them to drop completely out of sight.

I was continuing to take notes, despite knowing their legibility was suspect. My dad called it nearly coded handwriting. Nobody could read it but me…and Piper. She'd assumed she'd mistaken her translation, thankfully.

School had to be out by four o'clock, but maybe Piper had somewhere to go after school. Going across the way to the machine shop would give me a chance to interrogate two other "suspects." I could ask Danny about Hank and work up to asking them for alibis. I'd failed to consider that it might be difficult interrogating your own family.

At ten minutes after four, I walked over to the machine shop. Danny was working on a couple of bikes. My uncle was working on a Harley, but he waved at me.

"Heard you had some problems with Hank Jr." My uncle set down his wrench, possibly to impress the seriousness of his opinion. "You'd be wise to stay away from him."

"Yes, sir."

"Danny said you found some of them beasts near the Devons' also?"

I shrugged. "Some."

"Nothing you couldn't handle though, I take it?" My uncle did have a very direct stare.

"No. I know what I'm doing."

"There's more here than there should be according to Critch…and Jess." Since Danny's dad wasn't blood, he couldn't sense them like our other relatives. Must be disconcerting to hear this stuff secondhand, especially from Aunt Jess, his own wife.

"Yes. Far more than there should be."

"Any chance that's what is making folks behave strangely?"

"Possibly." And some folks were getting in over their heads in ugly craft they shouldn't be messing with.

"Will your daddy be along to help you?"

"He's caught up in something right now, and I'm a full Watcher-in-standing."

Danny and my uncle both waited for me to say more.

"If it gets to be more than I can handle, he said he'd come. But I can handle it."

Danny smirked and I wanted to punch him in the face. He had no idea what it was like to be a Watcher. Neither of them did.

And they were still waiting for me to say more.

I didn't much feel like offering information. I still couldn't believe that fiend went inside Piper last night. My dad had received the *Cliff's Notes* of the event. Outsiders wouldn't understand. I didn't understand, and I'd been there.

This small spit on the map was kicking my Watcher ass. A few fiends were one thing. Fiends and somebody with a death wish inviting them around? Hell, they were going to get themselves killed and take a few others with them.

But not Piper.

Really, only a damn fool of a Watcher would keep at this without help. It was tempting to be that fool. I had plenty of reasons—my pride being the biggest. Then, there was the thing squashing my pride. Short, sweet, and liked to count. Having my dad around could make things awkward, but I wanted her safe and counting her nights away.

I sighed. "The State Department has my dad tailing a foreign dignitary. They don't want an international incident due to fiends. So next week is probably the soonest he can be here."

They both returned to their tasks.

"Hey, ugly." I kicked Danny's shoe.

He snorted. "You're so ugly your mama takes you everywhere with her just so she never has to kiss you good-bye."

"You're ugly enough to chase snakes."

"You're so ugly you'd make a freight train take a dirt road." That was impressive coming from Danny. He'd probably gotten it from one of his sisters.

"You're so ugly your cooties keep their eyes closed." I'd picked that one up from his sisters. They were mouthy little things for their age.

Snorting, he dug into his pocket and pulled out a quarter. Danny held it up in the dusty sunbeams filtering through the window and said, "Can't turn off the lights like you."

"It's daytime. I can't do much, either. I'm just like you."

"Just like me. Now, that's a shame." He flipped me the quarter, purposefully making me jump for it if his smirk was any indication.

I snatched it out of the air and looked at it. "Nice goatee." Somebody had carved a goatee onto George Washington's face. I pocketed it.

"We've all got our secret skills," Danny said. "You come 'round to win quarters off me?"

"No. What time does Piper's school let out?" He'd graduated last year—he should know.

"1:55."

"So, she should be home."

He shrugged. "Hank says she sometimes gets home about when he does, but he plays sports. Who knows what Piper does."

I didn't offer up any information though I knew a shade

more than most about Piper. "Speaking of Hank, why do Hank and his father hate Piper?"

Both Danny and his dad stopped working.

"How'd you know they do?" my uncle asked.

I shrugged rather than tell them I was making an educated guess since Piper had an uncanny sense for who was a danger to her.

"It's on account of her mama," my uncle said. "Letty is local you might say—has family in town. She used to visit now and then when she was a teenager. I think Hank Sr. was interested, but she married Max Devon. Hank had been shut out by a man who'd never thrown a football in his life and wasn't from around here. Intellectual that man, Mr. Devon. Genius, really. Piper is just as smart. Hank Jr. was expected to impress everyone with his scholarships—instead it's Piper drawing the attention. Word is she can basically pick a college."

"And then she went and took that test again just to show how much better than us she is," Danny put in.

"The ACT? So, that's why they hate her? They're jealous?"

"No, 'cause the Devons act like they're so much better than everyone around," Danny said. "Her daddy makes a fortune at his job, you know. Piper doesn't even need a scholarship. She just wants one."

"It's not our place to judge." My uncle gave Danny a "hush-up" look. He was a little late in rising to her defense to my mind.

"I can't believe you're saying that after one of them called the cops for animal cruelty with those barn cats." A muscle twitched in Danny's eyelid.

My uncle narrowed his eyes further. "We don't know that for certain, and it's not our place to judge," he said again.

Okay. "What about Jared?" I asked. "What's he got against Piper?"

"What's it matter?" Danny asked. "Having a difficult time coming to grips with your girlfriend being a freak?"

I grabbed his head by the hair, and he yelped.

My uncle looked up. His worn and greasy hand tightened on his wrench, and his whole body looked stretched taut like his skin was too tight on him. Our gazes held, and I understood what Piper saw. He was the type of guy who you thought might kill under the right circumstances. He might or he might not find those circumstances.

"Piper is not a freak. Leave her alone." I let go of Danny's hair.

He rubbed his head while scowling at me.

My uncle relaxed. I knew he wasn't keen on his "wife's strange kin," but he didn't interfere. Though I sensed he also preferred not to have us around. Maybe that's why he'd asked about my dad. Maybe he didn't like having me here, let alone without supervision.

"You don't know nothing about nothing," Danny muttered.

I left before I insulted my uncle's hospitality more than I already had.

She'd been out of school for two hours. What did that mean? She knew where I was. We'd never settled that she'd come to my place, but I'd assumed. Maybe she'd assumed the opposite? Or maybe she wasn't ready to trust me.

Danny wouldn't be going out of his way to help me anymore, but I didn't regret setting him straight. I wasn't about to let him disrespect Piper.

Shoving my hands into my pockets, I walked to her place after grabbing my laptop bag from the house.

Her mom answered the door while drying her hands on a dishtowel…again and again.

"I was hoping to see Piper, ma'am. Is she around?"

"She called from school to say she had some studying to

do, said she wouldn't be home til supper."

Which I suspected in Piper's behavioral philosophy translated into the message she didn't trust me. I smiled at her mom. There were ways to get around that. I didn't give up so easily.

"My name's Gris Caso, ma'am. I'm staying in the farmhouse across from the Porters. Jess Porter is my aunt."

She tilted her head while she examined me, much like Piper did. Staring seemed to be a family trait. "Are you in school with Piper?"

"I've graduated. I'm actually in town on business."

She nodded as if I'd passed a test.

"Piper came over to the barn the other day because she was upset about her dog."

"Oh, I'm sorry. We've told her and told her not to go in there."

I shook my head. The last thing I wanted was Piper to stay out of the barn. "No, it's fine, ma'am. Really. I don't mind. Matter of fact, I took her out for lunch on Sunday."

Her jaw dropped. "That was you? Well, bless my soul, that girl mumbled something that sounded like Liss, and I couldn't figure out when she and Alissa Traven started up a friendship. I hope you don't think I'd normally let Piper head off with somebody I haven't even met."

I grinned. Piper had snuck me by her mom so she wouldn't have to get permission. "No, ma'am."

She clucked her tongue. "And on a Sunday. She'd gone to church earlier that day so I'd figured she could skip our Sunday meal, but…" She shook her head. "You know Piper's only seventeen, right?"

"Yes. I only turned eighteen a month ago, and she acts older than me."

She smiled at that. These Devon women might not be impervious to charm, but they *were* difficult.

"We went to Dick's and that was it," I added, hoping that'd help. My mom was this protective of me, and I was a gargoyle part of the time.

A soft gasp and she shook her head again. "And he didn't call me? Well, I've a mind to say a thing or two to him as well."

I cleared my throat. "Would it be all right if I waited for Piper? I wanted to see her. And I have some work that I can do remotely." I could get back to doing research.

"I'd love to have you stay for supper." And for an interrogation—her shrewd eyes said, but I'd expected that. "I'm sure she'll be home by then." She stepped back to let me by.

I tried not to smile triumphantly. I might've managed to outmaneuver Piper in one way, but I still had to convince her to trust me. That'd take a lot more work.

"If you'll just take off your shoes and put them in here…" She opened up a nearby closet.

I was glad I'd worn some of my better shoes and socks. This was nearly dressing up in my world. I put my shoes in a bin before looking around.

The house was spotless and very color-coordinated. Everything matched down to the littlest detail. There was nothing in the room I sat in that wasn't colored off-white, forest green, or maroon. The cherry wood table matched the frames on the wall to the exact hue. There were no family pictures, but I could see them in the adjoining hall, which apparently had a more relaxed color scheme. The couch wasn't comfortable, but it wasn't uncomfortable—it was merely another matching item.

"Your house is beautiful." Not a lie. It was beautiful in a very exact manner. Maybe it made sense that Piper saw her condition as darker since her mother's seemed straightforward. Clean and matching—and I *had* seen Piper's room, after all. Not that I was one to judge.

"So what is it that you do for work?" Piper's mom gestured at my laptop as I set it on my lap. If she didn't already know, she wasn't in the local gossip loop, which suited me just fine.

"My dad and I document the history of towns and supernatural events from a skeptical standpoint." An explanation I'd used so often I could say it in my sleep. None of it was a lie. Just vague.

"Well, shut my mouth, you're a writer?"

"Researcher into supposed paranormal events."

"Is that right? And you came here." There was a retreat in her body language and expression. She couldn't be worried that it had anything to do with Piper. She shouldn't be. Piper wasn't paranormal or supernatural. In fact, Piper's mom was currently allowing the biggest supernatural creature she'd ever meet to sit on her couch…her very exactly matching couch. I was the one thing in the room that didn't match. Of course, that basically described my whole life. I was one of those things that'd never belong.

"I came here on account of my family being in the area. As I said, I can work remotely." I wanted to ask Piper's mom about her family in the area. It'd be weird if she was related to the Beaumonts, and even stranger if she was somehow related to me through Critch.

Relief flooded Mrs. Devon's face. She was likely over-protective of Piper. If Hank and my cousin were anything to judge from, Piper hadn't met with much acceptance among those her age.

"You know, I haven't talked to your aunt for quite a while," she said. "I had no idea a person could make a living doing research like that, let alone y'all's family did it."

"Most of our jobs are for the local and federal government. My dad is working for an embassy right now. We investigate so they don't have to waste manpower."

She nodded. "Well that makes sense. Is it dangerous?"

I wasn't sure that anybody had ever asked me that, but it did segue into what I wanted to talk about. "It's difficult to predict, but I don't need to carry a gun if that means anything." It meant that I grew body armor and had talons that were more effective. "It seems like Hidden Creek isn't free from danger, though. Piper told me about your dog."

The shuttered look dropped back into her eyes—her brown eyes, not like Piper's mossy green ones. I wanted to go check out the family pictures in the hallway to see how much Piper resembled her dad, but I didn't want to act suspicious.

"She said you think an animal did it," I said.

Her mom sighed...a long exhale. "I don't. I never did. Piper doesn't think so, either, I take it?"

I shook my head.

"It's so hard to know what to do. I heard her screaming and I ran out there expecting...I don't know. She's never screamed like that. It was like I had a banshee in my front yard. I dragged her away and I just wanted it over, I guess. It hurt to see that. I wanted it to stop hurting for everybody, and the best way to do that was to pretend it hadn't happened. It was likely a prank—a horrible, sadistic prank." It sounded like she was trying to convince herself. She shot me a look. "Do you investigate those sorts of things?"

"Sometimes."

"Is that why you're interested in Piper?"

Finally. A question I could answer honestly. Somewhat honestly. "I'm interested in Piper because her smile lights up a room. She's sweet and the smartest girl I've ever met."

Her mother was much easier to charm if the brief pause in her hand-wiping was anything to go on, as well as the flushed look of pride.

"And that's why I'm worried about her. This thing with her dog...most people wouldn't think of killing something as a prank, not normal people anyway."

She nodded. "You might be right at that. I didn't know how to handle it. I didn't want people staring Piper down and asking her questions. Reckon we should've had the sheriff come, but I wondered if that'd be making a spectacle of Piper's sadness." Her hands worried the dishtowel, twisting it back and forth. "The timing made it suspicious. Piper is, as you said, smart, but some of the locals don't appreciate it. She was taking this test again, even though her score was much higher than everybody else's in Hidden Creek, and everybody, including Piper, had already sent their scores off. There was no reason for her to take it again, but she got it in her mind that she wanted to. She said she knew exactly where she'd gone wrong on the previous test. She even used her own money to retake it. People were talking, but Piper insisted… and, well, you've met her—you know how she can be."

I definitely knew how she could be.

"And I shouldn't say this, but I imagine you'll find out soon enough, being what you are. People around Hidden Creek are superstitious. Animals get killed and everybody around here wants to blame it on something supernatural." She pointed at me. "I'd appreciate it if you could prove this *wasn't* supernatural."

Piper's mother had the lay of the land all right. They hadn't called the sheriff because the situation with Phil Laramie already had people in Hidden Creek eyeing Piper. This would've added fuel to the fire. "It wasn't. I know it wasn't already. But can you think of who might've done this to Jester?"

She swallowed. "If you saw it, you couldn't imagine— you couldn't imagine anybody you've ever met doing that. It must've been a prank, a bet, a…drunken fool, somebody high on something. I think some drugs can make you do things you normally wouldn't. I don't know. You just can't imagine the blood. It was everywhere." She looked on the verge of gagging. Piper had mentioned her retching in the bushes.

"Maybe it was somebody her age? We ran across some of the boys from the school and they were…" How did one put this?

"Damn fools?" she supplied, startling a grin out of me.

"Some of them." Maybe she was right, and I was looking for a bigger plot with the dog. Though the grave-robbing on top of the dog killing and the curse pouches seemed like too much to be coincidence.

Then, there was Trina's disappearance.

Hell, there were too many unknowns.

"Yeah, well, the boys 'round here haven't really won her heart that's for sure. Sometimes I get the feeling she can't wait to graduate and get as far away from here as possible. The only colleges she's considering seriously are west coast ones. That was even before this thing with Jester."

I didn't know what to say to that.

"Piper hasn't received any threats before, has she?"

She paused and bit her lip as she stared at me. Piper and her mom were so cagey. I respected that, even if it was aggravating me to no end. "No, not that I know of—we would've called the sheriff if she had. I didn't even know where to start with this. There's been some vandalism. She says it happens to everybody, though, and, even then, she isn't one for talking about such things. Maybe you'll find out more and be able to keep my baby safe."

"I will. I won't let anything happen to Piper. And I'll find out who did this to her dog."

"She *did* go to lunch with you, and she's never given the fools around here the time of day." Which was her way of saying that her daughter didn't think I was dangerous or an idiot.

But, Piper didn't trust easily. In fact, I should've realized that. Why had I assumed Piper would trust me when I was there last night with next to no explanation? I wasn't thinking clearly, but I couldn't with Piper's long legs right there. I needed to concentrate on Piper and rein in these, uhh, needs.

"Well, I'll leave you to that," her mother said. It froze me until I realized she was referring to my work, not my lust for Piper.

"Much obliged, ma'am." I stood respectfully and nodded as she left the room. She was still rubbing her hands on that dishtowel.

Piper and her mom were something else.

I heard a low murmur as Mrs. Devon called on the phone in the kitchen. Then, her voice rose slightly in volume as she tore into Dick. Hopefully she wouldn't return anytime soon to toss me out of the house.

In the meantime, I opened my laptop. I needed to earn Piper's trust. I'd exposed some of her secrets without doing the same. I sat on the perfectly-matched couch and stared, unfocused.

My screensaver came on. A gargoyle slid up and down across my monitor. Gargoyles or grotesques once marked places that would welcome a Watcher's presence. A gargoyle on a building meant that a Watcher lived there or could be contacted through them. Eventually, they'd become a decoration. Now they were a part of history linked with superstition.

Few knew of us today, but we were known. We were still needed and well-paid. The world would always have its dark spirits that we could see, hear, and kill. Fiends outnumbered our reach, but they had a huge population to feed from. Tortured souls were everywhere.

I wasn't noble, though. I couldn't lie and say I was. The satisfaction I felt after killing a fiend, when its heart dripped through my fingers...it was monstrous.

There was a duality in me. I could command the darkness

to kill. I killed to save. Watchers were among the most deeply religious people on earth—while not being typically religious at all. We believed in evil. We had to. Light. Dark. Evil. Good. I contained it all inside this body that shifted from flesh to stone.

I was a creature encased in human skin.

I pressed a key, and the gargoyle disappeared. He was the myth. It was time to deal with my reality.

Chapter Ten

The library had one of the few remaining pay phones in Hidden Creek right outside of it, and this wasn't the sort of call I could make at home. I shifted from foot to foot as the phone rang. This was the first time I'd felt the absence of a cell phone. Mama had talked about getting me one, but who would I call? And I didn't exactly want everybody being able to get a hold of me. The thought made me feel hunted. I rolled a shoulder at the fifth ring. Anytime now.

If the place Phil was staying changed staff at a typical time, this would be the most chaotic moment. A breathless voice answered after the sixth ring.

"Yeah, I was hoping to visit my uncle Phil Laramie tomorrow. What time are visiting hours?"

"Uh." I could hear the click of keys and then she covered the phone to talk to somebody else.

"He said that I couldn't come when he was eating lunch. He hates when people watch him eat. It's one of those things of his," I said. "I don't know that I'd want people eating while I watched either, though."

"Well, I…"

"And I'm not supposed to wear any perfume either 'cause he said it made his eyes water. He said that y'all had a policy about that. That it was a fragrance-free facility and we'd both get in trouble, but I figured that was just him saying that. Is it fragrance-free?" I was hoping to overwhelm her with information so she'd slip up. It was kind of mean…the sort of thing I might need to cut myself for.

"No, but we do encourage people not to wear fragrances if at all possible."

"I knew it! So, when can I come see him?"

"What's your name?"

"Rachel Laramie."

"Your name isn't on our list for him, so I can't give out that information."

"Oh. Okay. I'll have my daddy call instead. Thank you."

I hung up. I'd call that a confirmation that Phil was still being watched. They wouldn't let him out to go kill a dog.

I thought it over on the drive home. I'd covered everything. I was making progress. So, why didn't I feel as accomplished and successful as I normally did?

Getting out of my car, I looked in our side yard for Gris's bike—which was silly and stupid. His bike wasn't on the side with our RV or the other side with the shed where I'd found Jester. It was just after five o'clock, and he wasn't lurking about hoping to catch me. I'd blown him off.

I was in control. I was always in control. I wasn't an emotional wreck waiting around to get my heart broken into pieces. It was better to feel this sting now as opposed to in a week when he'd done his good deed and moved on, leaving me this exposed bleeding lump of pain wearing all my secrets on the outside. And he would move on, make no mistake about that. Boys like Gris didn't beg to be with girls like me.

Maybe he thought he had some big secret, but it was probably just something to do with the way he got rid of whatever was in my room—some kind of ghostbusting thing—if there even was anything in my room, besides all those weird bags.

My brother's laughter greeted me as I slid off my shoes near the door and carried them to my bin in the front closet. There were shoes in the guest bin. Probably one of Dale's friends. His friend had big feet for a thirteen-year-old. 'Course my brother's feet doubled in size every year. I put my backpack in my room before walking into the dining room.

"Sorry I'm late. I got held up at the…"

Gris was at the table. With my family. Eating supper.

What the heck?

My mouth hung open.

"Close your mouth—you'll catch flies." Mama nodded at my chair. "Sorry we started without you, sugar. Your daddy has a meeting tonight and has to run."

Gris stood as I approached and pulled out the chair beside him for me. He was being all polite, and he was here. This wasn't the plan at all.

I sat down and stared at my plate.

"Gris was just telling us about a sea monster in a pond in Virginia," Dale said, shoveling food into his mouth.

"A sea monster in a pond?" I repeated. He was here. Gris was here.

"It turned out to be a publicity stunt." Gris sat down beside me. I could smell either his aftershave or cologne. The scent had a sharp, tangy bite to it that I liked, and he hadn't drowned himself in it, like boys sometimes did.

I looked from my plate to his. Gris's plate was empty, too. He'd waited for me to get home to eat. This was certainly not the plan. Should've known Gris wouldn't follow a plan.

Why did he have to smell so good? It wasn't fair. I didn't wanna follow the plan now, either.

Gris started dishing up food while he told the story. "There was a new restaurant opening right on this lake, and they wanted word of mouth to spread just a smidge faster. So, they'd rigged this thing on a timer. It was rubber, stretched cross a metal frame. It looked like a mix of a walrus, a tiger, and a giraffe."

Dale burst out into snorting laughs.

Gris scooped mashed potatoes onto his plate before passing them to me. There was a jolt inside me when Gris's arm brushed my shoulder.

I met his eyes.

Gris smiled at me, and our hands brushed on the serving spoon. Zings shot down my arm and straight to my stomach, where they jumped around.

"Hey," he mouthed.

My breath caught. Such a simple thing. But the way he looked at me was complicated. It was as if he was searching my face for answers, even as he was trying to tell me something. All that was in a single look. I was in over my head.

"The sea monster?" my brother prompted.

Gris looked away and I breathed easier. The cat had lifted its paw and the mouse had run off. Not that he scared me—no, I was scaring myself. I felt too much. Gris eroded holes in my walls.

"Problem was," Gris said, "they hadn't quite worked out the buoyancy versus the aerodynamic structure in time before the sightings started. They'd figured leaving valves for water to go in and out would make it easy to drag underwater after a short up and down appearance. Well, the air would get dragged in the front as it was coming up from the water, and so, when this sea monster dove, it would shoot air out the back making a loud and rather crude sound."

I knew what story Dale would be telling tomorrow at school. He was barely breathing from laughing so hard.

Gris shook his head with his lips firm as if fighting a smile. "In some ways it worked—word of mouth spread. Unfortunately, this restaurant was going for a family dining atmosphere, but they were serving Mexican food, and they had some difficulty turning off the sea monster, even after the restaurant opened. The whole first week it was open, the restaurant's monster would spray mist from its back end at anyone seated on the deck while letting out a monster of a sound."

I was glad I hadn't started eating as I covered my mouth with my hand and laughed.

• • •

"How are you?" Gris asked.

The others had left the table, though Dale downright vehemently protested his exile to his room for homework.

"I'm fine." I was eating the last of my food. Eating with a boy around was a slow process. I kept running my tongue along my teeth to make sure nothing was stuck. Then, I couldn't spill, and my hand felt shivery from having him around. Jem had spilled her cup, but it was okay for her to be excited about Gris being there. I'd just gone without drinking. Now everybody else was gone, and I'd never taken this long to eat, and I was dying of thirst.

"Is my cousin ever mean to you?" he asked right as I finally took a drink of water.

I nearly spit all over. "Pardon?"

"Your mom said she thought maybe your dog's death was in retaliation for you being so smart and surrounded by idiots. Being as I'm related to an idiot, I figured I'd ask."

I shook my head. "I haven't spoken to Danny for a good

long time, not since he graduated for the most part. He avoids me."

After I'd turned him down when he'd asked me out, Danny just frowned at me every so often and never spoke to me again. He wasn't as much a bully as his friends. Hank was worse. Hank sometimes tripped me, and he constantly pushed books out of my arms.

Gris was almost finished with his third helping of food. I'd never seen anybody eat so much. He must have some kind of a metabolism.

"My mama said that? About it being somebody trying to get back at me?" I asked when he went back to eating as if his plate was about to be snatched away.

He nodded.

He'd talked with Mama about Jester. I wasn't sure how I felt about that.

I set down my fork and clutched my fingers in my lap. What now? He was here. I was here. *We* were here.

"Let's go for a walk." Gris picked up both our plates and carried them into the kitchen.

Down the hall, Jem squealed as she took her nightly bath. My brother had music blaring from his room while "working" on his homework. Everything seemed normal. This was our routine every night. Supper together. Jem took a bath. Dale did his homework under duress. It was the same pattern, and that was comforting. It made sense. But tonight a boy who'd eaten supper with my family now wanted to go for a walk. This was all something that happened to normal people who led normal lives. Not Piper Devon.

"What are you doing?" I asked as he rinsed our plates and put them in the dishwasher.

"It's not right?" He gestured at the dishwasher. "I thought I had it figured out." He tilted his head. "It seemed a straightforward pattern."

"It's all in the right spot, except..." I reached in and flipped the knife, point down. "She swears that it dulls the blade, but somebody could slice their wrist open reaching for it. She'll probably change it back before she starts it up. It's not sensible, but it is what it is." Mama and I were in a constant silent war over whether the knives should be put into the dishwasher up or down. I was right.

"Walk?" Gris repeated, grabbing my hand and pulling me from the kitchen. He was holding my hand. This felt normal and healthy and sorta wrong on account of that.

"It's getting dark." It was that brownish part of the day when the sun was fading fast, but it hadn't reached the gray hour of dusk.

"I know. We won't go far. Your mom might scold me if she thought I was stealing you away. You can grab a flashlight if you're worried."

I ran to my room.

Mama popped her head out of the bathroom where she'd been singing a song to Jem about her boat and duckies. "I like him, sugar," she whispered. She glanced down the hall at Gris. She had this gooey "my little girl has a boyfriend" look stuck on her face. It was plain frightening. Hopefully she wouldn't say anything. Who knew what she'd say to Gris *now* if they were ever alone. I had to make sure that never happened. Ever.

I followed her gaze. I liked Gris, too, but I wasn't about to admit it.

Gris studied a family picture on the wall at the end of the hall with a smile crooking his lips. Did he think I'd looked funny as a kid? Well, I had, but he wasn't supposed to notice that.

"We're going for a walk," I told Mama.

"Don't stay out too late." She reached out to squeeze my hand. "He's nice, Pips. Polite and sweet."

My heart wanted to agree. It thumped and burned in my chest. Trusting it—that was a whole other matter, but I nodded at Mama before heading toward Gris.

"Ready?" he asked when I stood beside him.

"What were you smiling at?"

He'd been staring at a family picture taken seven years ago in a studio. I hadn't quite made it out of my awkward phase where my teeth were too big for my face. Plus, I was wearing socks with Mary Janes. It wasn't a good look.

He pointed at Dale. "I like how your brother looks like he's gonna bolt, and y'all have him pinned. It looks like a group hug and not like y'all trapped Dale."

That's exactly what had happened. Nobody else had ever mentioned it before. 'Course, it wasn't as if we had a lot of people in our house in the past. The picture hadn't seemed that obvious to me, but maybe it was.

"You're really good at reading people, aren't you?"

He opened the door for me and then took my hand in his. "My mom says I'm intuitive. I'd always assumed that meant too curious for my own good."

"It might still mean that."

Gris laughed. "It might at that." He shot me a look. "You look more like your dad."

I frowned. What did it mean when a boy said you looked more like a male relative? Probably nothing.

He squeezed my hand and pulled me after him across the yard.

It'd be so easy to accept this if I was a regular, everyday, average girl. A boy being interested. Him holding my hand. But I wasn't a regular, everyday, average girl.

"Why are you here—at my house, Gris?" I held up our joined hands. "Why this? I told you I'm not falling for your charm." I was, but he didn't need to know that.

"I thought we were going to compare notes. We're in an

investigation together, after all."

We'd reached the wooden fence that separated our yard from the dirt road that led to all the houses around. A patchy neighborhood was at one end—toward the area that looked like the bat's body if you'd seen a map online like I had. In the other direction, after our property, the road curved up. It meandered around through some fields and off on a few lone roads on its way toward where Gris was staying. Then, the road curved back toward Hidden Creek, the main part of town, and my school. We were on the outskirts of the town.

"So that's all it is—an investigation? And you're holding my hand, why? So I don't get lost?"

I liked having my hand in Gris's. It felt safe. Which was wrong! He was leaving. I was leaving. I waited for him to drop my hand since I'd called him on it.

He didn't. "I like you, and I'm worried about you," he said finally.

"What does that mean—that you *like* me? Like as an interesting curiosity?"

He smiled as he turned toward me. I'd felt comfortable staring at him while he was staring elsewhere. I looked down at his soft, worn T-shirt. It had a gargoyle on it. I traced the gargoyle with a finger. The stone image had a smirk on its face and its eyebrows were raised in a challenge. It was charming in the same way Gris was. Leave it to him to have a shirt with a cocky gargoyle on it.

Grabbing my hand, Gris pulled it to his mouth to press a kiss on it. His mouth felt good against my skin. Real good. The cut on his lip had healed, and his mouth was just lighter pink there. Mmm. His mouth was so soft and his hands were warm as they gripped mine. I should most certainly keep staring at his shirt.

"You're interesting, but that's not what it is. I've been homeschooled my whole life. Never attended public school or any school at all. I don't know how to do things in the right order or say the right things, Piper."

"There's a right order?" I wasn't even sure what we were talking about, but that seemed like a good place to start. Order was good. I liked order.

"There must be. I must be doing this all wrong if you didn't have any idea I liked you."

Gris couldn't do things wrong if he tried. He could sweet-talk a snake out of its skin.

"Like…as a friend?" Did friends hold hands?

He tipped my chin up with our joined hands, and his mouth touched mine.

Oh…so…like that. His lips were soft on mine and maybe a smidge unsure, though that was hard to imagine on account of this being Gris.

A window opened, and my brother shouted, "Get a room!" before laughing his fool head off.

I winced as I pulled back, but Gris was grinning.

"But you know about me," I pointed out.

His smile dissolved into a frown. "So?"

"No, I mean, you know *about* me. You know I'm not… right. You should be freaked out."

He shifted around so his back was to my house, and then he kissed me again. It turns out, there's privacy in kissing a tall boy. His lips were pulling kisses from mine, and I wanted to remember everything perfectly.

This time when he leaned back, he said, "You don't freak me out, Piper."

"You're so normal, though, and I'm me."

Gris shook his head, his charming smile once again stretching his lips. "I am so far from normal, Piper. I'm nearly the opposite of it. It's just as well I was homeschooled because I never would've fit in. Trust me, I'm not normal, either."

My heart dropped into my stomach.

"Whatever." I pulled my hands out of his and faced the fence. It was just like a person with no flaws to act as if he knew what it was like. He was an outsider by choice, and he'd probably never tested out what people thought of him. Until you got laughed at and bullied for just being you, you couldn't join the club.

Trust him?

That was a joke. He'd told me nothing, shared nothing. He'd charmed me into forgetting that. Here I was with all my secrets out in the open. He'd seen the cuts. He'd heard me counting in my sleep. Panic screamed in my head at that—loud and long. I clenched my hands together.

He knew too much. Far too much. I should go. I could politely excuse myself. Thanks, but no thanks. Not really the way I'd expected to end my first kiss experience, but if I wanted to avoid my first heartbreak experience—I needed to get on it.

Gris sighed and leaned up against the fence. "They're called fiends, Piper, and I can see them."

Chapter Eleven

If I told her about fiends, I could avoid telling her about me, and I had to act fast. She was yanking back emotionally at supersonic speeds. Piper was in a full-on retreat.

I cleared my throat. "They're like poltergeists, I reckon. Only they're not dead people. They're like dead souls that never were alive."

"Like demons?"

I shrugged. I'd seen signs around her house that Piper's parents were religious. "If you'd like. I've never had a full accounting of one to know where they came from. They're nasty creatures, though."

"So, they *might* come from the devil?" She scrunched up her nose.

"I don't know. They smell evil, in my opinion, but I don't know much beyond that."

"The sulfur?"

I nodded. "You don't usually smell that until there are

quite a few of them congregated. They cause and feed off nightmares and dark thoughts—generally at night as they live in the shadows and draw power from the dark. I can see them. I've been able to ever since I was a kid. My dad can, too."

"That's what is in my room at night? The monsters?"

"Yes."

She squinted out into the distance and tilted her head. Piper's thinking face was as sweet as they came. Despite us talking about something as gruesome as fiends, I kept thinking we should go back to kissing.

Her frown returned. "I don't believe you."

It's not as if I could fault her skepticism. Not really. Just went to show how smart she was. People who grabbed on to superstitions quickly were easily manipulated. Piper wasn't like that.

"Last night, did you sleep okay after I got rid of them?" I asked.

"How did you get rid of them? Machines or weapons or what?" It was amazing how she managed not to answer any questions, ever.

"I ripped out their hearts, and they dissolved." No need to mention the talons or being able to control darkness.

"You did that last night?" The pucker between her eyebrows was distracting. I wanted to smooth it out with my fingers. Or my mouth. "That's why you were in my room?"

"I was in your room because those sacks were drawing a ton of fiends there. Most left when I arrived, but two needed to be killed on account of them not leaving you alone."

"So, they're like ghosts that you can see 'cause you've got some weird powers? And you kill them by pulling out their hearts?"

"That's about right."

"Why'd my throat feel like it was on fire when I woke up?" she asked.

I was trying real hard to be honest with her, but this would require some skirting of the truth. "One of them dove inside you. It took me a while to get it out of you." I'd spooked it into her, and I didn't like to think of my hand in that.

Her breath caught. And for a moment, I was as worried as I'd been last night—it took *that* long for her to take another breath. Then, she exhaled and I let out my own huff. "I had a fiend *inside* of me?"

"Yes."

"And they *might* be demons?"

"You weren't acting possessed if that's what you're wondering. No pea soup puking or head-spinning."

She scowled at me.

"You kept shivering—like you were trying to get it out of you." That was a kind way of phrasing matters, but I didn't want her picturing a horror show.

Dragging her lower lip between her teeth, she worried on it while she thought. Finally, she asked, "How'd you get it out of me?"

I shrugged as if it was nothing. "It's just something I can do." I looked away. Maybe if I wasn't meeting her eyes, she'd stop prying.

She was quiet for another stretch. Her body froze so tightly and purposefully, it was amazing that, when I'd kissed her, after the initial surprise, she'd gotten all loose and soft. I'd cracked through the wall she kept around herself—for a moment, and I wanted to do it again.

"I knew they were there," she said. "Not that I could see them or anything, but my room gets frigid cold at night, and I could feel them around me, creeping."

"They've been there a while?" It was a question, but I was hoping she'd still answer it.

Piper wrapped her arms around her torso, squeezing like she was both emotionally and physically cold. I wanted to hug her, but she didn't seem in the mood to be touched, not until we settled this other thing.

"Yeah. A while. It started with dreams. Then, I started sleepwalking—like I was trying to get away from them." She gulped. "Sometimes I leave the house when I sleepwalk. I wake up here at the fence…or sometimes in my bed, but I'd have dirt on my feet. The night Trina disappeared, I was sleepwalking. My brother found me on account of me leaving the door wide open. It's all gotten worse since then—the nightmares and sleepwalking." A shiver ran across Piper's skin. "I started using a nightlight again 'cause it made those things in my room less intense. I wondered if I'd done something horrible, like the things I imagine in my head, and they were my penance." She gave me a penetrating look.

"I've seen nuns bedeviled by fiends. It's not that."

"Nuns believe in penance and in guilt and in sin."

"And in forgiveness and redemption." She wasn't letting go of this aspect to it.

She nodded, but I could see a hint of doubt lingering. "When they were still around after so long, I figured I was still paying. Maybe some things are never paid off."

Maybe that was a reason why she cut, a way to pay off these imaginary debts and keep her personal inner demons under control.

"Are they just around me?" Another look that went clear to my heart. In her mind, she couldn't draw the line between fiends being evil, but not solely attracted to evil.

"No, I swear, Piper. It's not just you. It's the whole town. All of Hidden Creek is downright infested with them. It's why I'm here. I came to figure out why this town is so bedeviled by fiends and to clear them out, but they keep coming. And they're not just focusing on people. There were a bunch in an abandoned mill also."

"Harpers' mill?"

"I guess. I don't know all the weird names associated with these places: Jones' old field, The Smiths' daughter's ex-husband's old shed. In my mind, it's the nasty abandoned mill filled with monsters and too much pointy, rotten wood."

She grinned. "It's haunted. Well, that's what everybody around here thinks. Maybe it's less haunted now if you cleared it out."

"I hope so, but I can't figure out why they were there to begin with." What was the motive in creating a haunted mill?

"Will those ghost things—fiends—be back tonight?" she whispered. "I mean, you took those sacks out."

"I might've missed some, and you might be pulling a few in on your own."

"Why?"

"Sadness and nightmares drag them in, and, as I said, it's possible someone killed your dog to make you more of a target."

"That's why I'm pulling them in? My dog?"

Damn, she didn't ease up. Piper never would walk the easy road or ask the simple questions. She was looking at me with this desperate vulnerability and this conversation felt like a minefield. I probably owed her the truth, softened and with qualifications. "Also, maybe you're just more prone to the emotions that drag them in. Older people are, too. They've lived long enough to gather regrets and sadness."

She looked like she was having some of those emotional thoughts right now. Finally, she nodded. "It's on account of there being something wrong with me—with my head. There's a darkness inside." Her soft laugh was almost a sigh, and not happy in the least. "Maybe I deserve them."

I thought of all the lines I'd seen on her shoulder. She'd been hiding this from everybody, even herself for a long time. If we couldn't talk about this, how could she ever cope? I wanted Piper's bedeviling to be over, and it wasn't only the fiends doing it.

"You're not dark, Piper. And you don't deserve to have them bothering you or giving you nightmares. Maybe getting rid of the sacks won't fix everything, but it might make it easier for you to control your thoughts and what you worry about."

I listened to her breathing as I waited for her to come to a decision. Inhale. Exhale. My arms felt fidgety with the need to hold her.

Piper licked her lips. "It might make it easier to fix me." She bit down hard on her lower lip. Her teeth turned it white before she released it, then it pinked before flushing red. It was hard to focus when she did stuff like that.

"There's nothing that needs fixing. You're just fine the way you are. Though it might be nice if you weren't hurting yourself to pay for things you can't control."

Her eyes flicked up to mine, and I knew I was right. It was all there in her eyes.

"I'm a freak," she whispered, meeting my gaze without flinching. She was such an odd mixture of fierce and fearful.

It was a challenge if I ever saw one, and I never back down from a challenge.

"Piper, I see ghosts wherever I go. I rip out their hearts and kill them. I'm a freak, too."

A smile spread across her mouth. It was a sunrise on a perfect morning. She was beautiful.

She took a step closer. "You are, aren't you?"

As far as I was concerned, that was basically giving me permission to kiss her again. I made for darn sure I blocked her family's view with my body. This time, I wrapped my arms around her. This time, her arms snuck up around my neck and held me. This time, she definitely kissed me back.

• • •

My great-uncle had been in the house again. I could smell him. It must be from one of his arthritis creams that contained sulfur. I couldn't imagine anything less than extreme pain driving a former Watcher to use products with sulfur in them. It pulled in fiends like catnip, and their brimstone bodies smelled enough like sulfur that it lingered around them. After a night killing a slew of fiends, the scent permeated my clothes enough I've wanted to burn them and be done with it.

I wandered around the house looking for loose latches, but there weren't any. I wasn't as worried about Critch getting in, but I didn't want visits from Hank going any further than my front yard.

The fact of the matter was I could see Hank killing Piper's dog. I wasn't sure if the grave robbing was connected, but I could see him doing that, too. He had the build for it. I could attribute all the violence to him—but not the set-up, the planning.

I flew to Piper's. I'd told her I would chase off any more fiends, and I might need to be in her room to make sure of that. After last night's experience, Piper was going to be the least bedeviled person in the whole wide world.

A few fiends already lurked outside her house. I took care of them as silently as I could. As the hours passed and there were still lights on, I went back to my place and retrieved my laptop bag and a shirt before returning.

When the last light, aside from Piper's, turned off, I pulled on the shirt and tapped on her window. She must've been waiting because she slid open the window soundlessly and gestured me inside.

"Why aren't you wearing shoes?" She stared at my feet.

I never did. Not at night. I didn't want to tell her why, of course, but I couldn't think of a logical excuse. Not with her there in only boxer shorts and a tank top.

"I don't generally wear shoes at night," I whispered,

setting my laptop on a beanbag in the corner.

"Are you gonna be comfortable? You could sit on my bed next to me."

She'd followed me over to the corner. My eyes darted between her and the bed. That was a fairly bad idea that sounded good. We stood there, facing one another. The air between us heated up as it went on.

My gaze focused on her mouth.

She licked her lips.

Then, with an exhale, she hooked my neck and pulled my mouth down to hers. There was an inevitability about us that I didn't want to fight. Nothing was as natural as enclosing her in my arms as her fingertips clenched into the skin at the nape of my neck. Kissing Piper was heaven on earth, and we weren't even using tongues yet. I'd never enjoyed kissing this much, and I liked kissing.

When we came up for air, I let her go—though I didn't want to. "I should definitely sit in the corner."

"That'd be best," she said breathlessly, nodding as she stepped back. Her eyes slid to the desk behind me. "Oh, I crossed Phil off my list." She picked up a pen and drew a line through his name.

"How?"

"I spoke with the librarian today and asked her more about him shooting the library. It turns out there's a plaque in the reference section saying it was donated by his ex-wife— she ran off with this estate lawyer. Also, I called the place he's being held and he's still there. According to the librarian, it's not the sort of place you can wander in and out of." Her hand hovered over the names. "Now, I'm down to nine names." She frowned. "I'm not crossing out Coach Laramie, though, 'cause he really does hate me." She wanted to. She wanted to be down to an even number of suspects again.

Finally, she put the pen down and headed toward her bed.

My eyes followed the sway of her hips. It was gonna be a long night.

"Maybe you should wear more clothes tonight," I murmured.

Piper eased open drawers slowly, then donned a T-shirt on over her tank top and sweatpants over her boxer shorts. She crawled into bed after making certain that metal flashlight was on her bedside table. She wouldn't need it. I intended to make sure she got a nice, long night's rest, free from fiends.

"I can't even remember the last time I was this warm," she whispered. "Gris?"

"Yes?"

"Just checking. I couldn't see you."

"I'll be here all night, sweetheart. I won't let anything get you."

"What if you fall asleep?"

"I don't sleep at night. Not usually. It's why I didn't go to public school. That and I wanted to be done with school faster." And my changing wasn't as deliberate as my parents might've liked when I'd been learning how to control it. My wings had sprouted for first time after a weird dream—an embarrassment few boys ever had to deal with. They shot straight through my pajamas and scared me to death. It would've been nice to have somebody my age to talk it through with, but it wasn't something I shared around. It was a centuries-old secret.

"Do you like being on your own like this?" she asked.

I remembered what her mother had said about Piper trying to get far away from here. I couldn't blame her for wanting to be away from prying eyes. I'd only had a few days of Hidden Creek, and the town was peeling back the layers of my secrets. I didn't care for it even a bit.

"No. Well, sometimes. I like not having to answer to anybody, but sometimes that just makes the whole thing lonely. I like my family, but my mom likes to run my life. My aunt is more casual. Since I got here, I've realized how quiet an empty house is."

"Did you interrogate your uncle and cousin like we decided?"

I pushed off the beanbag and sat on the edge of her bed.

She tucked the quilt shyly around herself.

"I talked to them about Hank and his dad mostly, thinking I'd get an idea about their thoughts while I did. I can't decide what to think of them. I can't see Danny's dad killing a dog— unless it was an accident or the dog was attacking somebody. But what you described couldn't have happened by accident."

Piper wagged a finger at me. "Don't fall for that."

"What?"

"You're making the evidence fit the suspects."

"I just can't see a clear motive for my uncle or Danny. On the other hand, Hank…"

"Yeah, but don't forget that plain, ornery meanness is a motive also."

"That's why I mentioned Hank and I brought up my great-uncle. Critch is not right. The more I talk to him the more I realize he's got some terrifying ideas." I wasn't going to go into those ideas. At least I'd settled, in my mind, that Critch wasn't implying Piper was my long-lost cousin with that comment about her looking like Tawna.

"I'll talk to Hank next, then."

"No, you won't. Bastard didn't think twice about jumping me with a group, and if he did kill your dog, he's dangerous alone, too."

Rather than agreeing, she said, "It doesn't sound like you crossed anybody off our list."

"No, but I did find out that Hank and his dad dislike you because they're both jealous."

"Of what?" She looked so genuinely perplexed.

"Because you're smart and beautiful, and Hank's dad once had eyes for your mom."

"Ew." Piper wrinkled her nose. "Sometimes I can't figure out why we moved here."

She'd ignored the first part of my statement, but the soft pink blush on her cheeks said she'd heard it.

"Tomorrow, you'll tackle Coach Laramie, and I'll keep looking at the other suspects," I said.

"Next time, you should find out enough so that we *can* cross them off. At least one of them." Her eyes darted to the list on the desk. It was killing her that it had an odd number of names.

"Maybe I'll eliminate two of them."

Her aggravated frown made me laugh.

"You could also add Critch's name."

"On which page? My list is still for suspects that might have killed my dog." There was a stubborn wrinkle between her eyebrows. It figured that I'd be attracted to a girl as pig-headed as me.

Leaning over, I kissed her forehead right above that wrinkle. "There. You're all tucked in. I could tell you a bedtime story."

She reached out and shoved my shoulder as I got up.

I dropped back down into the corner and opened my laptop. I tried to concentrate on the screen, but I could see Piper wriggling anxiously under the blankets. She glanced from me to the ceiling to the window. The darkness built outside as fiends approached. Humming softly, I wrapped the shadows around Piper while trying not to slip into form. It was a pain, and my fingertips tingled from my talons a few times before Piper's breathing lengthened and deepened.

I took off my shirt just in case I needed to transform. It'd been hard enough to bind the darkness around her without loosing the Watcher inside me. It'd seemed to settle her down, though. It settled me down, but maybe that was the Watcher side of me comforted by the approach of midnight—the deepest part of the night.

"Sixteen," Piper murmured, turning onto her other side where I could see a near scowl tugging at her lips. Even when she wasn't bedeviled, Piper was…troubled.

"Hush." I pulled the dark around her again.

My talons slid out. The night was deeper, and there was a presence prowling around outside. Crap. Fiends were coming. There might be something buried on her property dragging them near. I closed down my laptop and got to my feet. I wasn't about to transform fully if I could help it. I only needed my talons to get to their hearts. Transforming partway was tougher, but I could do it. As understanding as Piper might've been about things that crept in the shadows—that wouldn't extend to dating one.

The first few fiends I shoved back as they entered the room through cracks near the floor. Light specks freckled my vision from the amount of power it took to maintain a partial transformation. My body didn't want to be part Watcher and part Gris.

Two fiends snuck in at once, and I knew it was time to stop shoving them away and start killing. The first one was easy enough. I pinned it to the ground with one hand, while reaching into its chest with the other. The second fiend had made it to Piper before I could snatch it. To maximize my speed, so I wouldn't be repeating last night, I broke the restraint on my form. My wings slid out as I dove toward it. At full strength, I was a force to be reckoned with. I yanked it from Piper with the darkness and my talons all at once. Its heart dripped through my fingers and vaporized in the light.

Light!

The beam glinted off my talons. It was a circle on my thick, gray chest. The rush of adrenaline created a haze in my brain, as did the blood pumping through my veins from the burst of speed, power, and heightened awareness that came from my Watcher state. For a moment, I could only marvel at the gloss on my long, black talons before it occurred to me the beam of light was not good. Not good at all.

I looked up from my talons right into Piper's wide eyes. She was standing beside her bed and the beam of her flashlight blinded me.

Chapter Twelve

PIPER

One minute I was staring at something that seemed to be some mixture of man and monster and *snap,* I was staring at Gris who groaned with a twitch of pain.

"Gris?"

"Yes?" His voice sounded raspy and uncertain. A thin sheen of sweat covered his bare, upper torso.

My own breath quickened. It was impossible, but it was. I knew it was. I knew what I'd seen. "You were just a…what were you?" I kept the light trained on his chest. That had happened. I gestured with my free hand. "I woke up to this flash of ice crawling across my skin."

"A fiend got in." He winced in the light as if it bothered him, but maybe it was my staring—'cause he wouldn't meet my eyes.

"I turned on my light, and you were here, but you weren't you." It sounded ridiculous to my ears. I couldn't believe what I'd seen, but I couldn't deny it, either.

"Of course I was."

"No."

"It was just your imagination." Gris's eyebrows scrunched up as his forehead wrinkled. Even if I hadn't seen his eyebrows draw together, I could tell by his tone—trying too hard to be casual. He was lying his sorry tail off.

Ice shot through me, worse than the fiend's touch. It stole my breath.

He was lying to my face.

Worse—he was trying to make me think I was seeing things in order to keep it secret.

I knew what I saw. He could turn into something else. He had been partly a creature of some kind.

"So you're saying I'm crazy?" I clenched my jaw tight enough to break teeth.

I wanted to trust him so darn bad. I did.

Please, Gris.

Behind his eyes, I could see him running through options. His gaze was unfocused and his forehead was furrowed. I suspected the options he was considering weren't lie or tell the truth, but lie or dodge his way out with charm.

He looked at the window. "I ought to go. You need your sleep, and I ought to go." He headed toward the corner to gather his stuff.

Ouch. That stung in my heart. I wrapped my arm across myself and dug my nails into my skin. It didn't hurt enough through the sweatshirt. If it'd hurt enough, maybe I could be as casual as he was managing. Instead, I was all on display. I clenched tighter.

I couldn't believe Gris preferred having me doubt my sanity over actually revealing the truth about himself. I had too much pride for this. I firmed up my spine.

"Fine," I said. "Leave. But, don't come back. I won't want anything to do with you." It came out squeaky and hesitant, but it came out. The light from the flashlight in my hand was still trained in his direction, so I saw him freeze.

"Don't do this, Piper." He didn't turn around. "There are some things you don't want to know—that you don't want to see."

"The truth, you mean? So, it's okay for you to expose every part of my life and drag my secrets out, but that's just me, isn't it? Well, damn you, Gris. Damn you. And I won't even beg your pardon for swearing. I've a right. You even know what I say in my sleep."

"It's just counting. It's not the same."

"It's not *just* counting, and you know it."

I waited for him to do something—to say something, but he just stood there, staring down at the floor, his stuff in one hand, and his back to me. Finally, I realized he was waiting for me to relent, hoping for it. Maybe he reckoned I'd doubt what I saw if he was quiet long enough, still long enough. Hard to believe I'd thought he was different. I'd kissed *him* this last time. I was such a fool. A naive fool.

I sniffed and shook my head. I had too much pride for this. "Look, now we both know something about the other we'll never tell anybody. You can leave, and we'll pretend the other doesn't exist. We can do our own investigations. You can leave Jester's murder to me, and you can do…whatever else. As long as you stay away from me."

He'd probably be gone soon anyway, leaving behind memories that I'd worry over at night. Hidden Creek would poke at the wounds. But it'd only be a few months, and then I'd be gone. I'd blow out of here and forget Gris. Having somebody in the world who knew about me made me feel itchy and uncomfortable. I had ways for dealing with that, though. I threw a glance at my side table, waiting for him to leave.

"Is that what you want?" Gris asked, interrupting my

thinking. "Now that you know something dark about me, or think you do?"

'Course, I didn't want that. I bathed in the darkness every day. I breathed it. Lived it. My thoughts were all painted dark.

"No, but I'm not gonna let you lie to me and act like it's okay." That hadn't sounded so wishy-washy in my head. "And, apparently, you'd rather I believe I was crazy than know the truth. It's different when it's your secrets, isn't it?"

He turned with a fury in his eyes and his jaw tight. "So, you'll be going with option B, where I tell you everything about me, and you want nothing to do with me because it's ugly and unnatural? Sometimes the lie is kinder than the truth, Piper."

His anger made me take half a step back. "Yeah, that set of rules comes in handy when it's you and not me, doesn't it?" I liked things even. I liked things fair. This wasn't, either, and it wasn't the way I lived. My skin itched. My skin itched so bad. And the screaming in my head wouldn't quit—it was so loud. My mind was so crowded.

"It's something that comes into play when one of us is a monster and the other isn't."

I swallowed thickly. I was two seconds from bawling. Two seconds. I felt shivery and weak and tired of standing. "Fine, if that's the case, you may wanna tell me which of us is which. 'Cause I've thought I was a monster nearly my whole life."

The fight went out of him. His shoulders dropped, and he said my name on a sigh. "You're not a monster."

"I don't think you are, either."

"You will."

"I won't." I darn near growled. "Gris, when have you thought I didn't know my own mind? Either fess up or shut up and go."

One corner of his mouth hitched up. "Either fess up or shut up and go?"

"That's what I said."

His shrug was defeated. He dropped his bag on the ground. Gris's fists opened and closed at his sides before he exhaled thickly. "Fine. I'm a Watcher. One of us is born into my family in each generation. In other families, too, but it's kept secret. I can control darkness. I get rid of fiends in areas where they become a problem."

"You looked different."

"That's what I look like in Watcher form." He glanced down at the floor, refusing to meet my eyes.

"You had wings."

Shrug.

"You can fly?" I asked.

Another shrug. His mouth was set in a mulish line, as if any future comments would be similarly shrugged out.

I don't speak shrug.

"Change back."

"No!" he whispered through his teeth, his eyes once again filled with anger. It was so sudden that I took a step back, bumping against my bed, and almost dropping the flashlight.

"Why?" I blinked back sudden tears. I rarely cried unless something major happened. What was wrong with me? Well, besides the fact that Gris'd acted like I'd slapped him.

"I'm not about to change just to satisfy your curiosity."

The emotional punch in his words knocked the breath out of me. My heart wrenched. He didn't know me at all. Gris was all pretty words til it was about him. This wasn't even. If it wasn't even, it wasn't gonna work between us. If he believed I was just curious, it wouldn't have worked anyways.

"You don't know anything about me, Gris Caso."

I flicked off the flashlight and climbed into bed, yanking the quilt over my head. If I was gonna bawl my eyes out, I'd do it hidden underneath the covers. I bunched myself into a smaller target and started counting in my head. Two. Four. Six.

Eight. After one sniff, I felt the bed beside me tip as Gris sat down.

"Go away," I whispered. "Just go away." Crap. I could hear the watery sound of tears in my voice.

"No, Piper. I, uhh, maybe I shouldn't have said that."

"Maybe you shouldn't have." Another sniff, and I pressed my fists against my eyes to keep the tears in.

Gris rubbed my shoulder with light strokes. "My cousin hasn't seen me in my Watcher form."

"Yeah? Do you know what he says in his sleep? Do you kiss him?" I swallowed more tears before saying, "If you do, don't tell me 'cause that's so wrong."

Gris laughed softly. "Come out and talk to me. I swear I'll be nice."

"Will you show me?"

He flinched, making the mattress twitch. His hand stopped for a moment. Then, he trailed it along my shoulder. "We'll trade."

I waited. Trading might balance this out. If we both risked getting hurt, we'd be even.

"If I show you what I look like in Watcher form, you'll work on being okay in your own skin, too. I trust you—you trust me."

I ducked out from underneath the quilt. I could see his shadow in the dim light of my nightlight.

"You mean not…" I nodded at my shoulder.

"If that's what it means to you. Do you want to stop?"

That was the question, wasn't it? I'd never wanted to start, but it'd become a habit, and I couldn't break it—not without a good reason. "Yes. I think so. Yes."

"Then, your debt with the world is settled. You're good just how you are. You don't have to pay for being different."

"You want me to stop on account of it being creepy?"

"No, I just want you to be okay with being you. You

defined what that meant. It looks painful, but we all wear our past in some way." He leaned forward and wiped a tear from my cheek. "Trade? You promise?"

"I get the flashlight on."

He inhaled, appearing to consider it—but it seemed more for show. "Fine. You have to promise, though."

"What if I break my promise?"

"Then, I'm sure you'll have a good reason. Nobody has to be perfect."

I never do break promises. I might bend rules, but I don't break promises. "Just as long as you stick around this town." I wasn't making a lifelong promise to a boy who might bolt just as soon as he felt like it.

"There's a lot to do here, and I'm finding I like the scenery." He picked up the flashlight and put it in my hand. "You ready?" As he got to his feet, he pulled me to mine.

I turned on the flashlight and trained it on his chest again. "I'm ready. Show me."

It happened fast. One moment, he was Gris, really hot, tall boy. The next, a winged, gray creature stood before me where he'd once been. His skin was slick and hardened like he was made of stone. His already thin face stretched to a pointed chin, and his cheekbones were high and sharp. Though his eyes looked similar in both forms, the white portions were diminished and the black-brown parts were intensified and shiny. The muscles on his chest were more defined, and it seemed like he was wearing body armor instead of skin. Besides the bone-white framework of his wings, they seemed a lot like bat wings.

The muscles on his arms were thick, corded, and tapered down to his hands where long, black talons graced each finger. They looked elegant and sharp.

"Can I touch your hands?" I asked.

With some hesitation, he held out his hand. I looked over

his knuckles then his palm. The skin was so thick and hard. It seemed as if it would reverberate if I tapped on it—like a tortoise shell. The talons were smooth like river rock except for their razor-sharp tips. Looking down, I noticed his feet had short talons also, possibly for grip.

My examination had brought me closer to him. Heat radiated off of him. Also, a fizzy kind of energy hung around him like static electricity. I slid my free hand up his chest. Gris's eyes widened. He'd acted as if I'd be repelled or horrified, which was ridiculous. I was touching a creature that moments before I would have thought was mythical. My heart beat faster. This was like something out of a dream—a good dream. This was like a fairytale, and I'd never even believed in those.

Using the tips of my fingers, I traced the thickness of his muscled neck and his smooth cheeks. The curves of his ears had elongated to a more pointed shape. His mouth had the barest suggestion of lips. When my fingers skimmed his mouth, he closed his eyes. Was that painful for him? A humming sound came from his chest like a purr.

"Do you like that?" I whispered. "When I touch you?" I couldn't believe I'd dared ask that.

He nodded, keeping his eyes closed.

"Can you talk?"

Another nod.

"You don't want to, though?"

His jaw clenched. Wait one second, that's why some of this seemed familiar. "You were here that night. You spoke to me. You sounded different."

"Bad?" he mumbled, keeping his mouth clenched shut.

"Nah, just different. You were nice. It was the first time my monsters hadn't scared me. I couldn't figure out why you could talk and why I wasn't scared of you." I huffed out a laugh. "I really thought I was losing my mind that night. I wasn't scared of my shadows."

He opened his eyes, but kept them downcast. I turned off the flashlight and tossed it on my bed.

"You don't want to see me anymore."

"It's not that. It's making you uncomfortable, and I only want to touch you." My cheeks heated up in a molten hot blush. But then my fingertips and thoughts were lost in the wonder in front of me. Touching him was like touching magic. "Your whole body is smooth like the rocks in Hidden Creek." I finally dared to touch his wings. Bony lengths formed the top edge and three joints down into the actual wing, which was like a bat's. Another bone lined the bottom, which curved up into a thick muscle where it attached to his back, almost as if they'd slide behind his shoulder blades.

"Your wings remind me of…" It was likely rude to make comparisons. My mama hadn't taught me the etiquette on what to say if your boyfriend had wings.

"A gargoyle's?"

"Sorta. Only you look more like you, and you're wearing pants. Gargoyles don't wear pants."

He snickered. It was different from his normal deep laugh. It sounded raspier and a smidge more sinister, but that didn't bother me. Inside, he was still Gris. On the outside, he was different as could be, but everything on the inside was sweet and charming and Gris.

"Is it hard to fly?"

"It's a lot of work." The odd reptilian hiss whispered in his words. His tongue must be different. "It burns off a lot of energy. I'm always hungry."

My hands returned to the smooth planes of his chest. He was so strong. It must be difficult to go back to his human form when it came after this. Did he feel weak? If I could fly, I might never want to be human again. My hands slid in unison down across his stomach. The ripples of his abs were fascinating. A deep shudder ran through him again. When I reached the waistband of his pants, I asked, "This is why you don't wear a shirt or shoes at night?"

"Yes." The single syllable hissed out.

"Am I hurting you?"

"No, but don't go any lower."

Well, I certainly hadn't planned on it. I choked on an embarrassed laugh. I think the deep, rough rumbling I felt in my fingers was him laughing, too.

I skimmed my fingertips upward, across his chest, sketched his collarbone and then followed it out to his shoulders.

"One moment," he whispered. "You have fiends coming in."

I ducked closer to him, and he put his arm around me. Pressing my face against his smooth chest, I inhaled the scent of him—some Gris, plus something sweet and earthy that reminded me of the night after a hot day. In the dim light, his other arm stretched toward the window. I could almost make out the talons at the tips of his fingers. A pulse went through his body. Air or energy swept away from us.

"Shut my mouth, that was amazing," I whispered against his skin.

Gris froze. "It didn't scare you?" He seemed shocked. How could he be shocked that I was impressed? He had superpowers.

"Scare me? Don't be silly." I tipped back and used my hands to explore his neck and chin more thoroughly. His mouth felt too firm to be real. What would it be like to kiss him while he was like this? Would he think it was too weird? Would I think it was too weird? While I was still thinking about it, I touched his cheeks and forehead. He made that purring sound deep in his throat that got under my skin like an itch wanting to be scratched. He liked to be touched. I liked touching him. He was so smooth.

I hooked my hands behind his neck and pulled his mouth down while standing on my tiptoes. My mouth touched his and, for a moment, it was smooth and firm. Then, he yanked me tight against him while his hand slid into my hair, and he'd changed back to being just Gris.

"Piper, what you do to me," he whispered against my mouth. "I never…"

I wasn't sure what he'd planned to say, but I'd probably have agreed with it anyways. He held me tighter til my feet weren't actually on the ground, and his tongue nudged my mouth open. For a brief moment, I wondered if that's why he'd changed back 'cause he was self-conscious, and then I forgot everything as he kissed me so deep I felt like he knew everything about me now.

Chapter Thirteen

GRIS

A blond strand of hair fell across her face, and she wrinkled her nose in her sleep. I slid it back into place and let my hand trail lightly down her cheek. It must've tickled because her nose wrinkled up again, and she scowled at me.

Sitting on her bed, my back against her headboard, with her huddled up against my side all while trying to concentrate wasn't working at all, but hell if I cared. In fact, I couldn't bring myself to care if I ever accomplished another thing in my lifetime.

She fidgeted briefly before rolling away from me, and then she scooted until the curve of her back rested against my thigh. Then…the sigh. She sounded so peaceful now and then—which was odd in light of how often she moved in her sleep. Her fidgety, fretful nature didn't change just because she was sleeping.

I was about to say screw it and shut my laptop down when I saw an email from Dad. I'd sent him an abbreviated version of Piper's list—and included Critch. As interesting as her reasoning was, I wasn't putting either of our names on there… or my uncle or cousin's. I'd continue to investigate them by myself. My dad had more federal contacts, though—ones that could bypass the red tape of medical facilities and get into criminal databases.

Let me know if you need me. Wrapping up things here. Your mom's not taking her chick having flown the nest all that well. I think she needs a hobby. Or two. Maybe three. I haven't mentioned your "neighbor" Piper or she'd have found her hobby.

Okay. On to the important crap. Your list. That missing couple. I agree with you about the girl. No one who takes that many pictures of her lunches just walks away from the spotlight for no reason. No legal reason to stay hidden or under the radar—that all checked out. Then, there's the boyfriend. His landlord closed on his place, claiming his stuff to pay off rent—made a killing on selling it off. From what I've gathered, he had a first-rate man cave going on. The boyfriend is wanted in connection with some minor stuff by the police but he's always skated through. Something ugly happened. Not runaways, my gut says.

What do you know about Pastor Green? Phil Laramie is in that institution, and the pastor there in town is a frequent visitor. Still checking more sources. Keep me in the loop.

Be safe. Fly well, Dad.

"Eighty-eight," Piper whispered.

"Hush now." I rubbed the back of my hand across her temple. I walled the shadows around both of us while pushing against the perimeter of her room. Doing this periodically had seemed to keep the fiends away. Being this close to her was making it much easier. I wasn't even transforming. Of course, this was the middle of the night—the strongest hours for Watchers, but this felt like some control. Earlier, when I'd been trying to hide my transformation and keep the fiends out, it had all felt impossible.

I waited to feel some regret that I'd told her—that I'd shown her. I certainly wouldn't have picked tonight, but I didn't regret it. For once, it wasn't as isolating to have something monstrous hidden inside me.

Not only was she not scared, but she'd seemed amazed, in wonder. When she was touching me, I'd felt more powerful than when I was flying. My heart had been beating as hard as my wings against the sky and there'd been a rush—a huge rush. Then, she'd kissed me while I was transformed, and I could've done anything—anything. But I'd still wanted to be me. I'd snapped out of transform particularly fast; it'd stung my back as my wings tucked away.

Piper rolled toward me in her sleep. Her hand slid up my thigh but stopped right when I was starting to realize I'd best stop it myself. Her fingers bunched up in the fabric of my cargo pants, and she blinked awake.

"Hush, it's just me, remember?" I said when she squinted around.

"Oh, okay then." She settled back down on the pillow, closing her eyes. "You ask too many questions."

She probably wasn't awake enough to remember, but I decided to answer her anyway. "Even one is too many with you, Piper."

"So?" she grumbled. "What number was I on?"

"Eighty-eight, I think." I pushed little wisps of bangs away from her forehead.

"Ninety."

"Ninety-two," I added.

This caused her forehead to wrinkle in confusion. "Stop it."

"I'm helping."

"Ninety-two, ninety-four, ninety-six—"

"Ninety-eight." Yeah. I was plain horrible for teasing her.

"Nnnnnnngh," she complained.

I pulled the darkness tight around us.

She sighed and dropped back into a silent sleep.

See, other boyfriends couldn't do that. Not that she could brag about it. I moved her hand away from my leg and kissed her knuckles. I could do this. Piece of cake. I shoved a persistent fiend backward. I might have to kill that one.

With a sigh, I replied to my dad. *Not yet.* I could still handle things here on my own, and he might scare off Piper.

Then again, she'd come face-to-face with a monster and kissed it.

As suspected, there was one fiend out there who wasn't leaving without a fight. I closed my laptop and set it on Piper's nightstand. Sliding away from her was difficult— not physically—I managed that, but I missed being close to her almost immediately. I tucked the quilt around her, then turned, easing up on our wall of shadows.

The fiend rushed in, eager for a chance at Piper. Its heart was dripping through my hands within seconds. A second fiend followed suit, and a third met the same fate.

When I turned back, Piper was squinting at me. "That's amazing," she whispered.

No regrets about telling her.

A few seconds later, I slid back onto her bed, beside her. My wings were tucked away neatly, but I felt their presence, and for once, it didn't make me feel more separate and alone. I wasn't two creatures fighting for purchase in a single body. I was Gris, just as Piper was Piper. I was whole.

"Fifty-eight," Piper said.

"Sixty."

"Shuddup."

• • •

A familiar engine gunned in the early hours as somebody tore down the street in front of Piper's house. I hadn't killed a fiend in nearly an hour so I stashed my laptop below the bed and slipped out the window. I flew after the disappearing taillights of Hank's truck, which I recognized from when he and his buddies had brought me my new sledgehammer.

Hidden Creek was made up of winding dirt roads that curved and twisted all through the town. Flying a straight line meant I was waiting for him to arrive at the cemetery that was his obvious destination. A dark truck waited near the entrance under a copse of trees, not readily obvious, and Hank flashed his headlights as he went in, acknowledging them.

Hank didn't do confrontations without backup. I should've guessed as much.

Trees and benches peppered the old cemetery, their paths as tangled and convoluted as Hidden Creek's roads. I jumped from tree to tree, muffling my movements by drawing the darkness around me.

Hank made no attempt to be secretive or sly. He slammed out of his truck and stalked through to a bench near the robbed grave. Hank didn't sit at the bench. He paced beside it.

Odd place for a meeting.

The back of my neck prickled, and I swung around. Somebody was watching me as I watched Hank. I hadn't heard the other truck door open. If I had to guess, whoever was watching me had arranged the meeting and had already been here.

Either Hank saw my movements or felt the presence of

somebody else, too, because he stopped pacing and stared into the shadows near me.

This time, I pulled the darkness around me and disappeared into it while trying to be quiet as I snuck closer to Hank.

"Hey!" Hank squinted and produced a flashlight. He ran the beam across the tombstones and trees. "I know you're out there." The light hopped around, the tall grave markers creating sinister dancing shadows. A small critter of some kind skittered away beside me. Hank's light fixated on the spot where the rustling had sounded.

My breathing felt loud, even with the night providing a chorus of creatures that hunted in darkness.

"I'm fixin' to come find you and knock you into next week," Hank shouted. "You know I'm good for it. I'll do better than a broken nose—I'll break your whole damn face."

Could he tell I was out here?

Hank turned in a circle. "Hey, I'm not messin' with you." He waited a breath and then shouted, "And stay the hell away from her! If you know what's good for you, you'll stay away from her!"

Behind me, from where the truck had been parked, I heard a vehicle start up and rumble toward us. What now?

The truck shot through bushes and slammed into a tree, just outside the cemetery. One of the doors shot open, and Jared rolled out, screaming, tearing at his body, ripping his shirt off, not caring if his fingers scraped his skin as he did.

"Jared? What are you—?" Hank ran a couple feet toward him, then paused before backing away from his supposed friend. Jared writhed on the ground, nearly shredding his skin in his anxiety to get the four fiends surrounding him off.

The hell? Why were fiends attacking him?

Crouching, I looked back and forth between them. No way could I keep this on the down-low if I swooped in, but I also couldn't let Jared be killed right in front of me.

His screaming was turning guttural with blood.

Dammit.

"What did you do? I told you to wait!" Hank shook his head, then bolted for his truck.

Soon as he took off, I dove into the fight, yanking the fiends off Jared, whose defensive moves were slowing.

They didn't scramble away, but came back for more. They scraped me up as I killed them. I had to push out with my powers the entire time to keep them off me and the mangled body I was protecting. My phone was a casualty to the cause. It shattered into multiple pieces on a gravestone which seemed an appropriate demise. By the time I'd dispatched the final fiend, Jared was a moaning, nearly unconscious mound exuding sulfur, blood, and other bodily fluids.

I went to the smoking truck and peered inside. An empty syringe lay on the bench seat. Had he shot up with something that attracted fiends? Beside the syringe was a phone. Perfect.

Jared's wounds seemed ragged and bloody, but not life-threatening. I called 911 while still transformed and gave the cemetery as the address before dropping the phone beside Jared. My conscience was still squawking about leaving him, so I set off the car alarm and waited behind a tree until a slew of sirens arrived. I lurked in the trees, wanting to know what they made of it. They bagged the syringe and took Jared off in an ambulance.

The sun was rising by the time I made it back to Piper's house to retrieve my laptop.

Before heading home to sleep in my own bed, I sent an email to my dad asking him to overnight me a new phone and to find out what was in that syringe.

Chapter Fourteen

PIPER

I'd intended to confront him today. It was sensible, and I liked sensible things. I'd also forgotten that today was the day our entire Human Biology class went to the nearby college to look at a cadaver. Okay, so I'd intentionally forgotten — purposefully forgotten — and hoped the teacher would, too. Mr. Allen hadn't. That meant we had an hour and a half bus ride each way, but, other than telling Hank I wanted to talk to him, I didn't make much headway. Hank and Mattie had been memorizing the surface area of each other's tongues. It was too much human anatomy for me every time I glanced back there.

Everybody else in the bus had been talking about Jared ending up in the hospital. Nobody seemed to know why. 'Course there were rumors. Plenty of rumors. Ranging from a drug overdose to the newcomer to town, Gris, taking him down.

Hank was close-lipped about the whole thing.

Then, we arrived at the college and the panic set in. I'd explained to Mr. Allen that death and I…we didn't get along. Then, he told me this class trip was a huge percentage of my grade, and I made sure we agreed I'd still get credit if I passed out. He'd smiled when I'd insisted.

He wasn't smiling when I had to practically be carried out of the lab after fainting.

I lasted longer than expected. The counting helped. But I was still going to have to repress this good and hard.

The bus ride back to school was tedious and filled with snickering from all around me.

Hank likely hadn't killed Jester—though he'd looked far too interested in that dead body a couple of times. I'd seen Ben trying to make the cadaver's fingers snap. Dale probably would've accomplished it. He'd laughed when I'd said I was dreading this trip. He'd wanted to trade places. My brother was far too interested in dead things. For all I knew, Gris might be just as interested in dead things.

It felt good to slam my locker shut after collecting my books. Real good actually. I did it again. I forced myself to stop at twice. Partly 'cause if I'd done it three times, I'd have needed to continue on to four. Once you slammed your locker four times…well, folks worried about you and parents were called.

"Hey, Piper." Mattie walked up beside me. "Hank said to meet him inside the gym. Said he'd talk to you before heading out to the field."

I blinked. "He did?"

"He figured you were so persistent you'd just keep hassling him." She shrugged.

I'd been pretty considerate not to interrupt them until Hank was getting off the bus. "Uhh, thanks!" I called after her.

"Whatever." She turned around, walking backward.

"*Inside* the gym."

"Yes. Inside."

I darn near ran to the gym. Luckily, I was driving myself home, so I wasn't rushing to be anywhere. I stopped at the outside doors and yanked one open. All the lights were off, other than the emergency lighting. Dark. Very dark. I could do this. It couldn't be worse than watching somebody peel back a cadaver's face. I stepped into the gym, staying within the rectangle of light beaming through the wedged-open door. "Hank?"

No answer.

The air inside the gym felt unnaturally cold. Why was Hank meeting me in here when the locker rooms had outside doors?

"Hank?" I called again.

Maybe he just wanted to have a private conversation. If that were the case, my hollering wasn't lending itself to that. I dropped my backpack in the doorway to hold it open. As I straightened, I palmed my pepper spray from a side pocket, and stepped forward. My mama didn't raise no fools, and a face full of pepper spray might discourage a conversation, but I didn't much care. Underestimating a person's potential for violence wasn't a problem I'd ever had. While I didn't think Hank'd killed my dog, he wasn't exactly right in the head. Too many tackles during the football season. I'd once told him the risks of multiple concussions, and he'd pushed me down.

I took several hesitant steps forward and turned as the shadows moved. It was so cold in here. Why was it so cold? I sniffed, and the cold moved into my heart.

Sulfur. I was growing too familiar with that scent. There were fiends in here. "Look. Joke's over. I'm leaving." As I spun around, my backpack slid sideways and the heavy gym door slammed closed.

"Crap!" Not good.

A low laugh echoed, bouncing off the walls.

I rushed toward the weak beacon of the emergency light.

Wispy arms grabbed at me. I sprayed over my shoulder with the pepper spray and an unholy screech rent the air. I yanked free of the claws that seemed to come from all directions. I felt them. I felt the fiends. I ran for the gym door and banged into it as talons caught my skin and tugged on my hair. I fell out into the sunshine, tripping over my bag in the process, and sprawled out on my hands and knees, gasping. Who'd been in there laughing?

One of Hank's jock friends?

Coach Laramie?

Somebody else?

Black cleats stepped into view, and I looked up into Hank's grinning face.

"Who was that in there?" I asked, scrambling to my feet and brushing myself off. He didn't try to help me up. He wouldn't.

"Who was in where?" His smirk should've been slapped off his face long ago.

"In the gym. Don't tell me you had nothing to do with that. You pulled my backpack out of the door, you asshole." And I wasn't about to apologize for my strong language.

"It must've been the wind."

I snorted.

Inside, the locker room door banged open and closed.

"I should call the police," I said.

"I thought you wanted to talk." Hank shrugged and turned to leave.

"I do!" I reached out a hand to stop him, which ridiculous because we'd prefer to never touch…ever. It was a mutual sort of loathing.

Hank turned back around. "So, talk. You've got until coach shows up. He's running late."

I swallowed. "I want to talk about Trina."

"My sister?" His disinterest dissolved. "Why do you want to talk about her?"

"I think something bad happened to her."

"Why?"

Here went nothing. "I sleepwalk."

He blinked.

"I sleepwalk and the night your sister disappeared, I walked out to the fence. Now, I don't know what I saw or what happened, but I started doing it all the time. All the time, Hank. I think maybe I saw something and it's haunting me." Along with a bunch of fiends but I didn't add that.

His eyes narrowed, but he didn't speak.

"I need to know what you know about the night she disappeared. It might help us solve it."

"Us?"

I clenched my teeth. I knew him and Gris weren't going to be besties anytime soon. "You and me." Frak, a lie, and I couldn't even cut myself for it. I'd made that promise. "If we can figure out what happened, we can...have closure or something."

"Or find her."

I nodded quickly.

I felt somebody's eyes on me. The prickling of awareness made me roll a shoulder to ease the discomfort. Was somebody watching us? Or had whoever'd laughed in the gym come outside already?

"Nobody knows what happened to Trina and her boyfriend," Hank said.

"Was her boyfriend there that night?"

"Yeah, but my parents didn't mind him. Her previous boyfriends were real losers and stoned most of the time. Side-by-side, Troy wasn't half bad. Plus, he had a good pitching arm."

Uh huh, and that would matter to Hank's daddy.

"So, Trina didn't have any reason to run off?"

He shrugged. "She'd snuck out that night, but that was her thing. It was more fun to sneak out than ask permission. They were going down to skinny-dip in Hidden Creek. I heard her window open." He snorted in disgust, and his face twisted into a scowl. "She was laughing."

"She wasn't running off." It was a statement—not a question.

"No. She didn't take nothing with her. She kept a stash of money under a floorboard and it's still there. Or it was. I used it once I knew she wasn't coming back."

"Why didn't the police investigate more?"

"People see what they care to see."

"What did they find at the creek?"

He squinted. "Why would they look at the creek?"

"You said that's where she was headed."

Hank shook his head. "They assumed she'd left town. That's what my parents told them. It was basically good riddance in their minds. The police felt the same." His jaw went tense, and he closed his eyes. One second...two seconds...and he opened them. His eyebrows jerked together in a wince and then it was gone.

I stopped hating him. I couldn't. He'd keep hating me, but it was easy to hate somebody you didn't really know. I'd already known half of what Hank did, he did to impress his daddy. His daddy's expectations were unreal and kept raising each time Hank proved himself in any way. Now, I knew everything he did lately was colored by the bitterness that his sister had been judged and forgotten. He probably even resented his parents' preference of him, which hadn't helped anybody figure out what happened to his sister.

"Not that you'd care, freak."

It was a jab from a wounded animal. Aw, shoot. I'd really

enjoyed hating him.

Hank swallowed. "If you find out anything or remember anything, you owe me."

"Whatever," I said. That was what he expected. But I would tell him. It'd only be fair. "Hey, do you know what happened to my dog?"

He blinked. "Didn't an animal kill that stupid thing?"

"Did you see what did?"

His eyes flicked to over my shoulder for a split second to the gym behind me. "No."

I turned to look at the gym. He knew. Hank knew who'd been in there.

"Are we done here?"

"Hank, who was in the—"

"We're done." Whirling around, he strode toward the field. At the corner of the gym, he turned to look back at me. His mask of hatred was back on, even if it seemed softer at the corners. "You say anything to anybody…"

He disappeared from sight without finishing the thought. That was all right, I could've finished it for him. We all had these stupid parts we played, patterns that went on forever. I sorta liked that, even when I didn't. Even when they kept me up at night, it was still sorta nice that they were around. Patterns were like that.

It still felt like somebody was watching me. I didn't run to my car, but I walked faster than I ever had before.

· · ·

I drove to my house with the intention of walking over to where Gris was staying after I dropped off my backpack, but Gris was sitting on my porch. It was nice to be wanted. I liked being wanted. He smiled widely when I got out of my car, probably in response to my grin.

Dale was walking home from a friend's house just as I arrived. He rolled his eyes at my expression. He was at that age where PDA of any kind, from anybody, made him uncomfortable.

"Hey." Gris stood. He nodded at Dale. "What's up, Dale?"

Dale stopped and stared at Gris. "Jared's in the hospital. People are saying you put him there."

"It wasn't me."

Dale frowned, clearly disappointed.

Gris looked at me and then asked Dale, "You were hoping I had?"

Dale shrugged. "Well, he and Hank are always picking on Piper. I thought it was about time somebody stood up to them."

Gris's eyes narrowed. "I *have* stood up to them, and Hank better not be messin' with Piper."

There was something possessive about the way he'd said my name. I didn't need anybody fighting my battles for me, but, at the same time, it was nice to hear he wanted to.

"I've stood up to them, too," I said.

Dale snorted a laugh. "You're half his size, Piper. Your standing up puts you at shoulder level. You and Hank"—he shook his head—"it's like a fly going up against a giant. He just swats you down. The only one with any lick of control over him is Mattie, and she could do a lot better. A *lot* better."

I had my own opinion on why Hank sometimes listened to Mattie, and it was an opinion I wouldn't be sharing with Dale. He was too young. Plus, he'd had a crush on Mattie since he'd arrived at the school and she'd flipped her hair. Most boys did. Heck, if Gris went to school, he'd probably have a crush on Mattie, too.

The front door opened, drawing all our attention. Mama stuck her head out. "You'll stay for supper won't you, Gris?"

Gris smiled as if his wildest dreams had come true. "Count

on it, ma'am."

This pleased my mama to no end.

Dale had a one-track mind, and he asked Gris, "You really didn't put Jared in the hospital?" My younger brother looked so wholly crushed.

Gris shook his head, though his forehead was all wrinkled. He knew the rest of the story and wasn't sharing?

Mama's mouth dropped open. " 'Course he didn't, Dale. What are you thinking? Gris isn't like that, and I brought you up better than to think that of people."

Dale rolled his eyes and stomped inside.

Mama gestured after him with an apologetic look at Gris. "I don't know what's gotten into him."

Dale's music turned on full-volume a second later. Mama huffed and stalked after him for her hourly "Turn down that music. I swear you weren't raised in a barn, but it don't show" lecture.

Gris leaned in and pulled the front door closed. "I think it's funny that your mom thinks she knows what type of person I am." He kissed the corner of my mouth. "You reckon most people would find a gargoyle to be polite?"

I shoved him, playfully. My mouth felt all tingly where he'd kissed it. I wanted a lot more of that.

"How about you set your backpack down, and we'll go for a walk?" Gris suggested.

Last night's walk had entailed a lot of kissing, so I wasn't opposed to that idea by any means, but I had a better one. "I think we need to go check out Hidden Creek. The réservoir, I mean."

"I guess maybe I should grab my swimming trunks, then."

"Most people skinny-dip."

Gris froze and stared at me with his jaw dropped.

"We're not skinny dipping," I said quickly. "Hang on. Let me just put my backpack inside, and I'll explain."

Mama would have had conniptions if I just dropped it inside. She didn't like us cluttering up the front room, so I ran it to my bedroom. Before I went back outside, I checked in the front mirror to make sure I didn't have anything in my teeth. I looked pink-cheeked and bright-eyed…and goofy.

When I stepped outside, Gris was leaning against one of the porch's beams, watching the door for me. My heart did flips. He was waiting for me. Just me.

As we started walking, he grabbed one of my hands.

I tangled our fingers together. "It's not too far of a walk, but I don't like to take the road—it's not a straight line."

He nodded as he followed me into the field across from my house. I *knew* it was logical.

"What really happened to Jared?" I asked.

"What makes you think I know?"

I frowned. I thought I was figuring out his expressions. "Don't you know?"

"Yes."

"Well, tell me then."

"Somebody is messing with stuff way out of their league." He shook his head. "I followed Hank to the cemetery last night. I don't know who he was meeting, but whoever it was, they didn't show. Jared was there as back-up and must've gotten bored and decided to shoot up."

"With drugs?" My jaw dropped.

Gris grinned at my shocked expression. "Apparently Hidden Creek has some secrets."

"Do you think Coach Laramie knows?"

"Why would he know?"

"He's Jared's coach, and I've heard that he'd gotten in trouble at the last school he coached at. Everybody assumed it was either steroids or getting too friendly with students, but I don't know what's true."

"I haven't heard from my dad about what was in the

syringe—he's got connections that I don't have yet. But, in this case, it wasn't the drugs necessarily that put him in the hospital. There were fiends inside the truck with him. Jared drove his truck right up to the cemetery fence and rolled out, already getting attacked. They would've killed him if I hadn't been there."

"What did Hank do?"

"He left."

I gasped.

Gris raised his eyebrows. "I can't believe that surprises you."

"He was acting fine today. What kind of psychopath leaves his friend to die and then makes out with Mattie on the bus the next morning? Why, when I talked to him…"

"You talked to him? Piper! I thought we'd decided you weren't going anywhere near him."

"No, you told me, and I ignored it 'cause you were being overprotective. Besides, all we did was talk."

"I have reason to be overprotective. Somebody is gunning for you. Every time we turn around you've got more curse sacks in your bedroom. I can't even figure out when the culprit has the time."

"I've been thinking about that. It's on another list even."

We passed by the Porters' house.

"Well, that's not creepy as hell," Gris murmured.

I looked to find Critch staring out the window at us. "Don't profane," I said, drawing a smirk from Gris. "I can't figure out why you keep trying to stick him on my list."

"Because he belongs. He used to be a Watcher, up until I got the birthright. He figures I stole it from him." Clearing his throat, he said, "Okay, first tell me about your list of who might've gotten into your house."

"Well, that's just the thing—Mama is usually around. Though, she does take my sister to preschool in the mornings and stays in the foyer chatting with other parents."

"There's also during church. Your house would be empty then, I'd guess."

"I don't go every Sunday." I side-eyed him. "Do you?"

He tilted his head. "I don't. I could. I've just never affiliated myself with religion because I stay so busy. Being a Watcher has felt like a type of religion. I could go to church while I'm in Hidden Creek. I imagine that'd be important in this town."

I nodded, even as I groaned inside. Mama had asked me a few subtle questions about that, seeing as the Porters were in our congregation. If Gris went, I'd definitely have to go. "Maybe the sacks were a prank?"

He lifted my hand and kissed it. "No, something has gone sour in Hidden Creek. The sacks in your room, Jester, the grave robbing, Jared, all the fiends. Two of those were aimed at you, so somebody has it out for you. I'm almost certain they figured the sacks weren't enough so they killed your dog to set fiends on you."

"Then it is my fault Jester's dead." My stomach hurt just thinking about it.

"No. Not at all. You're in the way of something. Jester was in the way." He frowned. "If we could figure out why, maybe that'd tell us who."

"What's in those pouches that pulls them in?" I asked.

"They've been changing it up. The only thing consistent is the sulfur. Some topical creams contain sulfur. When elderly folks use them, it often makes them the first victims in a population. It's terrible. Whoever is messing around with those pouches might've killed Jester because I came to town, too. It stepped up their timeline. Maybe they figured it was only a matter of time before I started getting the fiend population under control." He ran a hand through his hair. "Though, if they thought that, they had a higher impression of my abilities than I've shown. Hidden Creek is infested with more fiends than all of Atlanta."

"Well, how many people around here know what you do?" He'd made it sound like few people outside of family even knew Watchers existed.

"It depends. I don't know what Danny told people." His smile was wry and frustrated. "Also, some people might just... know. There might be a whole line of Watchers here, without an active Watcher in it, but they'd know. Also, my dad wanted me to ask about a pastor here. Pastor Green."

I blinked. "Why? You think he's involved?"

"My dad says he's been visiting Phil, and local religious leaders might know about both fiends and Watchers. They did in the past."

"Oh." The stiffness in my body relaxed. It wouldn't have been right—Pastor Green being out for blood and evil. I needed a constant in this tilting world of myths and gray areas. "Of course he'd go visit Phil. That's just how Pastor Green is. He's spent time with everybody who's had problems. He even insisted on a proper search party after Trina disappeared." Though why that hadn't included the creek, I didn't know.

"And you trust that he's just being...Christian?"

I shrugged. "I'm not as religious as my parents would like me to be, but no, he'd never make my list."

"Ahh, your list. The one that had both our names on it."

"Mock all you want, but I know whoever killed Jester is on my list, even if I have some vague categories. If you're certain the sacks were put in my room by a person, that might help narrow our suspects down on account of not everybody has access to my room. Your uncle, Danny's daddy, he's not, umm, the right size to be going in my window, but he'd know how to jimmy a lock, I suspect, due to working on machines. Danny would, too, for the same reason. The coach doesn't live nearby so it'd be noticeable if he was around our house."

"There's my great-uncle."

I squinted at him.

"I'm serious," he said, seeming to sense my disbelief. "He's more logical a suspect than Danny's dad."

"Mr. Porter is farm-raised, Gris. I overheard him talking about going in on a cow with our family. My daddy couldn't turn down that offer fast enough, even after Mr. Porter offered to do the slaughtering. We don't eat anything that didn't enter our world by way of a Styrofoam, shrink-wrapped package."

"Critch is a former Watcher."

"He's also like a million years old."

"Eighty. But he was a Watcher."

He kept acting like that was enough, but what happened to Jester was a sight more vile than what I'd seen Gris do, and the way he'd described fiends—they weren't cute like Jester. "I will say that both Mr. Porter and the coach seem unlikely suspects for putting curse bags in my room." I winced. "Though, somebody I think put pouches in the gym today, and that might've been the coach."

Gris pulled me to a stop and turned my way. "What?"

"Today, when I confronted Hank, he wanted me to meet him in the gym. But when I went into the gym, Hank wasn't there, fiends were."

Gris took a step back before pushing up one of my sleeves to show light scratches. "Piper!"

I pushed my sleeve back down. "They're not that bad. I sprayed the fiends with pepper spray and then ran outside. I would've been fine if Hank hadn't kicked my backpack out of the doorway, leaving me in the dark gym with the fiends. Hank was waiting outside and that's when we talked."

"Maybe he set the fiends on you."

"I think it was somebody else. Somebody else was inside and laughing at me anyways."

Gris closed his eyes and inhaled deeply before opening

them. "I swear, Piper, you're going to be the death of me. You were attacked by fiends—probably these hopped-up, nasty fiends, right before you confronted a bully that might've killed your dog and, last night, left a friend to die."

"Well, I didn't know that then." I gestured with my free hand. "About him leaving Jared to die. But wait until you hear what I learned." I pulled him back into walking. We'd reached the woods leading to Hidden Creek, and it was kind of sweet to be holding hands and surrounded by all the trees with spring buds on them. "Hank said on the night Trina disappeared, she'd snuck out the window to go skinny dipping in Hidden Creek with her boyfriend, and she didn't take anything with her. She kept a stash of money under a floorboard, and she left it behind. That's important."

"You can't keep putting yourself in harm's way like this. And Hank, well, he's harm's way. He might have something to do with his sister's disappearance."

"He doesn't. Besides, as I said, I had my pepper spray with me."

"How do you know he's not a suspect?"

"He was too sad." Okay, it sounded dumb when I said it out loud.

Gris's expression seemed to validate my opinion.

"Well, how about he's not smart enough?"

"To kill?" Gris asked.

"No, he's not smart enough to make those curse sacks, and he hasn't really had the opportunity to put them in my room. He attends church, and he's at school when I'm at school."

Gris wiped his free hand down his face. "Anybody with access to the internet could look up instructions and make the sacks. They're not particular to a certain dark practice, and it's possible some fool might've just wanted to prank you, not knowing it'd draw fiends."

"But why kill Jester in that case?"

"They're sick and demented and it's unrelated."

"You really think that's the case?"

"No." He shook his head. "No, there's more connections than I'd care to see. The real question is: Do they know what they're doing?" He shook his head. "Maybe I shouldn't tell you this, but that grave they robbed was a Watcher's grave. It's possible they might be doing something related to that and not just causing mischief."

I gave him the flat stare that my mama always gave Dale when he fudged the reality of a situation. "Mischief? If they know they have y'all's super special bones, what might they be doing?"

He winced. "They might have found a method to open up a gateway for fiends to amass in Hidden Creek. Or it might be related to the birthright—though, if it was, I'd have guessed they'd be trying to kill me."

"And nobody's tried that?"

He shrugged. "Not with any success."

"Obviously," I said, my tone as dry as the desert.

We reached the outskirts of Hidden Creek and circled the murky réservoir. It was fully-surrounded by woods and the road we'd walked down to get to it had ruined more than one axle. The shade of the trees meant that the deep réservoir was cold and shadowed most of the year. Several of those trees had fallen during a winter storm, and the sun speckled the far side of Hidden Creek.

"Not much to look at, is it?" Gris gestured. "I'd expected something bigger. I could swim across this in about fifteen minutes."

"I'm sorry our itty bitty réservoir isn't up to your high standards, Gris. The creek that feeds it is over there."

"That tiny trickle? You sure you don't want to go skinny dipping?" Gris slid me a mischievous look.

"That water must be freezing, and do you even know how

filthy it is?" My cheeks felt hot just from the suggestion.

He laughed. We were talking about dark rituals, murder, and skinny dipping—and he laughed. "Why are we here, then?"

I shrugged and peered at the water. "I don't know. This is where Trina and her boyfriend were headed the night they disappeared."

"A year ago," he reminded me.

"Yes." Dropping his hand, I squinted at the water that now had sunlight flickering across it.

"What?"

Looking at a nearby tree, I said, "Hey, help me up into that tree, will you? I want to see something."

"You're going up into a tree?"

"Gris, I'm a Southern girl. I've climbed a tree or two in my lifetime." He helped me up, and I'm sure he smothered one of his charming grins as his hands lingered on my thighs. Brushing off my hands on my jeans—thoroughly—I looked down into the water from above.

"What do you see?" he asked.

"There's something reflective, but it's too deep to really tell. This was all in shade last year, though. We had a bunch of trees come down around here in November."

Gris swore.

"Don't profane."

He pointed at me. "Stay right up there. You hear?"

"In a tree? Why?"

"Because you're safe. And you might want to close your eyes."

"Closing my eyes while I'm up in a tree isn't very safe."

"Fine. Then you can watch me do some skinny dipping." He pulled off his shirt.

I closed my eyes. Most of the way.

Chapter Fifteen

The water looked cool and deep. Probably too cool for most people to swim in. But even if it was cold enough to freeze the balls off a pool table, I could still go in; water held darkness like the night did. Watchers could absorb enough to change partially, even during the day. I could use my thicker Watcher skin to keep me from freezing long enough to check out whatever Piper was seeing.

I stripped down to my boxers and dove into the réservoir. The water made my skin tingle. I wrapped the shadows around me. My skin felt slicker and my muscled form was much heavier, but I was stronger.

Keeping my eyes open, I plunged underwater. The world below the water opened up for me as bright as if it was no deeper than a few feet. The cold and the darkness likely prevented the locals from exploring down too far. It was about thirty feet, give or take, and murky since locals had thrown junk in. Not that this was unusual. Hopefully, whoever'd thrown that fridge there felt a stab of guilt, though.

Piper'd probably seen the car. I swam toward it. Not an old one from what I could see, and it didn't seem to be in pieces. It was an older car, sure, but not in such a bad way you'd think somebody would throw it in here instead of selling it for parts. Had somebody gotten drunk and crashed it? How long had it been down here?

I approached it from behind. The trunk and license plate came into view first. Tennessee plates.

Then, I knew exactly how long it'd been down here. It'd been down here as long as Trina and her boyfriend had been missing. Damn.

• • •

I wasn't the chattiest guest for dinner, but all that time I'd spent underwater helping the sheriff tow out the car had guaranteed I had an appetite, and Mrs. Devon's cooking wasn't to be missed.

I knew Piper wanted to talk about it. She'd gone running home to call the sheriff. My replacement phone hadn't arrived yet.

Piper was nearly vibrating in her seat beside me now. Her brother Dale had tried a few pointed questions before his mother had shut him down.

They knew it was Trina and her boyfriend. That had gone around the whole town before I'd even returned. Hidden Creek was turning out to be so much more than I'd bargained for. Any reasonable person would've asked for help. Hell, any reasonable person would have left town.

I wasn't turning out to be very reasonable.

When Mrs. Devon announced she was making cookies for dessert, but they wouldn't be ready for an hour, I gave in to Piper's pointed invitations to go for a walk.

She dragged me by our joined hands toward the barn, cutting across the field—due to her thing with straight lines. I could feel somebody in the Porters' place watching us. Either Critch or somebody else. Hell, it might be Danny's little sisters. I was getting paranoid. Hanging out with dead bodies could do that to you.

Just outside the barn, we both stopped. She stared at the patch of peeled paint, right beside the door with a focus that seemed like it could light the barn on fire. Then, with a guilty look back at me, Piper peeled a piece off.

"So, you're the one desecrating this hallowed ground," I said.

"Hush."

I winced. "Actually, forget I used that wording."

"Why?"

"Between the cemetery and the car—I've had enough to do with dead bodies as I ever plan to."

"Tell me about it," she said with a sigh that made me smile.

"Oh yeah?"

She looked downright traumatized. "My day before I met up with Hank was more disturbing than after, and that's saying something."

"How's that?" I knew she'd come home after her brother, and her mom had mentioned something about a field trip.

"Let's just say that I don't have a future ahead of me involving corpses."

"Well, you're limiting your career choices, but I think you might manage."

She shuddered. It was adorable. It got even more so as I watched her repeat that hay bale touching routine she'd done the first day we met. "Don't!" She held up a finger when she caught me watching her.

"I wouldn't dare."

"I like it here," Piper said as she touched the last bale of hay. After scrutinizing it, she leaned against it.

"I like that barn pixies like it here." I smiled at her confusion. "You, that first day. In that dress with your hair pulled back, you looked sweet and temperamental. Like a pixie."

"Pixies are temperamental?"

"Yes. Plus, you're much smaller than me. You seemed so tiny in this wreck of a barn."

"Have you ever swung from the rafters in a barn?" she asked.

I looked up. "In this barn?" Sometimes, her obsessiveness seemed to skip. How would she rationalize that as being safe?

She pointed up at the thick loops of leather on the rafters above the big mounds of hay. "I put those up so I wouldn't get slivers."

"Of course you did."

She climbed up the ladder to the hayloft while I watched her from below. In fact, she had my rapt attention.

"What are you looking at?"

"Your legs. You've got great legs, Piper."

"Gris." Her scolding tone made me grin and want to kiss her. She jumped to the first leather strap and hung, putting her exposed stomach at my eye level. Thin pale cuts feathered her skin, with a slightly pink line here and there. Another cut zone.

"Stop," she whispered, biting her lip.

I met her gaze. "It's fine, Piper."

"You're not acting like it is."

I had to. I had to be okay with it because it wasn't my place to judge what she did to survive. Stepping forward, I kissed her stomach, making her lose her grip. I wrapped my arms around her waist as I caught her, letting her drop down the length of my body. When we were nose to nose, I said, "We all carry stories on our skin, sweetheart. Your skin just happens to be beautiful without adding to it." I meant every word.

"Grisham," she said, using my full name. The lack of eye contact softened any rebuke. Piper pushed out of my arms before scrambling back up the ladder, avoiding my gaze. When she reached the second leather strap, she asked, "Aren't you gonna try it?"

"I'm not convinced those beams will hold me. I probably weigh twice as much as you. Besides, the view from down here isn't bad."

She kicked at me as I followed along beneath her—both because of the view and because I wasn't convinced those decaying boards wouldn't break.

"You should try it, Gris, it's like flying."

I laughed. I'd spent hours in and out of water, helping tow out a car of corpses because the sheriff's department couldn't handle the temperature or see the car. I should be grim and frozen. Instead, I was smiling ear-to-ear and warm from just being close to Piper, who was blushing again.

"I'll be the judge of that since I can tell you, with some accuracy, if that's true." I vaulted onto the platform, not even bothering with the ladder.

Piper cannonballed into a bale of hay and, a moment later, I dropped down next to her.

"You're right. That feels like flying."

"Really?" Her arched brows called me a liar.

"Yep, sorta." Leaning over her, I said, "Of course, this feels better than flying." I pulled her below me, lining up our bodies, and kissed her. The softness of her mouth was more exhilarating than a swift dive while in the air. I curled my hands into her hair. The strands felt so good between my fingers. Her gasp against my lips encouraged me to nudge her mouth open with my tongue and—

Swack!

I pulled back, looking around.

"What was that?" she asked.

"Stay here." I scrambled to my feet and ran to the open barn door. Peering out, I listened as I scanned the area. I didn't see anything, but if it was a gunshot, they didn't necessarily have to be that close. "I don't see anybody out there, but I don't know for sure what that was. Maybe a bullet." Sheepishly, I backed into the barn. If they'd been trying to kill me, I'd been standing there as a perfect target.

"Aren't gunshots louder?" Piper asked.

"Probably." Also, I just couldn't imagine somebody firing at us. "Let's go into that corner—out of sight." That way, I could listen to see if there really was anyone else out there. I was imagining things. It had to be a bird, or somebody throwing rocks.

Grabbing her hand, I pulled Piper over to the pile of hay in the corner. We sat down, side-by-side. I pulled our joined hands onto my lap, and my fingers traced the skin on her inner arm. I could feel the scratches on her arms from the fiends in the gym. Another place I had to check out. Hidden Creek was going to kill me from exhaustion.

"We should be able to figure out who is doing this or at least eliminate more suspects," I said. "I have experience dealing with the dark arts and you know this town better than anyone else."

"Not better than anyone else."

"You're always watching people. I bet you know more stories about this bedeviled town than anybody realizes."

"Does that bother you?"

"People being bedeviled?"

"No. Me watching people. Me watching you. Does that bother you?"

"Hell no. Stare your fill."

She actually laughed. "Don't profane."

Danny hadn't been entirely wrong about her staring, though, especially when you were keeping something from her—she stared through you. She had a real sense for when someone was lying. I couldn't figure out what it was. I brought her hand to my mouth and kissed her knuckles. I had to keep Piper safe. If it killed me, I'd keep her safe.

"Tell me about the car on the creek bed."

And she killed the mood.

I flopped down on the hay. "What's there to tell?"

"Obviously, it was them."

"I think they'll be comparing dental records, but I imagine it was."

She was staring at me. Specifically, she was staring at my forehead for some reason.

"What else did you see?" she asked—like she knew. The government could use Piper to get confessions.

"Nothing. Corpses. Rotting corpses." It was a bit mean, especially in light of the suppressed gag and the sharp shudder that worked its way down her body.

"You saw something else." Piper was still eyeing my forehead.

Oh hell, I couldn't really be that obvious, could I? "I don't see a fresh bullet hole." I gestured at the wall of the barn, attempting to distract her. "But it looks like this barn doubled as a shooting range at one point. It's more of a needle in a haystack than an *actual* needle in a haystack."

Piper went still and then shifted in the hay, looking down at it as if it was all needles and no hay. I hadn't even been trying that time. She wriggled closer to me as if she wanted to crawl on top of me just to escape the bale of needle-ridden hay. I smothered my smile just as she glanced up.

"Boys are so stupid."

"Girls are funny."

"So, tell me about the creek."

"It was nothing."

She sighed in exasperation and went back to staring at my forehead.

"I don't have a tell!" I said, sitting up.

"A what?"

"A tell. Something I do when I'm fibbing. I don't have a tell."

"Everybody does."

"What's yours, then?" I asked her. That would be good to know.

"Maybe I never lie." She even self-righteously lifted her chin to complete the picture.

"My mom used to say 'my cow died last night, so I don't need your bull.' Seems appropriate right now."

"I don't lie, Gris. It's not fair, and it's not polite. I don't lie." She was cute, even when she was lying about lying.

"You told me your name was Laura when we first met."

She grimaced.

"Whether it's because they're trying to hold back unpleasantness or they're out and out fibbing, everybody lies. Sometimes the lie is kinder." I leaned back in the hay.

"If I show you my tell, will you talk to me about Hidden Creek?"

For an hour, couldn't we be a normal couple? A normal couple—hiding out in a barn, hoping they hadn't been shot at? A normal couple—where one of us was a gargoyle? Hell, we were doomed. "I'd rather not. It was ugly."

"We're not keeping secrets from each other, and this'll make it even." Even. Piper used the word "even" where most other girls would use the word "perfect."

"Fine then. Show me yours, and I'll show you mine."

She blushed again at the innuendo. My mom would love her. Her voice was prim as she said, "When I'm nervous, I have a tic."

"A what? Like a bug? You have a bug?" I teased her.

She shivered and looked down at the hay like it was hiding critters.

I was terrible. I didn't deserve to spend time with a girl like Piper.

"No, not a tick. A tic. T-I-C. You know, a motion you do so often it's like a habit." She tucked a strand of hair behind her ear.

I moved my arms behind my head and relaxed. So far, this was the best part of today. "What is this tic?"

She pinched my side for being annoying. "It's with my hand. I…" She waved around.

"You what?"

"Oh, good grief, I tap my fingers together. That's all."

"I'll have to watch for that." I'd seen it. I didn't want to make her self-conscious, but I'd seen it. I grabbed her hand and kissed her fingers.

"We're even now. Well, after you tell me about the creek."

She was like a pit bull with a chew toy, and she was staring at my forehead again. "This is not even," she said when I didn't respond.

I groaned. "What do you want me to say, Piper? I went down into the water and found a car with bodies in it. It ranked low on the things I like about Hidden Creek."

I rolled onto my side and inched closer to her. She put a finger against my lips right as I leaned forward. "They've been there all this time?"

I pulled her close enough to kiss her neck. "Mmm." Piper smelled good. So much better than anything else I'd been around today. Her skin was soft as satin, too. I kissed up her neck and along her jaw.

"Was it disgusting?"

"Hmm." How she could still be talking about this when I was running my mouth across the skin just below her ear,

I didn't know. "Piper," I breathed her name. I wouldn't be ready to give her up anytime soon. I bit the skin right below her ear, making Piper jump. "You wanna know what ranks *high* on the things I like about Hidden Creek?"

"Mmm, yeah," she whispered on a breathy exhale.

"You. This barn with you in it. Piper Specials. Your mom's cooking." I paused and glanced toward her house. How long had it been anyway?

"She'll whistle when they're out."

Oh. Good. It definitely hadn't been a gunshot. I couldn't hear anything, and it wouldn't make sense for somebody to take one weak shot and then run off.

"Do you think it was an accident? The car, I mean?" Piper was chewing on her lower lip.

"I think they'll be doing autopsies." I smoothed my forehead out.

"Gris!"

"Laura!" Then, I shrugged. She wanted to hear it all? Fine, I'd tell her. "They had big holes in their chests."

"What?"

"Somebody had carved out their hearts. The water was cold enough that deep it sorta preserved them."

"That's disgusting." She gagged slightly. "Real disgusting."

I gestured between us. "Well, I'm sharing. I was gonna keep that to myself, but you like this sharing thing."

She was silent for a bit before turning onto her side and tracing my sleeve, above where the mark was. "What is this mark on your arm?"

"Each generation in our family, a Watcher is born. A mark appears on the arm of the chosen Watcher for that generation around the time they lose their first tooth. Shortly after that, the darkness seeps into our body at night and things happen."

"What things?"

"One night, you sprout wings in the middle of a nightmare,

and it damn near scares you to death."

"Don't pro…"

"Profane. I apologize. You're a funny one for rules and being polite, Piper."

"I am not." She punched me in the arm. "Why were you surprised you were the one to become a Watcher? Isn't your daddy one? Aren't you an only child?"

"Yes. It comes through my granddaddy's line. His brother, Critch, was the Watcher for that generation. But, the birthright could have jumped to one of my cousins instead of going to me."

"So, it'll go to your kids?" she asked in a whisper.

"It'll likely go to one of my cousins' kids and then move out of our line since I'm an only child."

"Why wouldn't it go to one of your kids?"

"Well, I'm not exactly normal, and I'm not sure I'm fully human. Gargoyles were modeled after us."

"So?"

"I don't think many girls are dying to spend their lives with a gargoyle. It's hard to believe my mom accepted it. I might not have any kids for it to go to."

She flicked me in the head. "You're not a gargoyle, idiot. You're you. You're Gris."

"I'm a freak inside."

"We're all a little freaky inside. You just happen to be able to fly."

I kissed her. I had to kiss her. Except kissing her, with her warmth pressed against me in the dark, made my body want to shift. My wings itched behing my shoulder blades. I pulled back abruptly. "Piper, I can't…" Hell, that'd been close. I sucked in a deep breath. And another.

"I'm sorry." She was breathing fast, too.

"It's harder to stop the change when it's dark."

"What?"

I dropped back into the hay with a sigh. "You almost wound up kissing a gargoyle."

"I wouldn't have minded."

Screw it. Groaning, I grabbed her, folding her into my arms, and I kissed her again—clear up until two loud whistles came from the direction of her house.

Chapter Sixteen

That night, Gris stopped by my room and knocked softly on the window. Rather than come in, he said, "I should probably stay out here."

I leaned out my window. Our front porchlight illuminated him, making his outline glow. Normally, I didn't much care for darkness, but he made it as warm as a fire-lit room. He was there without a shirt on again, and no shoes. It'd only been a day since I'd seen him changed, but it felt like a dream. It seemed impossible already.

"How did you get here?" I asked.

"Pardon?"

"Did you walk or ride your bike?"

I saw the quick flash of a smile. "I flew."

"I wanna see." I couldn't imagine such a thing.

His denial came so swift and firm that it startled me. "No."

I waited for him to explain. He didn't. The silence stretched out and filled with all the words we didn't say. Maybe he didn't figure I deserved an explanation. Maybe I didn't. I mean, who was I to him? A short pit stop in the grand tour of Gris Caso. I had to prevent my heart from investing in him. Once we solved Hidden Creek's fiend problem, he'd bolt out of here, anxious to see this town in his rearview mirror.

"Oh," I said finally—when somebody had to say something. I leaned back and put my hands up to the window to close it. "Good night then." Mama had drilled into us to be polite, and I was gonna kill Gris with politeness and then cry after I'd shut the window. It would be good practice—this shutting him out of my life. I was likely only a week from building my wall between my heart and Gris Caso.

"Wait. Just wait," he said, stopping my hands. I could see a war of emotions on his face in the dim light. "You don't make it easy to keep secrets."

"I didn't realize we still were." My tone was as prim as Mama's on Sundays. "But I don't know why I'm expecting even that much of a commitment from you. You could be gone tomorrow."

His hand enfolded one of mine. "It's not that, Piper. I'm just more used to keeping secrets than not keeping them."

"We've got that in common, then."

Sighing, he leaned back and looked at the front door. "Okay."

I scrambled through the window, and he caught me in his arms before my feet touched the ground. "Whoa!" He cradled me close to his chest.

"I wanted to see you, but I can't if I'm inside and you're outside," I said. "It's too dark."

"I know, but you're not wearing any shoes."

"Neither are you."

"I know, but it's different because my feet aren't cute."

I stared at him—tipping my chin down so he felt the full weight of it. 'Cause that's what a statement like that deserved.

"I'll have to change form to do it. I can't do a partial change to fly," he said, setting me down. "So, I'll look as I did last night."

"I don't mind." Watching him transform was like seeing magic. His wings surged out, catching moonlight. "That's amazing." I ran my fingers along his wings—the bones, the webbing.

Gris twitched as if it tickled slightly.

"How does it work?"

One swoop, and he was airborne. Six feet above the ground.

"Wow," I said.

He dropped down. "I might…"

"What?"

"I might be able to pick you up."

"Really?"

"Put your arms around my neck."

I did, hugging up to his body. This might be my only chance to experience this. He smelled like warm stone and Gris. He still smelled like himself. He put his arms around my waist, but the first swoop of his wings made me slip.

"Maybe if I held you and you put your legs around my waist," he said.

It was a bit awkward and…friendly, but it worked. And we were flying. We were flying. I wanted to scream, but not out of fear. It was as amazing and exhilarating as riding his bike—times fifty.

The airflow wrapped around us, caressing my sides. It was like dancing in the air.

Laughing, I tucked myself into his body as I stared at the moon above us. This was incredible. "Gris," I said.

There was an abrupt jerk and we tipped sideways before he righted us. "Say that again," he said.

"What?"

"My name."

I grinned. Silly boy. "Gris, this is unreal."

I tangled my fingers up in his hair—his hair that felt the same in either form. Even with all the changes, he was still Gris.

"Does it feel like swinging in the barn?" he asked.

I shook my head against his shoulder. "Take us that way, down that road."

"Why?"

"I'll show you. Right over there. That two-storey house with the clapboard shutters." I had him put us down beside a tree in their yard.

"We should get back," Gris said, looking around.

"Why?"

"Why? Because I'm not sure it's safe. Because Hidden Creek is trying to kill both of us. A good lot of reasons actually. Also, it's a school night."

I sniffed, even if he was right. It *was* a school night. "This is important."

"Is it? Where are we?"

I pointed up at the house. "Hank's house."

Chapter Seventeen

She had to be kidding.

"Oh, fantastic," I said. "Nothing says safe and cautious like spying on the family of a murder victim."

"Oh, hush, Gris. You know it's a good idea."

A good idea?

A *good* idea? "I should really take you home," I said.

"In a minute. I just wanna see what he's up to."

"Are your parents gonna check on you and be pissed?" It was my Hail Mary.

"No, I locked my door after I had Mama lock me in," she whispered.

Damn.

If she got caught sneaking out, she'd be on her own for this explanation. I should take her back and slide her cute little butt right back through her window. When had I become the voice of reason between us? It didn't sit right, but one of us had to keep her out of trouble.

Her toes wriggled in the grass, and she whispered, "Next time maybe I'll wear shoes."

"There's not going to be a next time, Piper." I wasn't dragging her to our suspects' houses.

"No. Of course not." Her quick agreement and her ramrod posture made me replay what I'd said. "I shouldn't have assumed. I mean, even if you *are* still in town." She wrapped her arms around herself.

Damn. I could be such an oblivious jerk.

"I just meant flying to someplace like this."

The sound of wood breaking drew our eyes to a window on the second floor. Somebody was breaking stuff—a lot of stuff. Something flew by the window and hit the wall.

Hell. I stepped in front of her.

With a huff of annoyance, she stepped around me. "It's just Hank," Piper whispered. She pointed at the driveway. "The only car here is his truck. I'm pretty sure that's Trina's room. His is on the other side and has the school flag hanging in it as a curtain. It's the *actual* school's flag. He stole it, Gris, and he has the *gall* to hang it as a curtain for everybody to see. Ain't that wrong? I think so."

Her outrage momentarily distracted me. She made me want to kiss her at the most inappropriate moments. This rush of a new relationship couldn't last, though. Part of it might even be because of the situation. Maybe it was just as well that both of us realized this was temporary.

Crash! Crap, he was shattering and destroying everything in his sister's room.

"Stay here." I transformed back to get a better look. Hovering isn't easy with wings as long as mine, but I was up there long enough to see Hank had trashed most of his sister's room. I landed right as a few fiends decided to approach us.

"Fiends. Stay put."

I pulled the fiends in and ripped out their hearts, rather

than wait for them to get closer. I usually waited for them to come to me, but not with Piper here. Everything was different with Piper—including hunting.

I transformed back, shaking out my arms and legs. Having Piper near me made for an adrenaline rush due to worrying over her.

"Wow." Her eyes were wide.

I tried to suppress my grin. The approval in her eyes… well, it wasn't bad. "He's up there shredding all her pillows." I gestured at the window.

"That makes sense. He's angry 'cause she's dead."

"I don't think that was really her choice."

"That's not the point. It's like you said with your ferret—it feels like you ought to be able to blame somebody or something when you feel out of control."

I watched her as she scrutinized the window. She could see into people's heads better than anybody I'd ever met.

Hank snarled and hurled something against the wall. Glass shattered.

"He didn't do it," she whispered. "He wouldn't have hurt Trina."

I was more concerned about the stuff done to Piper than the murder. Nothing could stop Trina from being dead, and it might have nothing to do with Jester's death, or the stupid fool playing with dark arts, but it just might. And Hank was a spiteful little hothead.

Piper tilted her head. "I don't think he did the other stuff, either."

"Jester?"

"Any of it. He's got too much of a temper for anything with a long-term pay-off—or anything that'd require cleaning up after. And I'm telling you, when I asked him about Jester, he wasn't expecting it. He'd have expected me to suspect him, and the fact that he didn't expect it means that I shouldn't suspect him."

"Okay," I said slowly. "Are you crossing him off your list so there's only eight?"

She nodded decisively.

Huh. I believed her. Her ability to read people gave her this edge I couldn't argue away. It was interesting that people around town had given her credit for things she hadn't done, but no one underestimated Piper. Her brain was a little, well, badass.

"Are we crossing off Jared?" I asked.

She tilted her head. "He might have done everything up until now. Though I don't think he's smart enough or any more cool-headed than Hank."

Also, she'd be down to an odd number again.

"I think I need to make another list. A list of names for those two categories at the end of my previous list."

"One was unknown enemy. By definition, you shouldn't be able to make a list of unknown people."

She shot me a dark look. "It'd be a longer list for sure—maybe a couple dozen names, but I could do it. But you'd have to tell me *everything*. Everything, Gris. Don't think I don't know you're holding things back."

I'd contacted my dad for him to get a list of dark crafts that might use hearts and the bones of a Watcher—especially crafts that might heighten the energy of fiends. Giving Piper any more information might put her in danger while she investigated the list. She had a limited awareness of how dangerous some of these players were. "I'll think about it."

The thud of his feet on the stairs was enough warning for me to grab her and swoop us both into the tree. Hank slammed through the back door and trudged down the street.

Piper squinted after him.

"Where's he going?" I asked. It was fairly late for him to be wandering off in a fury.

"To my house. Otherwise, he would've taken his truck. Mine is the only one farther up this street that you'd walk to." She said it matter-of-factly—Piper and her badass brain.

"Fine then, you stay here, and I'll go see what he's doing."

"In the tree? You're leaving me in the dark? In a tree? You can't be serious, Gris."

"You're a Southern girl—you like trees. Besides, you'll be safe up here. It's got a nice wide trunk. Just hold still."

"What if he wants to talk to me?"

"As pissed as he is? I'll head him off and tell him to screw himself." He wasn't getting anywhere near Piper.

I surged off the branch before she had more time to argue. She'd be safe on that upper branch from human critters and fiends. After the short flight, I dropped onto Piper's roof and flattened against it. With the night wrapped around me, Hank had no idea somebody was watching his every move. He stood at the fence. Fifteen minutes passed. He just sat there. His gaze searching the windows on the house.

Maybe he *did* want to talk to Piper, but he wasn't sure which window was hers. If that was true, he also hadn't killed her dog and stood beneath her window with blood on his shoes *or* put the sacks in her room.

Shoot, he'd been a good suspect, too.

But Piper had discounted him—and Piper could read people.

Kicking the fence, he muttered, "Stupid girl."

Who?

Trina?

Piper?

Another five minutes went by. Piper was likely pissed with me by now. Maybe I shouldn't have left her in that tree.

Just as I was considering going back to get her, Hank picked up a rock and hurled it at Piper's car window. *Crack.* Damn. I heard her parents waking up inside right as Hank bolted. I bolted, too—right back to Piper. Her parents would check on their daughter after somebody had smashed her car's window.

"Gris," she hissed with narrowed eyes when I reached her.

"We gotta go. Hank broke one of your car windows, and your parents will wonder where you are." I hauled her into my arms.

"There were bugs in that tree," Piper muttered. "I think it had a real nasty infestation going on, and you left me so high up I couldn't get down."

I thought of trying to hush her down but she was in full-on ranting Piper mode so I shielded us with shadows instead. We touched down outside her window. All of the lights were on in the house, and I could hear somebody in the front room's closet, probably her dad dragging on shoes to investigate. Her mom knocked on Piper's bedroom door and called her name right as I boosted her through the window.

"Bugs. Lots of bugs," Piper whispered. "I'm gonna need to take a couple dozen showers just to get the feel of them off my feet."

"I'm sorry."

She pointed at me with a finger that promised this conversation wasn't over.

Ducking down, I listened from below her window as she unlocked the door. "I'm fine, Mama. It was probably someone throwing a rock at my car…again."

"You're okay?"

"I'm fine. I'm gonna go take a shower," she answered.

"In the middle of the night?"

"Yeah, well, I had this nightmare I had bugs crawling all over me 'cause some idiot had left me stranded in a tree for over a half an hour."

"That's a very odd dream, Pips. You're sure you're fine?"

"In my hair! They were crawling in my hair and over my feet! My whole body itches. My arms! My legs! I swear they're still crawling all over me."

"Well, if you're sure you're okay," her mom replied.

"Plus, it was dirty in the tree. The bark had dirt all over it along with the bugs."

"Ew. Can we stop talking about this? You're about to give me nightmares. I might need to take a shower after listening to you."

I smothered a laugh as her mom walked off. The door opened, and her dad came out, carrying a shotgun. I built a black shadow wall around me as I flattened myself against the house. Even if he looked this way, he wouldn't see me.

Her mom's silhouette fell across the porch in front of the open door. "Piper said it was one of the windows on her car again."

Her dad swore, but went in that direction.

Above me, Piper's window slid open. She hung her head out and whispered, "Thank you for taking me out tonight," as her eyes searched for me. Her polite tone was at war with her petulant one.

Easing up on the darkness cloaking me, I touched her cheek while trying not to smile. "You're very welcome, Piper."

Growling, she looped a hand around my neck and dragged me forward to kiss me.

"Now, fly out of here before they catch you," she whispered.

Fly out of here? I flew as far as her roof and lay down on it. Eventually, the house quieted down again. By my estimation, Piper's shower was at least a half an hour long. She was good and clean by the time she opened her window and called my name.

I hung my torso off her roof. "Hey, sweetheart, you clean yet?"

She grinned. The scent of apples from her shampoo hung in the air around her. Yeah, I couldn't get any closer when she smelled this edible.

"Just checking. Good night."

Because I couldn't resist, I said, "Good night and don't let the bed bugs bite." Then a moment later, I was justified in adding, "Don't profane." The window closed slowly. Life was good. Life with Piper was real good.

Then, life got bad. Real bad.

My new phone shivered on vibrate right as I heard her settle into her bed. I pulled it out and answered the call.

"You want the bad news or the even worse news first?" Dad asked.

"Neither."

"I did some digging on the Beaumonts. Not only was Silas Beaumont killed in that house, but a couple decades later, Silas's nephew, Theodore, comes to stay in that same house. Now, old Silas had a niece living there, from a different sister, and the niece and nephew didn't necessarily get along. He tried to kick her out. She stood her ground."

"This would be Tawna?"

"Yes. Tawna turns up pregnant—which would have been grounds to kick her out back in that day as she wasn't married. But before she's tossed out on her ear, another animal attack kills Theodore Beaumont in that same house. Only this time, there were footprints walking away from the house. The police weren't sure if it was made to look like an animal attack or if it really was. So, two deaths in that house. First one, fiends most likely. Second, who knows."

"What happened to Tawna? Do you know if that was Critch's kid?" I asked.

"She disappeared that night. Never heard from again though she might've changed her name. It's possible when she had a child, the line might've continued—I don't know that we've nailed down that aspect of the birthright…whether they have to be born before their predecessor died. Obviously, if the baby was Critch's, our birthright didn't go that way."

"So, I'm living in a murder house. And I'm guessing the even worse news is that there are rites using Watcher bones?"

"There are, and the previous presence of the Beaumonts means people in Hidden Creek might not be as blind to our history as we might've thought…or wanted. Knowledge might've been passed down through families, and we didn't immerse ourselves in the dark sides of our gift. I have no idea what to do with another Watcher's bones, other than to bury them again. I'm emailing you what I've found."

That ought to make for some cheery reading. "So somebody might know more about me than I know about me?"

"Yep. Watch your back. If they need the bones of a Watcher for a ritual—they might want something fresher than old Silas. His 'best by' date may have passed, but I'm obviously not familiar with '101 Uses for Gargoyle Bones.' Be careful. I'll be there soon."

After saying good-bye, I hung up. That had killed the night. It couldn't get any worse than that. I was living in a murder house, I couldn't seem to handle going solo on a job, and I might have my bones stolen right out of my body for a dark ritual.

I learned four things during that long night.

First, it can always get worse.

Second, Piper might draw in fiends, with or without curse sacks. If I wasn't constantly trying to soothe her sleep, she tossed and turned all night. Fiends kept coming, drawn by the intensity of her emotional thoughts.

The third thing I realized was that sleepwalking was creepy as hell. When Piper walked out the front door with her eyes wide open, it took me some time to figure out she wasn't ignoring my questions on purpose. She walked out to stand by the fence while I was scouring my brain for everything I'd ever heard about sleepwalkers.

Everything I'd ever read referred to routine activities, but this didn't seem to be part of her routine during the day.

Her eyes were *wide* open. I'd always imagined sleepwalking to be something people did with their eyes closed and involved short walks. Piper stood out by the road for fifteen minutes, shifting from side-to-side. I kept saying her name, hoping she'd snap out of it, but she just stood there, eyes glazed, staring. In a person whose every movement was extra deliberate and controlled, this was so out of character that it was downright scary.

Finally, I couldn't take it anymore and guided her back to her own room. She climbed through the window and into bed. Her eyes closed as I tucked the blankets around her. I thought, *Finally, she's gone back to sleep* before realizing how ridiculous that was. She'd never been awake.

I found a third sack below her nightstand when I decided to check—a third sack that I'd swear couldn't have been there when we'd looked before. I'd checked under her nightstand. I had. I wasn't about to mention it to her—just in case I'd missed it.

I had to have missed it. There was no way somebody had climbed into her room again.

I was gonna make sure Piper was good and safe in the future—even if I had to stick to her like glue and stay in her room every night. If I had to be around her all the time, well, Hidden Creek wasn't all bad, and eventually she was going to college somewhere.

Though, the sleepwalking was definitely a bucket of ice on my raging hormones. She barely blinked. It was unnatural.

The fourth thing I learned from that night was, by far, the most disturbing. It outranked finding out how creepy sleepwalking is.

Somebody had buried a jar of the same ingredients found in the curse sacks. It was on the Devon's property, dragging in fiends. They'd congregated around the mound of dirt and dove, licking at it. I'd had to kill them even as I was digging. I kept putting the shovel down, transforming, and picking up the shovel the moment their hearts had sunk through my fingers. The newly dug hole and its size ought to have tipped me off to what I was digging up. I gagged when I turned up Jester's remains. Some sicko had used his grave to bury the jar, and it looked like they'd taken his teeth.

This monster had desecrated a grave after slaughtering a dog to plant a curse jar and take the dog's teeth. Another grave. A new grave. It seemed more disgusting to me than the other grave I'd spent time in. I was spending far too much time in graves. What in *the* hell, Hidden Creek?

This linked things up. The dog and the curse sacks and the fiends. Tossing something you'd found on a "black magic" website into your enemy's room was one thing, but once you dug up a dog's corpse to plant one…no, you knew what you were doing. I was out of my league. I'd dealt with loads of fiends. I'd visited fiend-plagued rest homes, where death hung like a constant specter in addition to the wispy monsters I hunted. Fiends screeched down the halls at nights there and the bedeviled shouted and shrieked. This was more disturbing than that.

This person was strong and malicious, and some of that focus on Piper had begun before I arrived.

Why?

Was she just an easy target, or had she actually done something to draw it?

When I climbed into the shower at the first rays of dawn, scrubbing the dirt of grave-digging from under my nails, I just plain wanted to forget the whole night. I tried to force my mind back to flying with Piper, but as I crawled into bed, my last thought was of Jester's souring body as I'd uncovered it. I'd been commanding the darkness since I was a child, but, now, my mind was full of it, bedeviled by my own visions.

• • •

I went to the diner again and ordered the Piper Special. Everything about Piper was growing on me. Well, not the sleepwalking thing, but I shouldn't hold that against her. If she was awake and doing it to aggravate me, that would be one thing, but she couldn't help it. She just…did it.

After I'd finished my burger, I ordered another one. I'd killed eight fiends the previous night in addition to the flying and the shoveling.

Actually, I wouldn't be able to eat another peanut butter burger if I kept thinking about the shoveling. I should've ordered Piper's burger with creamy peanut butter instead of crunchy. The sound of me chewing brought to mind the sound of that shoveling. Lucky for my stomach, I was hungry enough I'd be able to work past the texture.

Dick delivered this burger personally. "How is she?"

"She's better." She was, somewhat. She was doing better with this whole thing with Jester anyway, and that was probably what Dick was asking about.

"Heard you're around there a lot. Her parents are decent folk. They wouldn't let you sniff around her if you were a total perv."

"I reckon I'll take that as a compliment, sir." What did one say to that?

Dick wiped his hands in his apron and shouted, "Tony, take the grill," as he sat down across from me. "I mentioned before that Piper worked for me last year. She's real special."

"I think so. I like her a lot."

"I can tell." He snorted a laugh. "I caught you looking at her legs on the way in here."

I nearly choked on the bite of burger I'd taken. He'd seen that, huh?

Dick waved that away. "It's fine. You're interested in her in every which way, not like these other losers around here. I was glad she never took them up on it, and I'd warned them I'd spit in their food if they tried anything."

I set my burger down.

He smiled at my uneasiness. Did he have to bring up spitting in food while I was eating? A boy could starve with such helpful people around, and I suspect this was him being friendly.

"Piper's real observant. She notices everything and everybody. She kept track of what specials were most popular on some days and why. Piper has a system for everything."

He gave me this considering look as if he was dropping pearls of wisdom and making sure I was properly thankful. I was grateful for any help I could get, and he did make a mean burger.

"Not everybody appreciates somebody with that kind of observational skills, shall we say? This thing with Jester has me wondering if they think she knows something, has seen something. Maybe Jester was a warning." He tapped his fingers on the table. "You know, I mentioned to the sheriff about Jester, and it was the first he'd heard of it."

"Piper's mother didn't want to give the person who'd done it a chance to gloat. I believe they put out the animal story to diffuse that."

He sighed. "Sometimes the women in that family—well, they're too careful and examine things too much, if you know what I mean. Piper's mama is my second cousin, and that whole branch of the family tree is like that. It's part of their charm, but not everybody takes to it. And it can be aggravating in an emergency. Piper in a crisis, like a grease fire—now that's a sight to behold. She runs in circles. I have to keep four boxes of baking soda beside the grill nowadays thanks to her. Two wasn't enough. Three just wasn't right."

I grinned. "Four seems sensible."

Dick gave me a flat stare. "You've been spending too much time with her. I darn near embroidered that on her apron, well, one of her aprons; she had four when she worked here. Always had to be as pristine white as a bridal gown. That family has recipes for getting out stains like most people 'round here have for Mud Cake."

Okay, the sleepwalking wasn't that bad. I'd take that to get the rest of the wonder that was Piper.

Perhaps confiding in him wasn't a great idea, but on the other hand, he might help me get to know this place, and Piper trusted him. Leaning forward, I asked, "Do you know anything about Hank's sister?"

"Trina? I heard you found the bodies."

I nodded. "Did anybody have anything against them personally?"

He snorted. "I did. She brought her boyfriend in here right before it happened. I threw them both out. I heard he'd been selling drugs to teenagers 'round town. I don't serve those bastards. I've got a little girl. I reserve the right to kick out his kind. People are saying they were high and drove into the réservoir."

"People are wrong."

"Murdered?"

I nodded.

"What's going on in this town?"

That was what I was trying to figure out. "I think I ought to stop Piper from investigating. She might know more about this town, but it's not safe—especially if, as you said, somebody thinks she knows too much. I think she's out."

"Oh, to be a fly on the wall. You're going to catch layers of hell for that, kid."

"You don't think it's a good idea?"

"Son, it's a great idea. Just don't grow too fond of it. I am hoping you can keep the focus on you, rather than her. It seems like you can handle it." He stood up. "If you need any help keeping my girl Piper safe, you let me know."

"Can I get another burger with creamy peanut butter instead?"

He frowned. "You ain't gonna eat that one?"

"No, I will."

He raised his eyebrows. "Piper's mama cooks a mean spread. Is she not feeding you?"

"She is. I have a real high metabolism."

For a moment, I was tempted to tell him the truth: I was starving because I'd burned so much energy flying my girlfriend around, digging up a grave, and killing ghosts. It'd surprise him. I'd probably get kicked out, though, and one more burger might fill me up enough that Piper's mother wouldn't wonder how I was burning so much energy.

Dick nodded. "Fine then, coming up. Creamy peanut butter."

Piper sat down across from me right as my empty plate was switched out with another burger.

"Oh! Can you ask Dick to make me one of those, too?"

"With crunchy peanut butter not creamy?" the waitress asked.

"Yes." Piper gave me a horrified look, a look I'd reserve for the person digging up graves in Hidden Creek.

"I thought I'd try it this way," I said.

"It's not right."

"I'll take that under consideration." I took a bite. Crap. She was right.

Her raised eyebrows let me know she knew what I was

thinking. Her smirk ensured that I wouldn't say anything.

"How was school?"

Her fingers set to lining up everything on the table. "It was okay." I picked up her hand that was smoothing down the napkin over and over, and kissed it. Her cheeks flushed, and a smile crept up to the corners of her mouth. "I've been thinking we need to get more aggressive about our investigation, though."

"I think maybe it's time I take over."

She froze and pulled her hand from beneath mine.

"Things are getting dangerous, Piper."

"When you say 'take over' does that mean that you're in charge or that I'm out entirely?"

She was sleepwalking at night. Her dog's teeth had been robbed from his grave. We might've been shot at yesterday. I was being reasonable.

Lowering my voice, I said, "My dad's been looking into what they might want Watcher's bones for—along with other things, and it's not pleasant."

"I found my dog dead, Gris. Things haven't been pleasant all week." She enunciated each word very carefully.

It was safer for her this way. Clearly, my plan wouldn't meet with her approval if the obstinate look on her face was anything to go by. Her lower lip even stuck out. I wanted to kiss her. I wanted to taste that freckle in the corner of her mouth to see if it was my imagination that it tasted sweeter. It had to be—it was just a freckle.

"I'll be in charge," I said. If I kept her peripherally involved, I could keep an eye on her. Hopefully, she realized this was a huge concession on my part.

"What else aren't you telling me? I can tell something else happened between last night and today."

I rolled my eyes and went back to eating my burger. It's not like anybody said I had to share every single secret with her. Besides, last night sucked, and I didn't want to discuss it. Some things were best left buried, literally. Every time I thought of digging up that grave—my stomach twisted up. Call me a city boy or whatever, but no shower was long enough when you'd dug up a dog's grave. No shower.

Piper's gaze on me scalded like she had heat vision. Okay, maybe her staring wasn't always a good thing. I'd been cocky to think that.

I cleared my throat. "Found another sack in your room last night. There shouldn't be any more. I figure we must've missed it before. It was under your nightstand." There, I could tell her that. It was mostly true. I wasn't completely lying. We might've missed it.

When I glanced up, she was staring at my forehead. It was unnerving. It was like she could see inside my skull. I could imagine how this might annoy a person who wasn't also attracted to her. Crap, my forehead was all wrinkled, and I put conscious effort into smoothing it out.

"I talked to Coach Laramie today," she said.

"What did he have to say?"

She frowned. "He said that he didn't give Jared drugs and that if I implied that to anybody, he'd make my life hell. Then, he made good on that threat and made me sprint two miles."

"You accused your coach of drug-dealing?"

My question made her jump. Fine, it had been particularly loud, but I was trying to take care of her, and she was verbally attacking people we suspected of murder.

"You didn't go back into the gym, did you?" I hadn't gone by to clean out the fiends that'd been in there yet.

"No, but, I did ask the coach to laugh…like in an evil way, but it sounded more defeated than evil when he did it."

It was just as well her food was delivered because I had no response to something as strange as that. We ate in silence.

When I was done eating, I took a deep breath. "I apologize

for raising my voice." There, that was mature of me. I didn't mean it, but I'd said it. She was staring at my forehead again. It felt wrinkled again. Crap. Trust Piper to notice something like that. I smoothed it out—with difficulty.

"It's fine." Her cool tone implied something to the effect of "piss off," but I may've been paraphrasing. It was like she knew I wasn't telling her about last night. Maybe she *could* read minds. "Look, it's not like you've known me all that long. We just met a few days back. So, it's not like we have to share everything." Her fingers went back to rearranging stuff on the table. She'd folded her used napkin into a careful square and put it smackdab in the middle of her empty plate.

I waited for her to finish. She didn't. Was there a right answer here? There was. I knew there was. Her face fell when I didn't supply it. Maybe any response would be good enough to wipe that sad look off her face. What had she been saying? Oh, we hadn't known each other long.

"Right, we've only known each other a few days," I agreed.

Well, that was not the right answer. She swallowed and started chewing on her lower lip. How was I supposed to know I wasn't meant to agree with her? Why did she make a statement I wasn't supposed to agree with?

"Not to mention you won't be staying long," she said.

"I didn't say that."

"Oh, trust me, I'm very aware of what you're not saying."

"Piper."

She tucked a strand of hair behind her ear, murmuring, "At least I won't have to find a ride home this time."

Fine, I could fix this. I just needed to change the subject. I was intelligent and mature, so I said the first thing that came to mind, "You really do sleepwalk. It's creepy as hell."

Her face went ashen. Crap.

Chapter Eighteen

Well, I didn't need his flat, unwrinkled forehead as a sign he'd said something that was absolutely the truth as he saw it. It was all in the way he said it. He meant it. What kind of a person said that to somebody? I was tempted to snap at him, "Well you turn into something with wings and claws! Plus, creamy peanut butter? Are you kidding me? It's not even the right texture!"

He thought I was creepy?

I ought to be impressed this was the first thing about me he found creepy. I wasn't. I couldn't control my life when I was asleep. Letting somebody be around me when I wasn't in control—was a huge deal. He knew I talked in my sleep—and now this.

And I was creepy?

Creepy?

We were never kissing again and that wall between us was building right away. He could leave right now for all I cared.

Not to mention, it was obvious he was keeping things from me. It was written all over his face—or, at least, his forehead. I'd trusted him, and he was hiding something. Probably a lot of somethings. Why was I telling everything to somebody I'd only known a few days? Somebody just passing through?

"Your eyes are wide open when you do it." Gris gestured at his face. "I figured you were awake at first, and I kept calling your name. You weren't ever awake. You just stare and stare and—"

"And stare. I get it." Hopefully he got the subtext there. Oh, and screw you.

I thought we had something, but, no, I guess not. I'd come running here after finding the sticky note on his front door telling me he was here. I'd been dying to tell him about my talk with the coach. Maybe I shouldn't have told him. I was so obvious. I'd been like a girl with my first crush, which made sense, 'cause it was true. He was my first everything, but I must not mean a whole heck of a lot to him if he could say stuff like that.

I pulled a twenty out of my pocket.

There was probably a girl like me in every town he stopped in. I was another dumb hick who fell for it all. Him and his stupid charm—which probably worked on everybody—even me apparently.

Maybe it all was an act. Maybe the other girls knew his secret, too, and he took them flying. It was an original pick-up—I had to give him points for that.

"I got this," Gris said, waving his hand at the twenty I had in my fist.

"Fine." I didn't want him to pay for my stupid food, but I didn't care to be around him for a moment longer. "I have someplace to be."

"Where?"

I gestured vaguely over my shoulder. Anywhere but here.

He threw money on the table and stood with a sigh. "I'm a jerk, Piper."

No disagreement there. A jerk who apparently found me creepy. I crossed my arms and left the diner. If he followed me, fine. If not, fine. He'd better follow me, though. When I stopped at my car, I could see his reflection in the window behind me.

"So, I'll see you around then," I said. *Play it cool, Piper. Don't act like he hurt you.*

His hands slid onto my shoulders, and it felt nice, too nice to pull away right this second. They slipped down my arms before going around my waist as he hugged me from behind.

"Don't, Piper. I'm sorry. I've been stupid and said everything wrong."

I closed my eyes so I didn't see his face over my shoulder. I didn't want to study his face to see if it was the truth. It was tiring to always be on my guard. I needed somebody to tell secrets to. Still, he'd said I was creepy.

"Last night was an awfully long night, and I haven't recovered," he said.

He needed somebody to tell secrets to, but maybe he didn't know that. Maybe it was as hard for him to give up secrets as it was for me.

"You said I was creepy," I whispered. I felt a tear slip out of my eye, but I squeezed them tight so no more would escape.

He turned me in his arms. "No. I said sleepwalking is. You're not creepy at all, Piper."

That didn't sound different enough, not when the word creepy was stuck in there.

"It's different as night and day," he said as if he was reading my thoughts. His thumb brushed my cheek, wiping the tear that had escaped.

"No, it's not. If I told you something that you do is creepy, you'd be fine with it? What if I told you your flying is creepy? Or your claws? How would you like *that*, Gris?"

He froze. Exactly.

"You had your eyes open when you were sleepwalking," he said.

They flew open now. I shoved my hand into my pocket, yanking out my keys. That was his response? Seriously? The wall was going up. I was not going to be a casualty to this careless, stupid boy. Spinning away from him, I grabbed my door handle and pulled. My door didn't open. I yanked harder before glancing up. Gris was holding it closed.

"Wait, Piper. Look, I'm sorry—again."

"Is everything all right?" Dick walked out from behind the diner where he'd been taking a break.

"He's a jerk." I gestured at Gris, stomping a few feet away. His body was all warm and distracting.

"I am," Gris said. "I had a long night, and I've said criminally stupid things."

"No!" I growled. "You're not allowed to be nice. I need to hate you for a little longer."

Dick smiled, looking between us. I couldn't tell who he was siding with. "Do you want me to punch him, Piper?"

Did I? It was hard to say.

"It'd make me feel better," Gris said.

All the steam rushed out of me. "See, that's not any good then."

Dick laughed. "That's what I like about you, Piper— you're honest. I gotta go work on tonight's special, but I'm sure he'll let you run him over if that'll help."

The bell on the front door jangled as he went back in. It made me shudder. His previous bell was less…sharp. This one jangled on account of the bell being too small. It wasn't annoying me 'cause I was annoyed with Gris. It had bugged me ever since Dick'd switched it. I didn't like things changing, especially not noisy things.

"I'm worried about you, Piper. I don't want you involved because I don't know how to keep you safe. It's getting bigger—escalating."

"What do you mean?" There were things he wasn't telling me. I knew it.

He sighed. "There are more fiends. They're getting stronger. And whoever is pulling the strings most definitely knows what they're doing. They might know more about being a Watcher than I do. You don't gather the things they've gathered without a purpose. Without knowing what that purpose is, I don't want you getting caught up in the crossfire." His black hair curled at the tips and looked messy today. He ran a hand through it, messing it up even worse. "You're special, Piper, and I don't want anything happening to you, either from man or monster."

"I was involved before you even got here." I glared and pointed an angry finger at him. "And you need me." I could help him. If he'd let me.

He took a few shuffling steps forward. "Mm hm." There was that slow, sweet drawl. Oh crap. He was being charming. I thought I'd grown immune to that. Maybe he'd been plying me with kisses instead of charm. "I sure do. Finally, something we agree on."

I folded my arms tighter and frowned deeper. "Not like that. And I *can* keep myself safe."

"With your pepper spray?"

"It *does* work you know. Unlike your charm, which isn't gonna work on me."

"'Course not," he said, stepping closer. "I won't even bother trying it, then."

He'd better not—sure seemed like he might, though.

I dropped my gaze to the ground so he wasn't distracting me. I needed to think.

We knew each other's big secrets. That made us something to each other. Maybe we needed each other. We could watch out for each other. He knew about the darkness and what lived in the shadows, and I knew what lurked in Hidden Creek in the light. It was safer for us to be together. We could stop this from getting worse together.

As I stared down at my feet, I saw the tips of his motorcycle boots as he edged closer. I really ought to stop him, but I didn't. I didn't even try.

"It'd be safer for us to stay together," I said. "Logically, I mean. It's sensible." It wasn't just that I wanted him with me. I did, but it wasn't *only* that.

"Absolutely." He slid his arms around me. Mmm. He knew how to hold me just right—not too tight, but tight enough that I didn't feel like everything inside me would fly apart. "You can't leave me alone, Piper. I'll get into all kinds of trouble."

I rolled my eyes as I looked up at him. "You *are* being charming."

"A little." He kissed my forehead. "You seem to think it's one of my few strengths, so I'm going with it." His fingers traced my mouth in its determined frown. "Does this work on anybody? Or do they all just want to kiss you like I do?" He touched the corner of my upper lip. "Especially right here."

"I don't know. How about your charm? Does that always work for you?"

"You know, I haven't noticed one way or the other."

"Your other girlfriends never said?" I was holding my breath, but couldn't seem to stop.

He tilted his head. "I don't know that I've had any girlfriends. Just dates now and again. Of course I've never stuck around anywhere long enough to have relationships."

The first sentence had sounded good. The last had killed the buzz of the first one. It had killed it dead. My stomach was sour and heavy at the thought of this being a stopover in the life of Gris Caso. I was a stopover, too.

"You'll probably leave here soon enough," I said.

"Not soon. That is the one upside to this town—I've got a sort of job security so I can stay and date Hidden Creek's hidden treasure."

I snorted.

Leaning down, he whispered, "Piper, I can promise when I leave I won't want to, and every day I'm here I'll keep you safe and take you flying every night." His hands slid along my cheeks, cupping my face. He kissed right beside my mouth before his lips brushed up my cheek to my ear. "Sometimes, we might even leave the ground."

• • •

He was wearing that gargoyle shirt he'd worn before.

"What?" he asked as he climbed through the window.

"I like that shirt. It's like you're flipping off the world when you wear it."

"You like that?"

I nodded.

Gris yanked off the shirt and gave it to me.

The warm cotton sat in my hand, and I stared at it. "What?"

"It's yours," he said, sitting down on the beanbag in the corner. "I don't normally wear a shirt at night anyway."

"Oh." I pulled it on over the shirt I was wearing and fingered the worn material. It smelled like him. I'd never had a guy give me a shirt before.

"It looks good on you," Gris said, opening his laptop. "Go get your list."

Retrieving my list, I sat next to him on the beanbag. It squished inward, shoving me against him.

Gris put his arm around me. "Who's still on our list?" He narrowed his eyes. "You've added more pages."

"Well, I started extrapolating out on those final two list items, but I realized if we're looking for someone who has knowledge, means, and opportunity that limits our suspects. So, your theory is that it's either somebody from your line or from this other Beaumont line?"

"But they might not have the name Beaumont. Critch once suggested that everyone has changed their names."

I tapped my pen on my list, yawning. Being this close to Gris was making me sleepy—especially with his shirt off and his warm skin, heating mine. "Maybe it'd be easier to confirm that our suspects can't possibly be from this other line. We can try looking up their family history."

"You've got fiends outside," he said, yawning, too. He shook his head. "You're making me tired. Okay, let me up." He extricated himself, with difficulty, from the beanbag. Gris stood there, watching the window. "I'm going to turn off the light, other than the nightlight beside you so I can pull them in and kill them. I don't want them just hovering outside all night."

"Yep, that's nosy."

He grinned at me and turned off the light.

The change of skin to stone might never become less fantastic to watch. Nor would the strength in his movements or his fierce concentration. I was falling for a gargoyle. It was as bittersweet as the last day of summer. I should enjoy it while it lasted, but holding on to somebody planning out their good-byes stung even when it was good.

Then again, it all ended. It all failed. It all turned to dust. Protecting myself and holding too tight to perfect had given me peach-white scars and fewer memories that could make me smile.

Setting his laptop down, I stood up to get a better view.

When he was done, he turned to me and tilted his head as if considering me. "Does it bother you that I'm different in the dark?" he asked in his husky Watcher voice.

"I'm dark inside, even when I'm in the light." I waited for the words to make me feel apart and cold.

But Gris's half smile was admiring, warming me from head to toe. He was still here, even though I'd walked away from him twice. He made me want and that wanting didn't feel dirty or wrong—I felt alive. I wanted to step into the shadows and run my fingers across his hardened skin. I wanted that so much. I loved touching him. And, it felt powerful to know he trusted me with his secret.

"You're not dark inside." A second later, he whispered, "Step into the dark, Piper. With me."

It sounded suggestive and maybe a bit scary. I liked it. I took a step forward right as his hands came out and drew me into the shadows.

Chapter Nineteen

Gris

The nightmare was always the same. The clawing of a monster under my skin, trying to get out, as I stood in a crowd of people. I pushed against it, forcing it down, but it was going to break free at any second. They'd know. They'd all know.

Abruptly, I woke up to someone shaking me.

"Gris! Wake up!"

I blinked stupidly at Piper and tried to orient myself to the room. I was in the house I was renting, not Piper's room. I'd left there when she'd got up to go to school. I looked at the clock on the windowsill. "Aren't you supposed to be at school?"

Piper threw a look over her shoulder.

Right. Question.

She turned back to me and the panic in her eyes broke through my exhaustion. "Gris! There's a gas leak in your house. I can smell it."

I could, too, now. I woke up immediately. "Out the window,

Piper." I grabbed my laptop bag, looping it over my shoulder and shoved open the window. "C'mon! Out that window right this instant!" I scooped my phone from the ledge where it'd been charging.

She scrambled across the mattress and through the window.

I followed her out while punching 911 into my cellphone and grabbing Piper's hand. Yanking her toward a huge cypress near the barn, I said into the phone, "Yeah, I got a gas leak in my house. I don't know where it's coming from." At the cypress, I dropped all but the phone and gestured for Piper to stay.

After following the directions from the operator as well as turning off the gas, I jogged back to the cypress while pocketing my phone.

Piper was pacing, but she didn't look sick.

"You okay, Piper? Do you have a headache or want to throw up?" I grabbed her face in my hands when she didn't answer right away. Rubbing her cheeks with my thumbs, I said, "Piper, I know you don't like to answer questions, but you gotta tell me you're okay. I'm trying to figure out if you have carbon monoxide poisoning and we need to run you to the ER—wherever that is."

She shook her head. "I'm fine, Gris. I wasn't inside very long."

Sighing, I grabbed her in a tight hug. She was okay. Everything was okay as long as Piper was okay. I inhaled deeply, taking in the fresh scent of her apple shampoo. "Your hair still smells like you." I kissed the top of her head.

In the distance, sirens screamed our way.

Pop! Pop! Crack!

We turned toward the back of the house. The kitchen burst into flames, and several of the windows spider-webbed with cracks.

"You don't see that every day," I admitted.

"Should we do something?"

"I'm not sure what. It's not like I have a hose or even a bucket to hold water. The fire department is on their way."

"Should we go grab some of your stuff out of the house?" she asked.

"Nope. No way." Luckily, I didn't have much and the place wasn't heavily-furnished. My aunt wasn't getting that Halloween bowl back and, hopefully, they had insurance.

"But it's burning down, Gris!" I sensed the panic swelling in her and remembered what Dick had said about Piper's ability to cope in a crisis. Apparently I'd get to experience that firsthand.

"It's fine, sweetheart. You saw what I owned in the room I was sleeping in. I might go move my bike over here."

Smoke started pouring out patches of roof, so I moved us to a tree farther away.

"I suspected that roof might not have kept the rain out," I said.

"Do you think the house will explode?" Piper was starting to bounce around and get shivery.

"I think that only happens in movies, but we can move into the barn." I laughed. "This might be the only situation where the barn would be a preferable shelter."

"Gris!" She grabbed my shoulders and shook me. "Your house is on fire! It's on fire!"

I returned the favor, grabbing her shoulders, and made eye contact. "Dick warned me you weren't good in an emergency, and he wasn't lying."

"Shrapnel! Aren't you worried about flying debris? Or explosions or, or, or…" Wild-eyed panic had never made my heart burn like this. She might have been hurt because I was just so damn sure I could do it all on my own. I'd even been pushing her away. If she hadn't come in, I'd be beyond medium rare. What a stupid way to go.

"Nothing is going to happen. You got me? I'm here. And you're here. And we're going to keep each other safe. It's going to be fine."

She took a deep breath, and her eyes lost some of that panicked sheen.

I put my cell phone in her hand. "I'll go move my bike, and you call your mom and tell her that you're here, and you just saved my life."

"I'm not sure that's safe," she said as I walked toward the house.

"It's fine." The house was smoldering. I stopped and turned. "How did you get into my house?" I'd locked everything and checked it. Twice.

"The front door. It was unlocked."

Hell.

After we'd ruled out most of our suspects last night as belonging to the Beaumont line, I was facing the ugly certainty that my great-uncle was trying to kill me to take back what he viewed as his. If the smell of leaking gas hadn't covered it, I probably would have smelled the sulfurous scent of whatever cream Critch was using. Maybe that was what was driving him mad—he was creating his own source of bedevilment.

I called my dad while I grabbed my motorcycle boots off the front porch. It was definitely past time to call it. I couldn't handle all that Hidden Creek was dishing out.

"Please tell me this has nothing to do with another corpse," he answered.

"Nah, this time it was an attempt to put me six feet under."

"If this is your idea of a joke, Gris…"

If only. I pinched the bridge of my nose. "Somebody just tried to kill me in a fire from a gas leak."

"Somebody?"

"Pretty certain it was Critch."

My dad's sigh was long and loud. "Look, son—"

"I need you, Dad. Piper is right in the middle of this, and she's more important than my ego."

"I'm getting in the car now. Keep me updated."

Paramedics stopped by and confirmed Piper was fine. My aunt stopped by with lemonade and sandwiches. Several of the other neighbors came over to investigate, and more and more of Hidden Creek kept appearing, as well as the sheriff and his deputies.

"Strange that the sheriff is here," my aunt said.

"Not that strange. Where's Critch?" I asked Aunt Jess.

She looked startled. "I assume he's in his room. He's probably even asleep."

I snorted. Sure he was.

Aunt Jess joined her family who were hanging on the fence, watching their rental burn down.

"You okay?" I asked Piper again. The paramedic had said she was, but I needed to hear it again from her.

She punched my shoulder.

"It's a reasonable question," I said.

"It was the first two times."

"Well, you didn't answer the first two times, either."

She punched my shoulder again. "Why do you figure the police are here?"

I shrugged.

More police arrived. Firefighters went in and out of the smoking house.

"Do you think it's structurally stable for them to be going in and out? That doesn't strike me as very sensible," Piper said.

"They got the fire out quick, and there were enough holes in the walls and roof that I doubt the gas was as sealed up as it could've been." Piper was ramping up into a panic again. I slid my arm across her shoulders and tucked her into my side.

"It's okay. I'm sure they wouldn't go in there if it wasn't safe." Everything else was going to hell, but I had Piper grounding me with her cycling panic. Every time she said the word "sensible," I wanted to kiss her.

She started tapping her fingers at her side.

"I guess I'll be sleeping in the barn tonight."

Piper shuddered. "At least I cleaned out all the rusty metal and buried it over near the fence."

I stilled. "Are you pulling my leg?"

She shrugged. "I don't like the smell of rust. Plus, it wasn't safe having all that around. It was sensible, Gris."

There it was again. I dropped a kiss on the top of her head.

The entire town was staring us down. I could feel it.

"You'll probably go stay with your aunt's family, right?" Piper asked.

"Nah, probably not. I had a difference of opinion with Danny, and it might not be best." A vast understatement. "Keep away from my cousin and my Uncle Critch, Piper."

"All right. Danny hasn't spoken to me if he could help it for a while now. I doubt it'll be a problem. I've never spoken to your great-uncle. Ever. He's watched me from his window a few times."

"A few times?"

"Nine times—that I've noticed. When I walk past their house, he's stared at me from that back window. I guess that's where he lives? He's never yelled at me or done anything. He just stares. I've waved, but he hasn't waved back." She shrugged. "He's old, though. I reckon being old earns you the right not to be polite. I'm hoping so anyways. I'm looking forward to not always being polite."

"Just the same, stay away from him, too."

Several of the police strode out of the house and right in our direction.

Here it was. Here was where they told me that it was

arson, and my own great-uncle had tried to burn me alive. Hidden Creek really only had Piper going for it.

. . .

Dad would be here in a few hours, and then we'd be heading to the local police station to have a chat with them. It was what every boy secretly dreamed of—telling the police your great-uncle was trying to kill you because you'd become a gargoyle and he'd lost his wings. I didn't know how to handle it, so I'd told the sheriff I couldn't think of anybody who'd want to kill me, but I'd talk it over with my dad.

Dad had called several times from the road to ask, "Are you sure, Gris? Are you sure?"

No, but I knew I'd locked that door before I'd gone to bed. It'd saved my life that he'd left it unlocked. Piper wouldn't have tried to get in had the door been locked. She might've rang the doorbell, but maybe not. This had to end. If Uncle Critch was terrorizing Piper, too, then that went double. He might've even killed Trina and her boyfriend to "save them from bedeviling." Maybe he saw them when they were high and thought they were gone to the fiends. Who knew what Critch had gotten into his head? No, it had to stop.

When I finally made it back to Piper's side, it was to find her mom as well as Dick there.

"He'll stay with us tonight and then he'll be in your room tomorrow," her mom was saying to Dick.

They both turned to me expectantly.

I blinked. "Excuse me?" There was a huge crowd of people right outside the fence, and they all seemed to be leaning in toward this conversation.

"You'll stay in our camper tonight and, tomorrow, you can move into the room above Dick's garage," Piper's mom said.

They'd all but arranged my life without me. I wasn't sure

what to think of that. "I'm obliged to y'all, but I don't want to be a burden."

"You're not sleeping in your barn." Piper scowled at me. "It's too unhygienic. Anything can happen to you while you sleep." Her fingers snuck in-between mine, and she looked across the crowd gathered with what could only be called daring. It was strange having somebody on my side.

Her mom nodded.

Somebody and her mom were on my side. It sounded like a punchline to a joke.

"The room over my garage is sitting empty, gathering dust," Dick said.

"Not actual dust," Mrs. Devon said. She frowned. "Well, we can dust it if it has actual dust."

"And sterilize it," Piper said firmly. "A lot."

"I can pay rent while I'm here," I said to Dick. It'd be easier than trying to find another place to stay while I was dealing with the aftermath of what Critch had done. Nobody asked why I wasn't staying with my aunt and uncle, and I was grateful for that. Once the town knew about Critch, it'd spread like wildfire. They might blame us for every bad thing that'd ever happened.

Dick nodded. "I'll take your money."

Perfect. I loved working with reasonable people who understood a man's need to not be in debt. It'd also give Piper some space for when she found out about my great-uncle killing her dog—for whatever reason he did. If she wanted nothing to do with me after that, I wouldn't blame her.

I could feel Piper staring at me—in addition to the rest of Hidden Creek. I smoothed out my forehead. Sure, I was hiding stuff from her, but it was for her own good, as she'd know soon enough.

"My dad will be here in a few hours," I said to Piper.

"He can stay in the house in the guest room," Piper's

mom said. "It just doesn't seem right to have you in the house what with you dating Piper."

Piper groaned. "Mama!"

I fought a smile. I wasn't sure what she was about. We were standing side-by-side and holding hands. I was holding her hand in front of her mom. In some states, we'd have been halfway married at this point.

"Thank you, ma'am," I said.

Her mom nodded and glanced around. "How about we head home? You must be hungry."

Mrs. Devon knew the magic words. There wasn't much I wouldn't do for her cooking.

A portion of the house's roof collapsed—causing a collective gasp from everybody outside the fence—except Piper who shouted, "I knew it!"

Before we left, I went to my aunt and leaned across the fence. "Keep Critch in his room until my dad arrives," I whispered. "Even if you have to lock him in there. Keep him there."

My aunt looked guilty rather than surprised. "Why?"

I shook my head. I didn't want to say it out loud, let alone with the crowd around us. "Promise me?"

She frowned.

"Promise me, Aunt Jess. I told my dad you'd do it. Don't make me a liar."

"Jack agreed?" she asked.

I nodded.

"Fine then. I'll lock him in. He'll hate it. He'll rail, and he has a filthy mouth when he's in a rage. Maybe I'll send the girls to stay with friends til Jack arrives. It'd be better anyway. Better for everybody. Time to bring things to light." I had a feeling we'd end the day wishing they'd stayed the hell in the dark and kept quiet.

. . .

Three hours later, I was sitting on the Devons' front porch watching the road for my dad.

Piper dropped down next to me. "Are you going to explain to me what's going on?"

"It'll be obvious soon enough," I said, taking her hand. When it was obvious, she wouldn't want anything to do with me. I might as well enjoy these final moments.

She sighed and looked up at the dimming sky. "Full moon tonight."

I went still. "Is it?" A whole lot of the rituals Dad had come across involved the full moon. He wasn't sure how much was superstition and how much was legitimate since he didn't even think it could work. Not that he was willing to let Critch find out. Damn. Hard to believe it'd come to this.

"Yes. I have it on my desk calendar." She cleared her throat. "Are you mad at me?"

Her words broke my concentration on the road, and I turned to her. "Mad? Why would I be mad?"

"On account of what Mama said about us dating? I never told her we were dating."

I blinked slowly and continued staring at the burned house ahead. We were holding hands. Didn't that mean something to Piper?

"Do you *not* want to be dating me?" Crap, I'd asked a question. There was no way she'd answer. No way in hell.

"Do you wanna be dating me?" she asked, biting her lower lip.

"Yes. I thought we were dating—for as long as I'm here."

"I'm not sure if you can call what we've done dating."

"I tried to take you out to lunch, but you left me high and dry. I tried to take you skinny dipping, but you were having none of it."

The look she gave me would have turned anything less than a gargoyle to stone.

"Maybe tomorrow we could go on a date," she said. "So, we can *officially* call it dating."

"We could do that." I could see a decent amount of misunderstandings in our future, such as it was. She saw more layers than anybody could even imagine. "Also, after we start dating, we're exclusive. We're just dating each other."

She nodded. "For as long you're here." It sounded so much worse when she said it. Like the clock was ticking. Maybe it was and hopefully the next few hours didn't ruin everything. "What were the police wanting at your place?"

"They found out how the fire started. Somebody put a broken bottle end in the window, and it lit a bunch of rags that were stuffed around the gas valve behind the oven. They lit up when the sun hit the bottle."

"What kind of a person would do that?" Piper's green eyes were as wide as I'd ever seen them. "They tried to blow up the house."

"They tried to kill me."

"They couldn't have known you'd be asleep in there."

"People know, Piper. Either Danny has told them stuff about me, or they already knew." Especially the ones who were related to me. They knew better than most, I'd imagine.

"I can't figure out who'd do all these things. My dog, the grave, Trina and her boyfriend, your house…it seems like too much for any one person."

"Maybe it's not just one person." It had to be. It had to all be Critch—though I couldn't see him digging up the grave, the more I thought on it. He might want to, but he didn't seem strong enough anymore. Maybe he'd tricked Danny into doing it for him.

She turned to stare at me. Danny wasn't wrong. She did like to stare, and it was unnerving. I leaned over and kissed her. She kissed me back for a second, her lips softening against mine, and then she pushed back and looked all around.

"Gris! We're out where anybody can see us."

I smiled.

A door slammed.

We both looked up and across the way as Critch left the house, heading toward the barn, casting furtive looks around.

"Hell. Aunt Jess was supposed to keep him in."

What was he carrying? Could he do whatever ritual without actually killing me or having me present?

Piper followed my gaze. "Wait, that's not why you have me steering clear of Critch, is it? You don't really believe he's responsible for Jester's death, do you?"

I got to my feet.

"Gris, he wasn't on my list for a reason. I can tell you a lot of what happened—couldn't be Critch." She got to her feet, too.

"You can't underestimate him, and, technically, he'd fit into your unknown enemy category. He might—"

Shaking her head, she interrupted me. "No. The one thing I never do is underestimate somebody's ability to be harmful. Critch definitely didn't kill Jester. One hundred percent sure."

"He might be stronger than he looks. He used to be a Watcher."

Squinting, she considered that before shaking her head again. "I don't think he's strong enough, but I won't swear to it. It's Jester's barking. He barked at whoever came after him. He never barked at Critch. Ever. Even when Critch brought a bone for him out to the porch. I think Jester recognized that it'd unsettle your great-uncle and stop Critch from petting him. Dogs can sense that. On the other hand, Jester didn't much care for Danny or Hank. I figured, with Hank, that maybe he had the right idea. Dogs are smart, Gris. They know who's dangerous and who's not. I just imagine that might've been overridden by food." Her eyes narrowed further. "That had to be how it was done."

"I need to go after him—Critch, I mean," I said. "You're sure it's a full moon?"

"Of course I am. I'm also sure Critch didn't kill Jester."

"Maybe he's responsible for dragging in fiends and other folks around him were just…inspired by the bedeviling." Maybe either Danny or my uncle were involved and doing some of this. Maybe Danny had killed the dog. "I'd still see him as accountable for all that's happened if that's the case. As a Watcher, Critch knew the consequences." I started across the yard. "Stay here."

She didn't stay. Following me, Piper said, "Okay, so the fire was almost certainly Critch. He's the most logical suspect. There's a certain craftiness to it that fits his personality. He didn't just soak the area in gasoline and light a match—no, he set it all up cleverly to distance himself from getting his hands dirty. That's not to say the house fire had anything to do with you."

I blinked. "Well, why—"

She interrupted again, which was just as well because I'd been about to ask her a question. "Critch hated that house. He used to stare at it from across the way with this strange look on his face. If I had to swear, I'd think he loathed it."

"He does have some history with that house." I stopped at the gate and turned to her. "You really do need to stay here."

"If you think I'm not going with you, you're dumber than I thought."

I frowned at her.

She frowned right back.

"Piper, this is dangerous."

"It's not your great-uncle. Trust the list, Gris. Lists don't lie. And, no matter what, I'm coming with you."

I grabbed her shoulders. "Even if you're right and he didn't kill Jester, there's a whole lot that's happened besides that."

She cupped my face. "Gris, if killing Jester was to bedevil me and everything else is associated with fiends, aside from the fire, it's all the same person or persons. It's all about who wins if we lose. If you toss in everything that's happened with fiends from the beginning, who wins?"

Pulling away from her, I opened the gate and started down the road. There was a moment of hesitation behind me as Piper tried to decide whether to cut across the field or follow me.

She caught up to me.

"What do you mean who wins?"

"Well, what was your first brush with fiends? Jester's death?"

"Actually, the hell of it was, I passed that mill on my way into town. I nearly stopped and took them on, despite being exhausted. They would have slaughtered me. Critch was the one who sent for me. He knew I was coming in."

"So, did three other people on my list."

"He knew about the birthright."

"So, did three other people on my list."

My great-uncle had gone into the barn…or around the barn, but I hadn't seen him come out behind it. I stopped right in front of it to take one final stab at convincing Piper to stay outside. "Look, I'll immobilize Critch and we can discuss all your theories when my dad arrives."

She was staring at the patch of paint right next to the door while biting her lip. Sensing my gaze, she turned to me and clenched her fists at her sides. "I'm going with you. I understand 'crazy' better than you ever will. Maybe I can reason with him." Then, she stomped over to the door and opened it.

Stepping through the doors, I searched the dark interior for my uncle.

"He did come in here, didn't he?" Piper asked softly.

"I thought so." Great. He was gone. I wanted to throw something but I didn't want to scare Piper. Then her words niggled at the back of my brain. "Three people?" I asked. "What three people were on your list who fit this besides Critch?"

"Your aunt, Danny, and his father."

"You're including my aunt?" Aunt Jess had looked guilty earlier when I'd talked to her, but...no.

With a sigh, Piper stepped over to a bale of hay just past the light cast by the door. "Never underestimate a woman, Gris."

That's when the persistent itching on my back from my wings hit me. "Hell." I grabbed her just before her hand hit the bale and dragged her into the light.

"Don't profane, and what are you doing?" she asked, pulling her hand from mine. I grabbed her around the waist, holding her close to me.

In the silence, she heard it, too.

The scrambling and shuffling in the hay, all around us.

Piper shivered. "It's cold even in the sunlight," she whispered.

The fiends were crowded into this barn like somebody'd sold admission. I could smell it, that scent—sulfur. Critch had gathered fiends here.

Behind us, the barn door slammed shut and a large piece of wood bolted it closed.

Fiends dove toward me from all sides, their banshee shrieks so piercing that I winced and jerked. My skin hardened in an instant as I slipped into Watcher form. I shifted so quickly that my wings stung as they burst through my shirt. My shirt split all along my sleeves, and my clawed feet shot through my shoes.

Grabbing Piper, I jumped into the large patch of light left behind by the square window above us in the barn. I was back in human form in an instant, but not before I'd felt the brush of fiends' claws on my skin. This was bad. This was very bad.

Piper's breaths came in quick bursts. "So cold. They're here. I felt them." Her head bumped my chin as she looked up. "Gris, they're here."

Chapter Twenty

A shiver spooked through my body, and it was justified. I couldn't see, but I could feel Gris changing from his normal form to the other and back again. And they were here. Like the nights in my room, the monsters were out from under the bed and roaming.

"Gris?" What should we do? I glanced over at the door. That's part of what had seemed wrong when we'd walked up. The door to the barn had been open. It'd been closed earlier.

"There's a whole slew of fiends in this barn, Piper, and they're aggressive. I'm not sure what is setting them off, but— they're going to attack. They usually wait until night when they have more strength, but they won't this time." He sniffed. "That is *a lot* of sulfur." He groaned. "That damn mill. It's like that mill again—only there's more than twice as many."

I could smell the sulfur in the air now. It smelled like several dozen eggs had gone very wrong in the barn. "It does smell evil if that counts for anything," I said.

A low, deep laugh sounded outside the barn.

I shivered even as Gris seemed to relax. It was the same laugh I'd heard in the gym.

"Danny," Gris yelled, "what the hell are you doing? Quit being a dumbass and open the door. Critch seeded this place with something like he did that grain mill. It's gathered a bunch of fiends. Let us out. We need to round him up before he does something we can't fix."

Something wasn't right—beyond everything else—beyond the strange scent and the cold feel of the air. Something was decidedly wrong. When Danny didn't answer Gris right away, I whispered, "Gris, he's put up the missing boards."

"What?"

We were in the only solid patch of light in the whole barn. There were streaks from ill-placed boards and holes in the wood, but every last one of the boards I'd stacked behind the barn was back up. They didn't match up just right, so he hadn't hammered them up, but they were up nonetheless.

"He wins, Gris. It was Danny. Not your great-uncle. Danny put the missing boards back up to trap us. Critch definitely set fire to the house, but Danny did everything else. I told you my list was right! I told you!"

Another laugh from Danny.

"It can't be," Gris said.

"Danny, you son of a bitch, you killed my dog. I hope you rot in hell!" If ever there was a time for cursing, this was it.

Gris shouted. "Open the damn door."

"Now why would I do that? I'd have to go through the ritual again, and I'm starting to run low on ingredients. I already had to take on getting more beast's teeth, and that was a pain in the ass. Only it wasn't on account of me not being able to use anything with cloven hooves or feathers. But you always thought I was stupid."

"I never thought you were stupid. Shiftless and ignorant, but that's not the same," I yelled back.

"Don't aggravate him," Gris hissed under his breath.

"Yeah, well, nobody noticed the dogs, did they? The other missing dogs?" Danny yelled. "You lock a bunch of angry fiends in a barn to slaughter everything and nobody thinks anything of a few dumb mutts disappearing with the rest of the livestock."

"Jester was not a dumb mutt. He knew you were sick and twisted. Jester always hated you!"

"Well, you have your boyfriend to thank for that. I used all the beast's teeth at the mill—the one he didn't stop for, even though it was on the way to our place. He'd set out so late that the ritual might not have worked, but he didn't stop anyway. I figured he wouldn't be able to resist proving himself and he'd be tired and easy prey…especially since he'd ridden here. I'd gone to all the trouble to goad him into riding his motorcycle, too."

Gris groaned and slapped his forehead. "He did. He said my rustrocket wouldn't even make it here."

Okay, I hated to admit it, but that was clever.

Gris turned around, searching for a way out. Maybe if I just kept Danny talking.

"Then, I had everything with me at the mill when he finally got around to it, but nine fiends wasn't enough. Plus, I had to step everything up when Gris got interested in my business and in you, Piper. You were just supposed to die. You had one job. Do you know how long it takes to gather these creatures? I've been moving them around as I gathered them, and there's only so many empty buildings in Hidden Creek. It's a damn pain to manage. It's like herding and it's taking up too much of my time."

I gasped. "You had them in the gym! That's just plain not safe. Kids go to the gym!" He'd had them in the gym, and I'd stumbled into them.

Danny laughed. "That was so funny. I couldn't believe the luck of that. I almost had you."

"Why are you doing this?" Gris asked. It was a good question. Hopefully Danny'd answer it.

Danny was busy muttering. "Heart of the unwilling. Teeth of the beast. Bones of one who'd come before. Death of the last."

"Danny, whatever Critch has talked you into—this is a bad idea."

"Talked me into?" Danny asked. "You think this was all his idea? Do you have any idea how long it takes to drag something as complicated as this transference ritual outta him? I think half the time he was confusing me with some other Watcher from fifty years ago." He snorted. "The old coot once tried this ritual to transfer it to his girlfriend. I honestly didn't think he had it in him to bait you. He kept changing his mind. I was meant to be a Watcher. Then, I wasn't. Then, I was. I think it was the damn mutts. He has a soft spot for dogs. He's barely been speaking to me since that damn dog. I'm tellin' you, I was fixin' to strangle him. He'd interfere—except when I wanted him to. Then, you survived that house fire. I thought when I saw the smoke I might need to move on to your daddy on account of the ritual needing to be done *before* the last Watcher's death and not too far ahead of time, either. But you lived. And y'all are both here. It's fate."

"It's not fate. We followed Critch here."

That made Danny pause. "He's here?" A moment later, he yelled, "Critch, come out, come out, wherever you are."

I'd have sworn Danny wasn't ambitious enough to do all this planning. Honestly, despite our dire circumstances, I was a smidge impressed. He used to take ten minutes to decide whether he wanted tater tots for lunch.

As if he'd heard me, Danny said, "I wasn't sure I'd be able

to do it, but it gets easier every time."

"Every time you do what?" A swirl of cold air whispered around us, and Gris clutched me closer. "Don't go into the dark," he whispered. "Whatever you do, don't go into the shadows."

"Killing. I don't even have to work up to it anymore. Y'all are right out in the open," Danny shoved something into the knot in the wood.

Gris grabbed me around the waist and bolted into the dark, changing form as he did. Everything happened so fast that I didn't even start screaming until we were already in the air and the spot where we'd been was peppered with rifle shot. Cold claws grasped all around me nearly as tangible as Gris's talons pressing into my skin. A *rip* was followed by breaking glass and plastic. Screaming, I kicked my feet in the air as he carried me up, up into the darkness toward the long beam stretching to the single window.

"Dammit, Gris!" Danny slapped the side of the barn.

When my feet touched the light on the beam and Gris landed behind me, we tipped off-balance as he flipped back into human form.

"Whoa!" Gris said, grabbing the crossbeam and wrapping us both around it. "Hold on, Piper. Hold on."

"They can't fly?" I asked. "I thought they could fly or something." Could they get to us? The shadows had talons, bigger talons than Gris did.

"No. No wings. They can creep and jump, but not this high. We're safe up here." He shifted around as he examined our predicament. "Sorta."

Long scratches feathered across his upper arms and drops of blood pooled along them. The air swam in front of me as I stared at the bright, red blood on his skin. I could nearly taste the metallic smell.

"Piper!" He pulled my arms around the beam in a tight

hug. "You can't faint. I'm no good in the light and I'm not nearly as strong during the day. If you fall…"

"You're getting blood all over me!"

"Concentrate on that, then. I'm staining your clothes something fierce. Stains all over. Get mad. Get frustrated. Just don't faint because they're starving for the chance to kill us."

I couldn't faint. I couldn't faint. It was a long way down to the floor of the barn. A long drop with a short stop. Even if the drop didn't kill me, the darkness wanted a taste of me. I could feel scratches on my skin, too. If Gris hadn't been protecting me from the fiends with his body, I might be bleeding stains into my own clothes.

A snort from outside. "I'm hoping so. I was gonna make it quick, but y'all are fighting y'all's destiny. Those fiends should be good and riled, at least from the powdered bones. That and the sulfur—that's what makes them spitting mad and calls them. Once I started adding the bones to the curse bags, it was like ringing a dinner bell. I still might have to dig up Silas's nephew for more supplies. And grave-digging is a nasty business—though I reckon you know that now. How was that Gris? I stopped by and noticed you'd found my little gift." He cackled this time. As Mama would say, that boy ain't right. He should've been higher up on my list.

"What is he talking about?" I asked.

"Nothing." Gris snarled. "You only need me for your stupid ritual—why go after her? Why torment her? Was it because you knew I wouldn't let anything happen to Piper?"

"Oh no, getting rid of her was always part of the plan. I made a few mistakes the first time I killed. I'd only needed the one heart, but then *she* snuck out as if they hadn't just said good-bye. So I had to kill Trina, too, and the car was a mess by then. I'd thought—the creek, nobody will find them at the bottom. There I am, driving them to their grave, right by Piper Devon, with her staring, staring eyes—like my worst nightmare come to life."

"I was sleepwalking! I don't remember any of it."

Danny snorted. "I heard you did that."

"Hank told you I've been sleepwalking out to the fence since that night?" For some reason, I hadn't expected Hank to run around telling people all my secrets, but I should've.

Another patch of hush from Danny.

Gris held me tighter and leaned down to whisper, "I'm gonna figure out how to get us out of here. Keep him talking."

I nodded.

"Well, I didn't hear it directly from him," Danny said. "Maybe if I hadn't pissed him off, he'd have told me, and I'd have known you didn't remember."

"I reckon Hank might be pissed that you *murdered* his sister," I said.

"Don't be stupid. He doesn't know that. Although he might guess as much. Only a few of us here with the guts to do it. I might have to deal with him after I'm done here. I had to deal with Jared knowing too much already."

He might be killing everybody in Hidden Creek by the time the sun went down.

"I think I might be able to walk along this beam out to the window and jump out," Gris whispered.

The beam we were on was only eight inches across, and he'd need to make it twelve feet to the window. There was no way. Then, there'd be the fifteen-foot drop from the window where he'd break both his legs, right before Danny shot him while he was down or the fiends ripped him to pieces. I might be overly careful, but that was plain ridiculous. "No, you can't."

"I might be able to."

"No. Gris, we can wait up here. Somebody is bound to come looking for us eventually."

He groaned and whispered, "We can't. The fiends tore

my pocket and my new phone is in a hundred pieces down there. Nobody knows we're here. The sun is going down, and it's taking the light with it." He didn't need to say what would happen when we ran out of light—we'd be trapped on the beam for sure. The arctic temperature of the barn and the scratches and blood all over him said that. "Plus, I'm not sure my cousin won't try to shoot us again. But it's gonna be okay, Piper."

I was less than certain of that.

Gris sniffed and then exhaled sharply. "Gasoline. I can smell gasoline."

"In a second, you'll smell smoke," Danny said. "I wasn't planning on burning this down, but somebody left me some gasoline."

Critch. That's what he'd been carrying.

"It's funny," Danny said, "did you know this old barn used to have bats in it? I guess it does again, Grisham."

I could see the spark near the back wall of the barn where Danny was. Danny was whistling as he walked around the barn, and the back wall started to crackle and pop. I wasn't even sure it needed the gasoline. This old place was a pile of matchsticks.

Gris and I were holding onto a crossbeam in the light, and Gris shifted from foot to foot, looking around, making the beams groan. I tried to shut out the fear of us plummeting to our deaths 'cause, quite obviously, we were going to burn to death. If I had to choose, I'd pick the plummeting to our deaths option. Then again, somebody would have to clean that up, and that didn't seem right. Burning to death was probably much cleaner. Maybe.

Gris grabbed me by the shoulders. "Hold tight to these beams, Piper. You hear me? Hold tight. Don't let go."

I nodded and blinked. Behind him, the barn was starting to smoke, and the air was already feeling hot and thick with it.

Gris tore off the remains of his shirt and dove toward the ground. I screamed, but there was a flash of movement in the darkness he'd flown into. He'd changed. He'd changed. He was okay. He was fine.

"What's going on?" Danny shouted right as Gris tore clear through the side of the barn. A second later, Gris was back with a still-shouting Danny. I could see them moving through the barn below me.

Then, they were in the patch of sunlight below the window. Both were covered in bloody scratches.

"What are you doing?" Danny yelled. "Now we're all gonna die!" He coughed as the smoke filled the barn. Even the sunlight was about to be blotted out by smoke. I wasn't sure what that meant for the fiends. If smoke was the same as shadow, there was nowhere we'd be safe. "You're going first, though." Danny dove toward Gris and the two of them grappled.

Reaching down, I yanked off my shoe and threw it at Danny's head. My aim was perfect, clipping his head, right above his ear.

Danny looked up. Gris shoved him off, straight into the darkness.

I was glad I couldn't see well. Danny's screams were enough. He screamed and screamed. These were the same creatures in my room night after night. I might not ever have a good night's rest again. I tried to cover my ears, but I needed to hold onto the beam. Horrible. Horrible. As much as I hated Danny, shudders racked through me as the noise went on and my fingernails tore into the wood from the beams. Tearing. Ripping. And the screams—the wet and ugly screams—and then they stopped and the silence was so much worse.

"Gris?" I gasped. Let him be okay. Please, let him be okay. My world was jack-knifed and a wreck from what I'd just heard. I couldn't breathe. I couldn't. Gris had to be okay.

"We need to get out of here," Gris shouted to me.

And I exhaled shakily. Alive. He was alive. My eyes stung from the smoke. It was hard to keep them open.

Gris coughed below me. "I can probably get outside again, but I'm not sure I can get up there. If I fly into the dark, they'll tear my wings off—they're *that* mad."

"Don't go into the dark." Having heard what they'd done to Danny—I might never go into the dark again. There were large patches of light he could bolt between, now that he'd broken in and out of the barn. "Don't you *dare* fly back up here."

"If I thought I could get to you before they did, I would. I just don't…" He coughed. "Can you climb along the beam to the window"—he coughed again—"and jump out?"

"I can try." I took a quick look down. "It's only eighteen steps." I was right above one of the hay bales I used to touch.

"I swear I'll catch you."

"You better." I took off my other shoe and threw it. No use for it now. I could do this. It was a long way down, but if ever there was a time to just embrace all the dark things that might happen and do it anyway…this was it. I took my first step, sliding my foot along the eight-inch beam as I did. Seventeen more.

"I'm outside. Keep coming," Gris called, coughing.

I took another step and another. And another.

"Talk to me. Tell me you're okay," he said.

"What am I supposed to talk about?" I took another two steps, coughing. My throat burned.

"Whatever the hell you want to talk about."

"Gris, my mama would've washed your mouth out for that!" I took another two steps.

"Really? My dad would've let me get away with anything in the Bible before I got my mouth washed out, that's for damn sure."

"Gris!" I took a couple more steps. I was gonna give him a piece of my mind when I did get outside. It was hot inside the barn and my eyes were starting to water like a garden hose. I coughed. Behind me, more wood crackled and popped.

"Yep. My dad lets me say whatever the hell I want to as long as I'm not in a lady's presence."

I took another two steps. Oh, he'd be hearing from me about this. "Just 'cause I'm in the barn, I don't count? Is that what you're saying?" It was getting harder to talk, and I stopped to cough.

"Yep. Do you want hear all the words I'm allowed to say? I can list them off." And he did. He swore and he swore.

I sped up and took several more steps.

He laughed. He *actually* laughed. "I can see you now."

That was good 'cause my eyes were watering so bad I could only see a blur ahead of me.

"One more step, and I'll need you to jump so I can catch you."

"Two," I coughed out, feeling around for the edge of the window. I took the last two steps. They were small. Apparently I stepped differently on a wood beam than when I was on the ground.

"I can see from the look on your face that I'm about to get a fierce lecture—the likes of which I've never received. I'll count for you. You gonna jump on two or four?" he asked.

"Four." I gasped out the word. The air was so hot and thick.

"One…two…three…four…"

I jumped and crashed into Gris's arms, elbowing him in the face and tipping him off balance so we fell to the ground. He didn't seem to mind 'cause he hugged me tight against him. I coughed into his chest and took in lungfuls of the much cooler air.

"Are you okay, Piper? Tell me you're okay."

I kept coughing. I figured that was answer enough, and mostly all I could manage. I felt like I'd been standing *in* a campfire.

"Danny?" A voice asked from behind our sprawled bodies, and I squinted my eyes open enough to see Danny's daddy with a rifle in his hand. He wasn't pointing it at us, so that was good.

"In the barn," Gris said, gesturing.

"Is he dead?" his daddy asked.

"I think so. I'm sorry, sir…I…"

Gris's uncle shook his head once and said, "I'll just go make sure" and headed toward the barn, cocking his gun.

"What does that mean?" I tried to whisper, but the coughing and my croaking voice made it louder than was polite.

Gris shook his head and held me tighter, dropping onto his back with me in his arms. In the distance, there were sirens again—heading toward another fire here. Maybe Gris had the right of it with the swearing. Hidden Creek would never be the same after this. It might be worth swearing over. I wouldn't do it, but it might be worth it nonetheless.

The barn crackled, popped, and smoked, and Gris hugged me tighter as our nightmare burned to ashes behind us.

Epilogue

GRIS

It was Piper's idea to tell the police that Danny had died when he'd changed his mind and come into the barn to save us from the fire. The lie didn't sit right with her, I could tell. I'd had to hold her hand to stop the tapping.

My uncle told the police he'd seen his son trap us in the barn, and he'd already been sure Danny was behind some of the other mischief in Hidden Creek.

My uncle said "mischief," but I'd have used the words malicious violence—especially since we'd told my aunt and uncle what Danny was after and about his killing spree.

It'd been a long week since then. A long week where I'd hardly seen Piper. Well, I'd seen her, but not without other people around. I'd kissed her on the cheek once in front of both our parents, but that was it. I hadn't kissed her—really kissed her—for a week.

Here we were, in Piper's room, a whole week after my cousin'd tried to kill her, acting like total strangers. I leaned against the wall beside the window she'd just let me in. Piper stood a few feet in front of me, her arms wrapped around her middle, looking both defiant and unbearably fragile.

"So the Porters are moving?" She licked her lips, and the gloss shone in the light, making her mouth sparkle like magic.

"They don't feel right staying here with Hank and his family after what happened with Trina. My aunt and uncle knew Danny wasn't right and had suspected he had something to do with a few of these things. They'd planned on confronting Danny with my dad's help." My dad had arrived with the paramedics. His horrified expression as I told him everything said that most rookies didn't typically face death to that degree. Dad said he was proud of me, but he would have been less proud of me if I'd gotten my stubborn ass killed. "I like to believe my Aunt Jess didn't know about the murders and believed that an animal killed your dog, but we didn't ask." I hadn't wanted to ask. Sometimes you wanted that ignorance.

She nodded her acceptance. "Your great-uncle is staying, though?"

"He says he wants to watch over the house." Though he hadn't been specific about which house now that I thought on it. "Dad reckons he's harmless enough without Danny here. They've hired somebody local to keep an eye on him." And I'd be keeping an eye on him while I was here.

"Mattie's mama," Piper said. "She used to work as a home health nurse. She's keeping watch over him."

"Yeah, I think that's about right."

Piper twisted her fingers in her lap. "So, that's it then."

"What is? You mean with Critch?"

She lifted her gaze. "No. I mean with you. You'll be leaving."

I couldn't for the life of me tell what she thought of that. Her eyes were solemn, but dry. "Is that what you want?"

Abruptly, Piper took off the sweatshirt she was wearing, revealing a tanktop. She pulled the right strap aside on her shoulder and pointed to a pale white line. "That was my first cut." Her fingers travelled along to a different pink cut. "This was my last cut I've done. Everything in between are payments against my debt for living."

"Piper."

"Gris." She leaned forward slightly. "I want, Gris."

"What do you want?"

"I want to live. I want to take chances. I've cut to pay for things I've done wrong. I've cut to pay for being happy. I feel like I've been paying for that my whole life, and I want... more. I'm not fixed. I'll still be like this, but I want to quit avoiding life 'cause I don't want to pay for it. I *want*."

"Do you want me?" I held completely still, despite my heart pounding. If she said "no" because I'd waited, holding back, keeping my options open...

"How much will you cost me?"

I exhaled. "I'm free."

She shook her head. "No, you're not. If I take a chance on you and you leave right away 'cause you've got a more exciting offer than Hidden Creek can extend, there's a cost." She rubbed her shoulder. "I keep all these transactions on my skin. I'm not saying that I'm not interested, but I want to know ahead of time."

I'd been reckless since I'd arrived in Hidden Creek—with our lives and with Piper's feelings. This last week had taught me how empty the value of that wandering independence was. "I don't want this to end. I can continue renting the apartment from Dick and use this as my home base. Also, there are still fiends in town." This town was still crawling with them, despite my best attempts.

"So, you'll just stay here in town?" She raised her eyebrows, her skepticism obvious. "Indefinitely?"

"No."

Piper nodded, her jaw tightening.

"It'd be boring here without you, and I've heard valedictorians tend to jet off to fancy colleges."

Her whole face brightened and she straightened up. "I found out my test score online."

"On your ACT?"

"Yep, three points higher. I got a thirty-four this time."

"Thirty-four out of thirty-six, right? That's fantastic." Piper and her badass brain.

Piper grinned, blushed, and wouldn't meet my eyes. "Thirty-four *is* a good number."

It was nice and even. Part of me was curious if she'd retaken the test to get an even number. I could see her doing that.

"I decided I'm, uhh, going to focus on Georgia State and Loyola and sending them this higher score. I should be able to get a full-ride with them."

My gaze caught on the college brochures on her desk. Georgia State wasn't so far from my parents' house. Loyola was in New Orleans. Neither of them was on the other side of the country like her mom had said she'd been planning on.

"You mean, in addition to the others you were sending applications to," I said.

Her chin tipped up, all defiant again, like she was staking claim on this section of the United States. "No. Just them. Right now anyways. That might change. It might not. I mean, they're both close. I thought being close to home might be nice."

She would be close, but not close enough for me. I could live in an apartment in New Orleans or stay with my parents in Atlanta. If that's what she wanted.

"It would be nice. There are probably a lot of fiends in New Orleans."

She smiled. "There might be."

This was better. "So, what would you be majoring in?" I asked to keep her talking.

The question somehow made it through her guard because

she said, "Psychology or maybe math. I haven't decided."

"Psychology might include some anatomy classes. Anatomy classes usually involve working with cadavers. I've heard how much you enjoy that."

Her eyes widened with a look of horror.

I laughed.

She threw a pillow at me. "Gris!" Her horrified look shifted to staring at the door.

"I've muffled the noise," I said.

"You can do that without changing?" she asked.

Under the guise of returning her pillow, I sat down beside her on the bed. "Yes. When it's this late at night."

Wrinkling up her nose, Piper asked softly, "How come you haven't told me not to tell anybody about you?"

"Because I trust you." I feathered my fingers across her fist clenched in the blankets atop her bed. "I've missed you this week. I've wanted to see you every day. You're not the only one who wants things." I wanted to be right here, right now. Preferably holding her, kissing her. But I worried that everything had changed. Blown to hell by my birthright and Danny coveting it. There were also those dark moments in the barn. I'd jumped through the side of the barn and pulled Danny back in with me. The fiend's shrieking had blended into his shrieking. Then, I was there, and I'd had to get Piper out. Nothing else mattered.

This last week she'd been the only tangible thing for me. My future was hazy—other than I wanted Piper in it. Sensible, beautiful Piper with her logic and control. I probably didn't deserve somebody as amazing as Piper, but I still wanted her. I wanted her, body and soul. I needed her in the same way.

"You missed me?" she whispered.

"Every moment."

Like the sun breaking from behind clouds, her wide smile shifted something inside me, dispelling the darkness left over from Danny's death and all the unanswered questions. She flipped her hand and held it open, waiting to see what I'd do.

"You know, we never really got that date." I took her hand. "Mostly on account of you not hunting me down to go skinny dipping."

Piper rolled her eyes. "There were dead bodies marinating in that water. I wouldn't even put my toes in there if you dared me, Gris Caso."

"How about I take you out to the movies tomorrow night instead?"

"Or you could take me flying right now, as long as you promise not to ever strand me in a tree again."

Not one to miss an opportunity, I got to my feet and used my powers to blink out all but her nightlight.

Piper gasped, rewarding my showing-off.

I let go of her hand and pulled my shirt off. Rather than tossing it aside, I put it overtop her tank top.

She looked down at the shirt before meeting my gaze, her eyes full of questions.

"I like you wearing my shirt, and it's a little cold outside." After slipping off my shoes, I shifted into my Watcher form before reaching for her hand.

Getting to her feet, instead of taking my hand, Piper ran her fingertips along my hand and up my arms before wrapping her arms around my neck. Standing on her tiptoes, she said, "Gris, I missed you, too," and pressed a soft kiss on my mouth before dropping down to her heels to look at me.

Piper stared straight into my soul, without flinching.

I stared back—and her darkness saw mine.

A gargoyle and a pixie. Who'd have ever guessed?

"So are we going on this date or are you all talk?" she asked.

Pulling her along with me, I opened the window. "Hell no, I'm not."

"Don't profa…" and the rest was lost in a gasp as I dragged her into the sky with me.

Author's Note

I chose to give Piper the same type of obsessive-compulsive disorder that I have because it's a lesser known set of symptoms. Piper has purely/primarily obsessional OCD also known as Pure-O. People with Pure-O often go undiagnosed until much older because they don't have the commonly known symptoms. Like Piper, I thought that I was going insane for much of my teenage years. Like Piper, I'm a cutter, though I haven't cut for many years.

When my daughter was diagnosed with OCD, it required me to accept my diagnosis. As this was a secondary diagnosis for her, a family history was the only way she'd be able to qualify. That day, when I stated unequivocally that I had severe OCD, my impression of the disorder changed. I looked at my daughter, who was a toddler at the time, and recognized that what she had—and what I had—was not dark. It couldn't be. Since then, I've spent a lot of time trying to spread awareness of what OCD looks like from the inside. I've mentored those struggling with it. I've talked to people dealing with self-harm. I've cried with parents who've lost children to suicide and

OCD.

I've attempted to create a realistic portrayal of the condition from my experience, but OCD is a broad spectrum of symptoms. If you or someone you love might qualify for a diagnosis or you'd like more information or a consultation, contacting someone in the medical profession is a great place to start, or the International OCD Foundation is also a fantastic resource at: https://iocdf.org/ There are also resources for those struggling with self-harm, and You Matter is an informative starting point.

Acknowledgments

I don't know that it's ever possible to recognize everyone who helps take a story from an idea to publication and this book is especially difficult in that way. So many people had their hand in this.

First of all, my family has put up with a lot from me, not just in relation to this book. My husband, my kids, and my extended family have pitched in or been sounding boards. They are such a wonderful support system. My husband saved my life again and again when I sunk deep into the destructive side of my condition. My siblings especially helped with this and in grounding me when my own OCD roared. My mom's quirks became Piper's mom's quirks—and I should probably admit that I never figured out her dishwasher pattern. Also, I know I was a rough teen to raise at times, but I love you and Dad.

So many betas read this, in addition to editors. Tina Sandoval, Britt Marczak, Trysh Thompson, Sarah Jolley, Tasmin, and Jay Donovan all helped improve this book. Brittany provided a much needed sensitivity read and Jay's moral support cannot be undervalued. Special thanks to Chelsea Hundley for helping with editing at a crucial point. I know I'm missing beta readers because I ran the cutting scenes by a lot of people. I'm sorry if I didn't mention you.

This is the book that brought Sarah Yake into my life as an agent, and then I got all feisty about where it should go. Thank you for sticking it out with me, Sarah.

The editors and staff at Entangled are some of the finest and most intelligent people I've ever met. Kate Brauning's commitment to clarifying the best in a story without sacrificing its heart is evident in every email. I submitted this to her because she wanted an "own voices" novel, and she's stayed true to allowing my voice to be heard.

Finally, we lost my thirteen-year-old dog to cancer while I was in revision of this book. It felt like losing a piece of me. While he couldn't read this even if he was alive, I can't go without acknowledging that Nanaimo was a source of solace when my world was on fire. When my OCD was bad and my paranoia was high, I knew he was watching over my kids and I could sleep. Many thanks, old friend…and I hope they have the squeakiest toys in heaven.

About the Author

Wendy Laine is the penname of author Wendy Sparrow. Writing is in Wendy's blood, as are equal parts of Mountain Dew and chocolate. Wendy has been telling tales since she was a child with varying amounts of success. Her parents clearly anticipated her forays into the paranormal because she heard "The Boy Who Cried Wolf" over and over. She lives in Washington State with a wonderful husband and two quirky kids and is active in Autism and OCD support networks. She can usually be found on Twitter, where she'll talk to anyone who talks to her and occasionally just to herself.

Also by Wendy Laine, writing adult fiction as Wendy Sparrow...

PAST MY DEFENSES

THIS WEAKNESS FOR YOU

CRAZY OVER YOU

ON HIS LIST

FROSTED

CURSED BY CUPID

Discover more Entangled Teen books…

ATLANTIS REBORN
an *Atlantis Rising* novel by Gloria Craw

In a few days, I will be Laurel clan chief—and it doesn't come lightly. My human family thinks I'm dead, and the only person I can count on is Ian, who I know has my back and who I want to give my heart. Gathering the fifteen clans of Atlantis is more tasking than I thought. Especially since they're proposing we create hybrids. A dangerous decision. If I can't change their minds, then the descendants of Atlantis could disappear forever.

THE WISHING HEART
a novel by J.C. Welker

The bejeweled vase Rebel just tried to hawk now has every magical mobster in the city hot on her tail in a game of cat and mouse in a world she never knew existed. But freedom could unravel a love like Rebel has never known, or it could cost her her heart…

OTHER BREAKABLE THINGS
a novel by Kelley York and Rowan Altwood

According to Japanese legend, folding a thousand paper cranes will grant you healing. Evelyn Abel will fold two thousand if it will bring Luc back to her. After a car crash got Luc Argent a second chance at life, he tried to embrace it. But he always knew death could be right around the corner again. And now it is. A road trip to Oregon—where death with dignity is legal—is his answer. But along for the ride is his best friend, Evelyn. And she's not giving up so easily.